CLOSING TIME

"Phoenix Force should be on Libyan soil by now," Barbara Price said. "That was the pilot of the Galaxy. They're clearing the area. Still at 25,000 feet and heading back to Aviano air base."

Brognola turned to check out the map pinned to the wall. The Galaxy had taken off from Sardinia, making its final leg of the flight. Once over Libyan soil, Phoenix Force would make their high-altitude jump, coming down in the predawn darkness.

Price's voice, low and steady, interrupted the Fed's silent reflection. "Striker confirms he's in position. On standby to move the moment we hear Phoenix has gone on the offensive."

She leaned back in her seat, shaking loose her mane of hair.

"Now all we can do is wait," she said.

DON PENDLETON'S
MACK BOLAN®

STONY MAN™

NUCLEAR
NIGHTMARE

A GOLD EAGLE BOOK FROM
WORLDWIDE®

TORONTO • NEW YORK • LONDON
AMSTERDAM • PARIS • SYDNEY • HAMBURG
STOCKHOLM • ATHENS • TOKYO • MILAN
MADRID • WARSAW • BUDAPEST • AUCKLAND

First edition November 1995

ISBN 0-373-61903-0

Special thanks and acknowledgment to
Mike Linaker for his contribution to this work.

NUCLEAR NIGHTMARE

NUCLEAR
NIGHTMARE

PROLOGUE

Los Angeles, California

Orchard leaned forward from the rear seat of the car and prodded Burton on the shoulder.

"Don't lose her now," he snapped. "We've wasted too much time already."

"Easy for you to say," Burton replied. "Driving in this L.A. traffic is no easy trick."

"Yeah, I heard it all before," Orchard said. "Just quit beefin' and drive the damn car. For the money you're being paid, this tail should be a breeze."

Sitting beside Burton, the ponytailed Cribbins gave a soft chuckle. "Hey, don't upset him, or he'll quit and go home."

"I don't quit," Burton said, anger tinging his words.

"Sorry, mate," said Cribbins, the British member of the team. "Make a strategic withdrawal, I should have said."

Realizing he was being set up, Burton grinned.

"Hey, Orchard, what are we down for next?"

"Damned if I know," he answered. "Let's take things one at a time."

Ahead of them the station wagon they were tailing pulled out of the traffic and cruised into a gas station, pulling up beside a pump. Burton almost missed the entrance and had to turn the wheel hard. He rolled the Dodge to a stop next to a Coke machine and climbed out to feed coins into it. Returning to the car, he handed cans over to Orchard and Cribbins.

"She nearly lost you that time, buddy," Cribbins said between swallowing the chilled drink.

"Her time's coming," Burton grumbled, not attempting to conceal the malice in his tone.

"No funny business," Orchard warned. "You know our orders. Snatch them but don't hurt anyone."

"I wasn't thinking of hurting them," Burton grinned. "Not the girl, anyhow. I wouldn't hurt her."

Orchard tapped him on the arm. "Don't even think about it. Now cut the crap and let's get this show on the road."

They waited until the station wagon was gassed up and the woman had climbed back behind the wheel, then Burton eased the Dodge back into the traffic behind her.

"Where the hell are they going?" Cribbins asked.

Orchard, who had more patience and had been watching the freeway signs, said, "Knott's Berry Farm."

"You think?" Burton asked. He watched the signs now as the station wagon took the Beach Boulevard exit. "That's it. Knott's Berry Farm."

"If they get inside there, we'll waste all damn day," Cribbins said.

"So we don't let them get inside," Orchard said. "We take them before they leave the car."

"Oh, sure," Burton crowed. "How do we do that, for Christ's sake?"

"Like this," Orchard said as Burton slowed with the crawling traffic.

He eased open his door and slipped from the car. He walked casually along the sidewalk. The slow-moving traffic was easy to keep up with.

"What the hell is he doing?" Burton asked.

"Playing a blinder, son. Playing a blinder," Cribbins said, his lean features breaking into a wide grin.

Ahead of them Orchard had drawn level with the station wagon. Bending, he raised a hand as if greeting someone inside the car and, without haste, opened the front passenger door and slid in beside the driver.

"The son of a bitch," Burton breathed. "He did it. The mother went and did it."

"Just keep your eyes on that station wagon," Cribbins said.

His eyes flicked back and forth, checking the sidewalk in case anyone had seen Orchard's move. No one seemed to be taking any notice. Even so,

Cribbins maintained his watch until they had rolled another fifty yards along the street.

"Stay close," he said to Burton, who seemed to have calmed down now and was maintaining his position.

As ORCHARD PULLED the car door shut, leaning across the front seat with his left arm across the backrest, the tanned, attractive woman behind the wheel shot him a scared glance.

"Keep driving," Orchard said tautly.

His right hand slid under his sport coat and came out holding a Beretta 92-F. He held it low, aimed at the woman.

"You know what this is, so don't do anything stupid."

From the back of the station wagon the pretty teenage girl said, "Mom, what does he want?"

"Nothing to worry about, dear," the woman said. "Just do whatever he says. And that goes for you, Bobby."

The blond twelve-year-old boy slumped back in his seat, his expression one of disappointment.

"Good," Orchard said. "Now get us back on the freeway and head north. No breaking the speed limit. Keep it steady. You wouldn't want to be responsible for the death of some traffic cop, now, would you, Mrs. Hanson?"

Orchard received her full attention this time. The use of her name told her this was much more than just a simple robbery.

Stella Hanson was no fool. Nor was she under any illusions. She now knew that this had something to do with her husband, Walter Hanson, who did strictly classified work for the government.

She fought the desire to yell and draw attention. The moment she considered that, she dismissed it as both reckless and useless. All it would get her, and the kids, would be a bullet from the gun pointed at her.

For the moment all she could do was comply with the man's requests.

As they rolled along the ramp toward the freeway, Orchard glanced in the rearview mirror and saw that Burton was behind him. He leaned back, relaxing, pleased that the first phase of the operation had gone smoothly. Now all they had to do was drive to the house near Carmel and move to phase two.

They had been driving for almost an hour before anyone spoke, apart from Orchard to give directions.

The blond teenage girl, an image of her mother, suddenly said, "What are you going to do with us?"

Orchard turned to stare at her. Frightened as she was, the girl refused to look away.

"All I want you to do is send a message to your father. I need him to do something for me, and the only way I can convince him it's important is by letting him know I have you three under my protection. If he does what I ask, there'll be no trouble."

"What if he refuses?" Stella Hanson asked.

Orchard smiled a cold smile that matched the bleakness in his eyes.

"In that case he'll have the unpleasant task of identifying your bodies—that is, the parts they manage to find after I'm done with them."

CHAPTER ONE

Stony Man Farm, Virginia

Hal Brognola, his unlit cigar slowly being chewed into oblivion, slouched in his seat at the head of the big table in Stony Man's War Room. His gaze moved from man to man as his combat teams assembled for their briefing.

Able Team was already complete. Carl Lyons, the team's commander, lounged back in his seat, impatience shadowing his features. Lyons had little time for waiting. He was a get-up-and-go character who hated to be kept on ice. Sitting next to Lyons was Rosario Blancanales, the team fixer. His way with words and manipulation had earned him the title of Politician. But there were occasions when his sense of humor got the better of him. Especially now, when he sensed Lyons's growing irritation.

"Hey, Gadgets," he said, "you got any of those relaxing tablets on you?"

Hermann Schwarz, the third member of Able Team, glanced at his partner, frowning. Then he saw Blancanales's thumb indicating Lyons and guessed what he was up to.

"Left them in my other suit, Pol."

Blancanales shook his head. "Then let's hope we get out of here before he blows."

Lyons looked across at the grinning pair.

"Ho, ho, ho," he muttered. "Working with you two, it's surprising I'm still sane. Hal, how much longer? I need to take this pair out for their daily exercise."

As if in answer to Lyons's question, the door to the elevator slid open and David McCarter, followed by Calvin James, entered the room. Yakov Katzenelenbogen, Gary Manning and Rafael Encizo were already seated at the table, so Phoenix Force was now complete.

"Sorry to tear you guys away from whatever you were doing," Brognola grumbled.

"So you should be," McCarter snapped, dropping into a seat.

The British Phoenix commando wore a taut, grim expression. He looked distinctly unhappy, edgy. From the pocket of his baggy jacket he produced a can of Coca-Cola, which he placed on the table in front of him.

Without a word Brognola glanced at Katz.

"He's trying to quit smoking again," the Israeli explained.

The Fed nodded. "That's good." Inwardly he was thinking, God help anybody who gets in his way.

Reaching for the folder on the table, Brognola tapped it and brought the meeting to order.

"Okay, guys, I'll take this a step at a time."

Turning, Brognola touched a button in a small panel near the edge of the table, and one of the blank television screens on the wall flickered to life.

"I had Aaron set this up via his computer system and feed it through. I think you'll pick up the information easier from this."

Brognola used a hand control to advance the series of computer graphics.

"What we're looking at here is a layout of a proposed antimissile system that the U.S. is developing with the cooperation of NATO member nations. The system is designated as Theater High-Altitude Area Defense. Known for short as THAAD. Incoming missiles are spotted by satellite detectors and early-warning aircraft. Information is relayed down to mobile operations centers. The centers are linked to three sets of mobile missile launchers, which give the defense shield three strikes before a missile hits.

"The first strike can be ranged as far as a hundred miles out and as high as 120,000 feet. If that fails, the second upper-level launchers get their turn. If the missile gets through the initial defense shields, the third and final strike is left to the lower-level defenses. These are short-range missiles, with a twenty- to thirty-mile range and a ceiling of 30,000 feet. The whole system is linked to the operations center and takes its orders from there."

Brognola flicked the graphic displays back and forth as he explained the system, answering the questions fired at him by the Stony Man teams.

"Are these systems fully mobile?" Katz asked.

Brognola shook his head. "Not yet. But when they are, they'll have designated areas to cover. According to the technical people, they would be in constant contact with the early-warning planes and be able to monitor incoming data from the military satellites while on the move."

"How advanced is the system?" Blancanales asked. "I mean, how close to being operational?"

"I've had conflicting reports on that," Brognola said. "One guy I talked to said he was confident the THAAD systems could be put in the field right now. A more conservative view is that there's a lot of work to be done yet."

"Where does NATO come into this?" Gadgets asked.

"The concept is expensive to develop. Once the system is fully tested and proved, manufacture will become easier. The idea is to spread out the cost and the manufacturing bases. The combined NATO alliance will share everything. The systems will be identical.

"With the end of the Cold War and the breakup of the Soviet Bloc, there was an early feeling that the mass nuclear deterrent was no longer needed."

There was a low but blatant grunt of disapproval from across the table. It was followed by the hiss of released gas as David McCarter broke the seal on his can of Coke.

"You don't agree, David?" Brognola asked.

"Bloody right I don't," the cockney rebel exclaimed. "I'd be surprised if any of the others around this table did, either."

Carl Lyons leaned forward.

"Not very often do I agree with McCarter," he stated, "but this time I'm afraid I have to. The day I believe the Soviets have turned into nice guys is the day you can retire me."

"Come on, guys," Brognola said evenly. "The Russians aren't the only villains in the world."

"Look, Hal," McCarter said, "I'm not saying the whole damn country is full of bloody hard-liners. There are a lot of decent Russians who want the same thing as most Americans, Chinese and British—a quiet life, a chance to bring up their families in peace and to be left alone. On the other hand, there are enough of the other kind of nuts still on the loose who'd jump at the chance to start the Cold War again. Or even a hot one. Look at the state of Russian politics. Nationalism is rearing its ugly head again. The creepy buggers are hiding in the shadows, just waiting for the chance to take over."

"You might very well be right, David," Katz said. "But I believe we've strayed away from Hal's statement. How about giving him the chance to finish?"

McCarter snatched up his Coke and took a long swallow, muttering to himself about nicotine withdrawal and the problems of dealing with head-in-the-sand idiots.

"I'm as aware as anyone of the dangers coming out of Russia," Brognola continued. "But as I said, there are others we have to look out for. There are plenty of missiles in the hands of unfriendly governments, being supplied from a number of sources, such as the proliferation of hardware being sold by the North Koreans to Iran and Libya. The Koreans have been pushing sales of their No Dong ballistic missile pretty hard and successfully. It has a four-hundred-mile range. Intelligence sources have informed us that longer-range missiles will be marketed in the next year or so.

"The only good point at present is the fact that the North Koreans haven't managed nuclear capability yet. Their missiles are purely high explosive."

"Let's not forget biological warheads," Manning said.

"And sophisticated guidance systems," Schwarz added. "The way things are going, a missile can almost be dropped right into your bathroom window."

"You'll be safe, then, David," Calvin James murmured. "Not very often you use yours."

The Brit's scowl was an ugly expression to see.

Turning back to the television screen, Brognola brought up a series of photographs. He ran through them, putting names to faces and giving the details of their occupations.

At that moment Barbara Price entered the room. The beautiful woman, as intelligent as she was attractive, filled the role of mission controller perfectly. Her coolness in the middle of crisis situations had earned her the respect of the Stony Man combat teams. With a brief nod to the seated group, she sat beside Brognola, placing a pile of folders on the table.

"Hey, I recognize that guy," Encizo said, pointing to the stone-faced Asian who came on screen.

"Han Nor," Price said. "Talk has it lately that this man is the prime mover behind the North Korean sales of their missiles. Supposedly a roving ambassador for his country, intelligence has placed him in the company of Libyans and intermediaries for the Iranians. This is purely agency Intel. We don't have any hard proof yet, but the feeling is that Nor is the main man behind proposed missile sales for North Korea."

"You'll each receive hard copies of all the photographs with bios," Brognola said. "They all need checking out."

"I assume the reason we're here," Katz stated, "is that a threat of some kind exists. Is it directed at the THAAD development program?"

"Precisely," Brognola said. "What we have is a growing series of incidents that are becoming more than just irritants. With a massive cooperative effort such as this, there are bound to be interested parties who have negative feelings about it. They range from the antinuclear lobby to those agencies willing to carry out sabotage in various forms. Various security agencies, here and in Europe, have compiled details of the ongoing problems that have been hitting the THAAD project over the past few months. The consensus is that if the escalation continues at its present rate, the security of the entire development could be set back to an unacceptable degree.

"That situation cannot, and will not, be tolerated. My orders have come from the top, guys. The President is not prepared to sit back and allow this to happen. He wants it stopped, here and abroad. The THAAD system is too important to be jeopardized. Apart from the need and the cost, the system is an important link in retaining the cooperation and the confidence of our allies. We need them as much as they need us. Like it or not, we're all in this together."

"As usual," Price said, "we have arranged as much help as we can from foreign governments. Making them all aware that we have to stamp on these problems hard and fast provides you with a fairly wide brief to run your missions as you want to. But let's not forget it isn't too smart to step on too many toes."

She handed out the folders she had brought with her. Turning to the television screen, she brought up a particular image.

"Walter Hanson is a top-line cybernetics engineer. His particular genius lies in the development of the THAAD control and command systems. His work has been of vital importance to the project since its inception.

"He's employed by CyberPlus Industries and has an office at the company building in Silicon Valley, but he works mostly at home, where he has his own computer setup. He's so good at his work that CyberPlus was happy to allow him his freedom as long as he came up with the goods. This is the way he's always worked. If anyone tried to stop him, he'd up and quit. He's too important to the project to let that happen. Since the THAAD development, he's had around-the-clock protection at his house."

"But?" Lyons asked, glancing up from the file he was studying.

"During the past couple of weeks his work has begun to slip. Hanson has always delivered on time. Now his output has slowed. People have noticed errors creeping into his programming—the kind a beginner might make. The trouble is, if anyone challenges him, Hanson will likely quit. So his superiors have kept quiet about it and worked around the errors, in the hope it's just overwork and fatigue, something he'll get over. Obviously if it continues they'll have to do something drastic. The problem is, if Hanson is removed from the project, it would take months for anyone else to pick up on his calculations and program input."

"Do we have any indications as to why this has happened?" asked Gary Manning, the burly Phoenix Force explosives expert.

Brognola shook his head.

"As far as we're aware, nothing has changed. Outwardly, Hanson is behaving as he always has. But those he works with believe *something* has happened to affect his work."

"Maybe he's been bought off," Blancanales suggested. "It's happened before."

"We have to explore all angles," Price said. "That's your primary task, Able Team. See what's making Hanson act the way he is. All his background details are in the file."

"We can have his bank account checked," Lyons suggested. "See if he's been depositing money above his salary."

"If he is taking bribes, surely he'd have the sense to open a separate account," Calvin James said.

"Point taken," Brognola said.

"I guess so," Lyons accepted.

"If Hanson is deliberately sabotaging the project, I don't believe he's doing it for money," Blancanales offered.

"Why not?" Price asked.

"What I'm getting from his file doesn't go along with betraying his work for money. Hanson is already on a damn good salary. He owns two houses, three cars, a powerboat. And according to the file, his wife, Stella, is wealthy in her own right."

"Maybe he wants more," Encizo said.

Blancanales shook his head. "I really don't think so. The guy is no dollar freak. He's turned down two offers in the past year from big corporations. They were offering to triple his present salary. If the guy didn't want big bucks legit, why would he go for it dirty? It wouldn't make sense for someone with his track record."

"I'm inclined to agree with Pol," Brognola said. "There's something else behind Hanson's behavior. That's what I want you guys to check out."

Lyons stood, followed by Blancanales and Schwarz.

"We'll check in with the Bear," Lyons said. "See if he has anything to tell us about Hanson."

"Keep in touch, guys," Barbara Price said as Able Team filed out.

"So what do we handle?" Katz asked on behalf of Phoenix Force.

"There's an upcoming field trial of THAAD being run by a combined NATO force of military and civilians. The test is being held at a training ground in France. I want you there to keep an eye on things. As far as anyone is concerned, you're there as security for the U.S. contingent. Arrangements are already being made, so you'll be expected. Your contact will be Eric Talpern, a liaison officer attached to the CyberPlus technicians on-site. This will be the first full field trial of the THAAD system in Europe. The United States wants it to go well. There has been some resistance to the development and suggested deployment of the hardware. If the trial ends in disaster, it would give the detractors fuel for their next meeting.''

''So we keep our ears and eyes open in case someone tries any funny business?'' McCarter said.

Barbara Price handed out more files to the Phoenix team. ''That's about it,'' she said. ''If anything unusual occurs, put a lid on it. With a minimum of fuss, of course,'' she added.

''Easy to say,'' Encizo pointed out. ''Not always easy to do.''

''Understood and accepted,'' Brognola said. He glanced at Katz. ''At least *try* to keep from creating too many incidents.''

The Israeli smiled. ''Hal, you know as well as I do that we never go looking for trouble. But we have to put up some kind of resistance if the opposition starts to get rough.''

Price laid another folder in front of Katz. ''You'll find all your travel arrangements in there—passports and visas, identity cards, the relevant documents of authority. There's money, plus photographs and bios of personnel you'll contact. You leave tonight in a U.S. Air Force transport taking some equipment over for the trial. You'll be met at the other end by Eric Talpern.''

''Liaise as usual with Barbara,'' Brognola said. ''I'll be around if you need me.''

The big Fed pushed up from his seat, stretching his bulky frame as Phoenix Force trailed out of the War

Room. He crossed to pour himself a mug of coffee from the ever-present pot in the corner of the room.

"Barbara...?" he began.

She faced him, arms full of the paperwork she had collected from the table. Despite herself, she was unable to keep the concern out of her voice as she spoke.

"Nothing," she said. "We still haven't heard a thing from Striker. Forty-eight hours since he touched down in England, and all we've had is a call to say he'd arrived. Since then not a damn thing."

CHAPTER TWO

Silicon Valley, California

"The latest intel from The Farm has Walter Hanson at a symposium in San Jose. Some conference on the application of computer technology for the next century. Hanson is presenting one of the papers."

"Sounds enthralling," Schwarz remarked as he coasted the car in and out of the Santa Clara traffic.

Able Team had arrived in the area an hour earlier, courtesy of Stony Man's resident pilot, Jack Grimaldi. He had flown them in using one of the Sensitive Operation Group's aircraft, depositing them at a small airfield in Palo Alto, where they had picked up a waiting rental car.

Now they were on their way to CyberPlus Industries in Santa Clara to commence their investigation into Walter Hanson's off-line behavior.

"Hanson being away could work out for us," Blancanales said. "It allows us to talk to his associates without him being around."

Lyons grunted something in acknowledgment.

"What?" Blancanales asked, sensing Lyons's distance.

"If Hanson is deliberately sabotaging the work on THAAD, what's behind it? We've tossed out money. So what else makes a man try to wreck important government work?"

"Maybe he's gone over to the other side. Sold out his loyalty. Money wouldn't necessarily come into that kind of betrayal," Schwarz observed.

"Okay, that's one reason," Lyons accepted. "What about blackmail?"

"You figure he has something to hide?" Blancanales asked. "Like he's gay, or he likes to play the horses and he's up to his ears in debt?"

"It's happened before."

"Sure," Blancanales agreed. "But this guy has money enough to pay off his debts."

"Maybe he's into some kind of sex thing," Lyons suggested. "Young kids. Bondage. Group sex."

"Maybe he's on drugs," Schwarz threw in.

"Come on, guys, we could make lists all day and still not come up with Hanson's particular hang-up," Blancanales protested. "Let's ask some questions first and see what we get from that."

CYBERPLUS INDUSTRIES occupied a sprawling box-like structure with windows made from dark glass to hide whatever went on inside. Schwarz halted the car at the gate and got out to speak to the security guard. He produced the ID prepared for Able Team by Stony Man and gave the name of the man they were supposed to meet. The guard phoned through to the main building and confirmed Schwarz's credentials. After getting all three Able Team members to sign in, he gave them lapel badges and directed them to the main building. Schwarz parked in one of the visitor slots.

As Able Team climbed out of the car, a tall, spare man came out of the main building and crossed the parking lot to meet them. He was tanned and wore his dark hair in a close crop. Conservatively dressed, wearing a neat shirt and tie, he looked more like a business accountant than a computer designer.

"Saul Caplan," he said by way of introduction.

Carl Lyons took his outstretched hand.

"I'm Randall," he said, using his current cover name. "This is Martin." Blancanales nodded. "And Lester." Schwarz said hello.

"Let's go inside," Caplan said.

He led the way into the building and through the reception area. As the members of Able Team followed him along a brightly lit corridor, they looked through glass panels into an open-plan work area where over a dozen people were concentrating on monitor screens, fingers busy at keyboards. Caplan paused midway along and showed the team into a large, spacious office. There was a computer workstation adjacent to Caplan's large, cluttered desk. He gestured for them to pull up chairs and sit down.

"Anything I can get you before we start?" he asked.

Lyons shook his head. "Time's not on our side, Mr. Caplan, so I'd prefer to get straight down to business."

Caplan gathered his thoughts.

"I presume you're aware of the situation, and Walter's background?"

"Yes."

"Walter is a brilliant man. To say he's eccentric is not being fair to him. He has work methods that are a little out of the ordinary. But when you're dealing with the complexities of cybernetics, who can say what's normal and what isn't? What I'm trying to explain is that Walter produces the goods. There's no question about that. It's just that he likes to work the knots out in his own way. Nine to five is not a consideration where Walter is concerned."

"Fine," Lyons said sharply. "He's a nice guy and a genius. But right now he isn't producing the right kind of goodies. Am I reading things correctly?"

The manner of the interruption didn't faze Caplan. He smiled indulgently, almost as if he were tolerating Lyons simply because he had to.

"Discrepancies began to show up in Walter's work a few weeks ago. His figures would not correlate with the rest of the equations he had already set up in the mainframe."

"Did this interfere with the progress of the development?" Schwarz asked.

"Not immediately," Caplan explained. "Walter was always ahead of the project with his input. It meant that the rest of the team had his figures to fall back on as they moved through the computer layouts. So there was always a week or so lead time before they started to incorporate the latest data.''

"So how did you catch on?" Blancanales questioned.

"As the project head, one of my functions is to take Walter's input and break it down into workable sections for the groups involved. We have about six teams, each working on separate sections of the design. Walter would submit his data, and I would analyze it and split it into component parts, put it on disks for each section and eventually distribute those disks to the teams as they reached the end of a particular task.''

"So you were the one who noticed the discrepancies," Blancanales said.

Caplan nodded. "The points were small at first. I even let a few slip by because the figures had been manipulated to actually make sense. Until something didn't gel because, for whatever reason, Walter's calculations became too big to incorporate. That's when I started to backtrack. And found that his data just didn't make sense anymore.''

"How would this have affected the project?" Lyons asked impatiently.

"If the data had been fully integrated, it could have wiped out the progress of the past six months. It would have had a cumulative effect. The teams working from Walter's figures would have simply taken the information and added it to the system makeup. By the time we got to the production stage, we would have been developing something that simply would not have worked.''

"Did you speak to Hanson?"

"I was about to when your people contacted me from Washington. The timing was close. I was told to step back and not say anything until your people had a chance to check things out. Walter being away for a few days had given us all a breathing space. Look, I don't know what's going on, but if Walter has a problem, I want to help. He's not just an employee. Walter is a good friend.''

"Right now we don't know any more than you, Mr. Caplan," Lyons explained. "We only took the assignment yesterday.''

"I hope Walter hasn't done anything stupid," Caplan said.

"So do we," Schwarz said.

"He has too much to lose," Caplan said. "I don't mean his work. I'm worried for his family. He's devoted to them.''

"Perhaps we could talk to them," Blancanales said. "Try to find out if they've noticed anything strange in his behavior.''

Caplan shook his head. "Right now Stella Hanson and the two kids are vacationing in Los Angeles. Walter sent them off weeks ago because he knew he'd be tied up on the project during most of the summer. Stella and the kids are just touring around while school's out.''

Lyons glanced across at his partners. He didn't say anything, but they caught his interest in Caplan's words.

''What about the people Hanson works with?'' Schwarz asked. ''Any point in speaking to any of them?''

''You're welcome to talk to them,'' Caplan said, ''but I don't believe they could tell you anything more than I have. To be honest, he's had less contact with them over the past six months than with me. But feel free to talk to any of them.''

Lyons stood.

''We might come back after we've made a few other inquiries,'' he said. ''Thanks for your assistance.''

Caplan led them back along the corridor.

''Are all those people in there part of the THAAD project?'' Lyons asked, indicating the employees on the other side of the glass wall.

''Yes,'' Caplan said. ''That *is* the THAAD project.''

''Tell me something,'' Lyons said as they reached the far end of the corridor. ''Who's the girl at the third desk—the black-haired one?''

''Jennifer Sayato. Why do you ask?''

Lyons gave a grin. ''My type, I guess. She's very attractive.''

Caplan took a second look at the slim woman busy at her keyboard.

"I suppose she is."

"Well, thanks for your help, Mr. Caplan," Lyons said. "If we have to come back, I'll let you know in advance and we'll try not to interfere with your operations too much."

He led the way back through the reception area and walked directly to the car. His partners sensed the mood of urgency that Lyons was exhibiting. Once they were seated in the car, Lyons told Schwarz to start up and drive off.

"What the hell is going on?" Blancanales asked as Schwarz rolled the car out onto the highway.

"Find somewhere to park where we can see the parking lot," Lyons said.

Schwarz pulled the car over to the curb and cut the motor. He turned to stare at Lyons.

"What?" he demanded. "All that 'she's my type' crap. What did she do? Flash at you? Or was it something else we missed?"

"She watched us walk in. Took a really close interest in us. And she did the same on the way out. None of the others did. It just made me curious."

"So she likes to know everyone's business," Schwarz said. "Some people are like that."

Blancanales, sitting in the rear, leaned forward. "He's right, Gadgets. I noticed her watching us on the way out. Didn't pay that much attention to it. But she was taking a good look at us."

Lyons opened his door.

"I'm going to find a pay phone. Maybe the Bear can come up with some background on this Jennifer Sayato."

"Why are we waiting here?" Schwarz asked.

"It'll be lunchtime in a couple of hours. I'd be interested in seeing if Sayato takes a drive. It's a long shot but we need some kind of a break. If she does take off we can follow her. If she goes to her beautician, I'll give in gracefully. If she makes a connection, you guys are going to hate yourselves."

AT TWELVE-THIRTY two things happened to push Able Team's investigation into high gear.

Carl Lyons had left the parked rental car to make his follow-up call to Stony Man. Aaron Kurtzman had promised to have the information he required by then.

Lyons was returning to the car when he saw Blancanales leaning out the rear side window, gesturing for him to get a move on. As the Able Team commander slid in, Schwarz gunned the motor and cut across the highway, pushing his way into the traffic.

"See the red Porsche with the black soft top?" Schwarz said. "Our mark is driving it. She came out of the building like her skirt was on fire. I'd say she was in a hurry to get somewhere."

"Did you pick up anything from The Farm?" Blancanales asked.

"Jennifer Sayato is twenty-six years old. She attended UCLA, majoring in mathematics and technology, then went directly into computers. If she has any strong political views, she keeps them to herself. There's nothing outwardly to indicate what her convictions are— Never been openly involved with any extreme movements or spotted with anyone who might be considered a risk. She's clean, according to her records."

"Sounds too good to be true," Schwarz said. "Could be she's a lot smarter than she looks."

"Or dumber," Blancanales suggested.

"You don't get to drive a Porsche being dumb," Schwarz said.

"Okay, okay," Lyons snapped. Let's stay on her tail and quit the cross talk."

"Anything else you got to tell us simple grunts?" Blancanales asked.

"I've got Bear checking out the current status of Hanson's vacationing family," Lyons said. "Apart from all the things we talked about, what's the other way to get to someone?"

"Family," Schwarz said.

"Right. So I asked Bear to run a check on the Hansons. Most likely Stella Hanson is paying her way around California by credit card. If Bear can get a fix on her via her bank, we could trace her movements."

"Or lack of them if she's been snatched," Blancanales said.

"Smart thinking," Schwarz said.

They trailed the red Porsche for the next thirty minutes, until it pulled into the parking lot of a classy restaurant. Schwarz parked across the street and they watched Sayato hand over the car to the parking attendant. Without a backward glance she entered the restaurant.

"Who goes in to check what she's up to?" Lyons asked.

"It'll have to be me," Blancanales said.

"Why you?" Schwarz asked.

"Because I'm the only one dressed well enough to get inside a place like that."

Lyons frowned. "What's wrong with the way I dress?"

Blancanales didn't answer, but his silence was more telling than words. He climbed out of the car and crossed the street.

"Stay with the car," Lyons told Schwarz. "There's a pay phone up ahead. I'll call in and see if the Bear has anything new."

Schwarz nodded. He settled back in his seat and watched the restaurant.

Blancanales reappeared within five minutes. He strolled out of the restaurant with the air of a man who had all day to waste. He crossed the street and walked around the parked car. Opening the door, he climbed in and settled back in the rear seat.

Schwarz took the silence for as long as he could. He swiveled in the seat and leaned over to stare at Blancanales.

"Well?"

Blancanales nodded. "We were right," he said. "She's in there."

"Funny," Schwarz replied. "Now quit the clown act and tell me what you saw."

"The girl, plus her lunch partner."

"So she was meeting someone. Nothing criminal in that."

"I didn't tell you *who* she was meeting."

Schwarz glared at him. "Don't play hard to get, Pol."

"Her partner is none other than our principal player."

"Walter Hanson?"

"The same."

"He's supposed to be in San Jose." Schwarz smiled. "So Mr. Computer Whiz is playing around."

"They looked nice and cozy together. That might be an act for the public."

"Meaning?"

"I don't know," Blancanales said. "For all we know they might just be playing footsie with each other. Or maybe the girl is part of whatever has Hanson sending in bad homework."

"Here's Ironman," Schwarz said. "Let's hope he has something we can get out teeth into."

"So who's in there with her?" Lyons asked as he entered the car. "Walter Hanson?"

"Son of a bitch," Blancanales said tightly. "You knew all along, I suppose?"

Lyons shook his head. "Only a guess. But it might tie in with the info I just received from Aaron."

"About Hanson's family?"

"It looks like they might be missing."

"Another guess?"

"The Bear traced Stella Hanson's credit-card number. He tied that in to her bank account and went back over her transactions over the past few weeks. Caplan said she and the kids have been on vacation in the L.A. area recently. The transactions agree with that—hotel and restaurant bills, visits to Universal Studios, and the NBC center to see the taping of a comedy show. Same thing all around L.A. and Hollywood. They've been having one hell of a grand tour. Took in nearly every sight there is to see."

"I sense a *but* on its way," Blancanales said.

"The whole thing stopped just over two weeks back. Dead cutoff. No more transactions of any kind. It's like Stella Hanson and her kids just dropped out of sight—until two days ago. Someone started to make cash withdrawals."

"But you don't think it was Stella Hanson?"

Lyons glanced at Schwarz. "No, not after two weeks' complete silence—no hotel or motel stops, no more theme parks, no restaurants, no gas. Just cash withdrawals. All in the same area.''

''Where?'' Blancanales asked.

''Quite a stretch from L.A.,'' Lyons said. ''Carmel.''

''Hey, she's on the move again,'' Schwarz said.

Jennifer Sayato had emerged from the restaurant. She waited while her car was brought around front, then climbed in. She left with a squeal of tires, making a sharp turn that took her across town.

Schwarz put the rental car back into the stream of traffic and stayed three cars behind the bright red Porsche. It was an easy car to follow.

''She's not heading back to CyberPlus,'' Blancanales said.

''Let's see just where she is heading then,'' Schwarz said.

''Stony Man is doing a rundown on anything unusual that might have happened in the Carmel area over the past week,'' Lyons said. ''Just in case.''

The Porsche led them across town to a sprawling industrial area. Schwarz hung way back as they left the main highway and found they were on the quieter roads that wound in and out of the industrial area.

''She's pulling in,'' Lyons said, indicating where the Porsche had turned in through an open gateway.

Schwarz braked the car and the Able Team warriors sat and watched the Porsche cruise across the freight yard of what appeared to be a deserted factory unit.

"An interesting spot for a lunch break," Blancanales observed.

"She's out of sight," Lyons said. "Let's move in, Gadgets."

Schwarz drove along the road and in through the sagging gates of the site. A weathered sign hanging askew beside the entrance showed that the place was for sale. The state of the sign indicated it had been that way for a long time. Keeping close to the perimeter fence, Schwarz rolled the car up to the front of the main building and brought it to a stop.

"On foot from here," Lyons said as they climbed out.

They took a few moments to check their handguns and make sure the extra speed-loaders were in place.

With Lyons in the lead they moved to the corner of the building.

The Porsche was parked near the next building. The vehicle was empty.

"Cover me," Lyons said, and sprinted across the open space between the two buildings. He crouched in the shadow of the Porsche and waved for the others to join him. From there they broke clear and flattened themselves against the wall.

"Look," Blancanales said, pointing to a couple of cars parked farther along the building.

Lyons turned back to the single door that was the only access to the building in this section. He touched the door and it swung open.

"It's watch-your-backs time, guys," he whispered, then ducked inside, the barrel of the big Colt Python tracking ahead of him.

Blancanales and Schwarz crowded in behind him.

There was a narrow passage running ahead of them and a flight of wooden steps leading to the next floor. Footsteps sounded on the floor above their heads.

"That answers my next question," Schwarz said.

"I hate stairs in setups like this," Lyons grumbled.

They were all aware of the dangers associated with climbing confined stairs in threatening conditions. If the enemy caught them on the narrow flight, it could mean trouble.

Despite his misgivings, Lyons pushed his way to the front and went quickly up the stairs, the Python held two-handed. Blancanales went next, and Schwarz brought up the rear, keeping an eye on the stairs behind them.

The stairs came to an abrupt end, opening onto a large, bare expanse that looked like a production area. Now it was unoccupied except for a couple of computer stations, a few chairs and several people gathered around the equipment.

One of the people was Jennifer Sayato.

The group was engrossed in some task, bending over the monitor screens.

Lyons held up his left hand, cautioning his partners to slow down. He moved away from the stairs, allowing Blancanales and Schwarz to clear them. The trio spread apart, covering the group around the computer desks.

"Been a busy day for you, Miss Sayato," Lyons said.

The reaction from the group was instant, not totally unexpected, but surprising in its ferocity.

Most surprising of all was the fact that Jennifer Sayato led that response and hers was the most alarming reaction.

The pretty, dark-haired young woman, turning around at the sound of Lyons's voice, brought an Uzi with her. She opened fire as she completed her turn, and a spray of lethal slugs stitched the wall inches from where Lyons had been standing an instant before.

The Able Team commander, along with his partners, had dropped to the floor, so the volley of shots coming their way found nothing but empty air.

Two of the four men in the group also turned on Able Team with weapons identical to Sayato's.

Within the space of a few seconds the vast room echoed to the blast of gunfire. Apart from Sayato's initial burst, the shots came from the weapons of Able Team.

Lyons fired first, his closely spaced shots thundering loudly. A pair of slugs, hurled from the muzzle of the Python, caught the slender woman chest high. The impact of the slugs picked her up and threw her backward, into the figures still seated at the computer desk. Her frail form twisted violently, her brief scream of protest as her life was ripped from her lost within the crash of shots from Blancanales and Schwarz as they took out their respective targets.

Lyons, rising, saw one of the seated men reach for something on the desk beside him. The man kicked his chair back and turned. A heavy automatic pistol gleamed in his fist, and he started triggering it, laying down a senseless fusillade of shots that went everywhere.

The Python thundered once. The Magnum slug hit the wild-firing gunman in the head, tearing his skull apart and dumping him on the floor in a bloody sprawl.

The surviving man at the computer desk threw his hands in the air and stayed very still.

Blancanales and Schwarz covered him as they crossed the room.

Lyons checked out the sprawled bodies, first clearing their fallen weapons away from outstretched hands. All four were dead. Lyons stood over the crumpled form of Jennifer Sayato. The black hair was streaked across her face. In death she looked even younger than her years. But no longer pretty. Her features were fixed in a rigid grimace, eyes still wide open in shock. Blood had splashed up across one cheek and her blouse was soaked from the ugly wounds caused by the massive Magnum bullets.

"Now what the hell is this all about?" Lyons said loudly, wanting to move on from the ugliness of sudden death.

Schwarz was bending over one of the computers, peering at the screen.

"Looks like they're making copies of data disks," he said. He picked up a couple of disks. "These are marked CyberPlus."

"Where did you get them?" Lyons asked the lone survivor. "Who passed them to you?"

The young man glanced at his dead companions, then switched his gaze to the armed and grim trio who had taken life so easily. His thin face was already a bloodless mask, and his eyes showed the terror that was building inside him. His fear manifested itself as a dark stain that rapidly spread across the front of his wrinkled pants. Beneath his shirt, his chest rose and fell in trembling spasms.

"Please don't kill me," he begged, his voice breaking as he tried to force out the words. "Jesus, don't kill me."

"Then answer the question," Lyons snapped. "And don't give me any cause to hurt you."

"Jenny brought the disks. She got them from Hanson. Walter Hanson."

CHAPTER THREE

Bordeaux and Aquitaine Regions, France

A late-afternoon curtain of rain, drifting in from the Bay of Biscay, greeted Phoenix Force as they arrived in France in a U.S. Air Force transport. The plane trundled along the runway of the Aerodrome de Bordeaux Merignac, following the official vehicle to a remote corner that had been allocated to it.

Turning away from the window, David McCarter zipped up the collar of his leather jacket. His foul mood, brought about by his attempt to stop smoking, was not helped in the least by the sight of the rain.

"Only one thing I hate more than France is when it's bloody well raining in France," he declared. "Can't we go back?"

Katz pushed up out of his seat and picked up his flight bag with the hook of his prosthesis. As he passed McCarter's seat, he leaned over.

"No, we cannot go back, David. And don't try to kid me you want to."

McCarter scowled at the Phoenix commander. "How can you be so smart and still live to such an old age?"

The Israeli's laugh followed him along the aisle.

Turning into its appointed parking slot, the transport came to a gentle stop. Katz stood at the hatch and waited until the air crew opened it and dropped the steps. With the rest of his team close behind, Katz exited the aircraft and stepped onto French soil. The first thing he noticed was the chill in the breeze that was pushing the rain across the tarmac. The cluster of administration buildings in the distance showed through a soft haze.

A dark blue Citroën cruised in the direction of the parked transport, turning in a wide circle and drawing to a halt only yards from Katz. The rear door opened and a spare, middle-aged man with thinning sandy hair climbed out. He wore light brown corduroy trousers and a beige waterproof coat. Glasses with thick lenses made his pale eyes appear large, almost owllike, and when he moved, his actions were slow and deliberate.

Mr. Greenburg?'' the man asked, approaching Katz and taking his proffered hand. "Eric Talpern."

Katz nodded. "My companions. Mr. Browning." McCarter nodded brusquely. "Mr. Maple," at which Gary Manning inclined his head awkwardly. Katz indicated Rafael Encizo. "Mr. Lopez. And, finally, Mr. Ivory."

"Welcome to France, gentlemen. Sorry we couldn't have arranged some better weather." Talpern indicated the car. "Please. Make yourselves comfortable. It will take us just over an hour to reach the hotel. I'm sure you'll like it.''

"Is it warm and dry?" McCarter asked.

Talpern, his hand on the front-passenger door handle, glanced across at the Briton. "Very much so," he said.

"Good," McCarter growled ungraciously. "I like it already."

Phoenix Force's selection of luggage, which included aluminum weapons cases, was removed from the transport plane and deposited in the Citroën's trunk.

As they settled inside the spacious car, Talpern spoke to the driver in accomplished French. The Citroën rolled off across the tarmac.

"It won't take us long to clear you through customs," Talpern explained. "We have special dispensation for you—which isn't easy to get in France."

In fact, it took only twenty minutes for Phoenix Force to pass through French customs and get back to the car. They sat back as it cleared the airport gates and picked up speed on the road.

"How far have you been briefed on our operation?" Katz asked Talpern.

"On a need-to-know basis," Talpern admitted. "It was made clear to me that you have wide-ranging powers and I have to cooperate fully without asking too many questions."

"The nature of our work does make that necessary," Katz explained. "However, Mr. Talpern, we are not here to make life uncomfortable for anyone within the project.''

''Unless they're up to no good,'' McCarter said blatantly.

Katz glared at him and McCarter retreated back into his corner.

''Excuse Mr. Browning. He doesn't travel too well. Flying leaves him a little testy.''

Talpern glanced at McCarter, then back to Katz.

''Tell me if there's anything you need and I'll do what I can to arrange it.''

''Thanks,'' Katz said. He settled back in his seat. ''I presume you have been made aware of the THAAD situation.''

Talpern nodded. ''We all know about the problems that have been upsetting the project. To be honest, Mr. Greenburg, sabotage—in any shape or size—is something we can do without during this field trial. The system is pretty well on-line, but at early stages like this you have to check out every aspect of the hardware. This trial is supposed to benefit us in two ways. First, it will demonstrate THAAD's effectiveness. The technical crew will monitor its performance and record data for analysis. And the trial is also meant to give our European partners a reason for maintaining confidence in the project.''

''Quite a package for one day,'' Calvin James said.

''If we don't have any interference, I'm confident the trial will be a success,'' Talpern said. ''But if the system has been tampered with ..." He shrugged in conclusion.

"What security arrangements have been made?" Encizo asked.

"We have four U.S. Marines on loan to us. They are responsible for physically guarding the two sections of the system being tested—the mobile control unit and the actual missile launcher. The French would not accept responsibility for security. Their view is that they're doing us a favor letting us use the Legion's training area at Les Causses, so we have to look after the hardware ourselves."

"Typical French," McCarter grumbled. "Always want to benefit from a deal without having to commit themselves too deeply. And *we* go and build a bloody tunnel under the Channel to bring them closer. If that isn't nuts, I want to know what is!"

"Browning, I don't think this is the time for airing your grievances," Katz admonished, despite Talpern's faint smile. "What is the timetable for the trail?" he inquired.

"Tomorrow will be taken up by final equipment and system checks. If everything is found to be satisfactory, the actual trial will take place the following day. The U.S. Air Force will launch an unarmed missile that will be targeted on a point within the trial area. The launch will be from over two hundred miles away. Once the missile is airborne, THAAD will begin to radar search for it from both ground level and satellite detectors. The moment the missile is locked onto by THAAD, the defense system will take over. We have three chances to stop the incoming missile.''

''I presume safety factors have been introduced,'' Katz said.

Talpern nodded. ''The incoming missile, as I said, is unarmed. However, it will also be fitted with a destruct package so that if the test proves unsuccessful, it can be destroyed in midair by the Air Force. The destruct device has also been duplicated.''

''I'd like to have a look around tomorrow,'' Katz said. ''We don't intend to interfere with the actual test procedure, but in order to function correctly we will need access to all areas. In case of an emergency, we need to be able to operate without interference and without prior consultation.''

''I understand,'' Talpern said. ''I was given a thorough briefing on your operation techniques. As far as I'm concerned, you have my blessing. However, you may find our hosts are not so compliant. As well as the French representatives from the manufacturing companies involved, there are also a couple of junior ministers from the government who have their own security people with them. And there are a number of French military personnel, as well as Italian, British and American.''

''A mixed bag, by the sound of it,'' Calvin James said.

''How are they all getting along?'' Encizo asked.

"Good question," Talpern replied. "It's difficult to tell sometimes. The British and the Americans don't appear to be having any problems. But when the French and Italians come into the picture, you can feel the tension."

The drive through the Bordeaux Region was pleasant. Renowned for its wine, the area contained rolling pine forest, dotted with lakes, and many vineyards. Here and there were tiny villages. Ancient châteaus clung to wooded hills, reminding the passersby that little had changed in this sleepy corner of France.

Later they passed across into the Aquitaine Region, where the landscape remained virtually unchanged.

The rain had stopped by the time they reached the hotel. It was situated in a converted château, once occupied by French nobility. Standing in acres of its own grounds, with meandering flower gardens and wooded slopes, the monolithic building still looked the part.

The Citroën drew to a halt outside the main entrance, and Phoenix Force climbed out, claimed their luggage and followed Talpern inside. He led them to the reception desk and signed them in. Keys were passed over by the dark-haired French receptionist, who, for no apparent reason, kept catching McCarter's eye and smiling at him.

"Hey, man, I think you may have scored," James said as he trailed after the Briton.

"If you weren't black you'd be green with envy," McCarter replied, slinging his bag over his shoulder as he started up the stairs, the aluminum weapons case in his other hand.

James glanced back over his shoulder to where the receptionist was checking the message tray at the desk. He sighed, then turned back to stare at McCarter's lean, disheveled figure just ahead of him.

"A chick like that going for McCarter," he said to himself. "What waste."

YAKOV KATZENELENBOGEN, clad in his robe following a relaxing bath, stretched out on his bed and picked up the telephone. He asked for a line and dialed the international code and number that would link him to Stony Man. He listened to the distant sounds of the connection being made, passed from point to point via satellite links and scramblers. Finally an echoing voice asked for identification.

"Mr. Greenburg for Mr. Ash."

Hal Brognola came on after a short delay. His distorted voice was still recognizable.

"I take it you arrived safely?"

"Yes. We begin in the morning. I should be able to update you then."

"Any problems?"

"None so far."

"I'll talk to you tomorrow."

Katz replaced the receiver. At least now Brognola knew that Phoenix Force had arrived safely.

Katz stretched lazily. He glanced at his watch. He could rest for a while before dressing and going down to dinner.

He wondered how Able Team was doing.

And Mack Bolan.

Had they come across any resistance during the course of their own missions?

Or were they, like Phoenix Force, finding little to concern themselves with at the present moment, and using the precious time afforded them to its best advantage?

The lull before the storm?

Katz couldn't give an honest answer. But he could take an educated guess—which would have caused him to admit that he found the air of peaceful reserve nothing if not unsettling.

LEAVING THE BATHROOM of the suite he was sharing with David McCarter, Calvin James heard the Briton's grumbling tones. McCarter's mood was proving to be harder on his friends than on himself. It was evidence of the bond between the members of Phoenix Force that McCarter's companions could actually put up with his aggressiveness.

As he entered the bedroom, James saw that McCarter was slumped in one of the low armchairs, fiddling with the TV remote control, furiously switching from channel to channel and berating the French networks for not showing programs in English.

"I suppose they show French-speaking programs all the time in England?" James remarked casually.

McCarter threw him a look that could have killed.

"Of course they bloody well don't," he shot back. "But we're not in England. We're in France and they don't have any English-speaking channels."

James crossed to his bed and started to get dressed, trying to make some kind of sense out of McCarter's twisted logic. He gave up quickly.

"Hey, we're due downstairs in twenty minutes," he called to McCarter.

"All right, don't make a case out of it," McCarter snapped, switching off the TV. He flung the remote aside and stalked off to the bathroom, shutting the door with a crash.

Fifteen minutes later James tapped on the door.

"Hey, you okay?"

"I'm fine," McCarter yelled. "Go ahead. I'll be down in a while."

James slipped on his jacket, adjusted his tie and left the room.

He met Gary Manning and Rafael Encizo in the corridor. As the three of them made their way toward the stairs, Katz came out of his room.

"Where's David?" he asked.

"Still in the shower," James said. "I hope it's cooling him off. He isn't the best company at the moment."

"Sooner he gets back to smoking those damn Player's, the better for all of us," Manning said.

"Give him a chance," Encizo said. "It can't be easy."

James grinned. "For him or for us?" he asked.

McCarter was still under the shower, trying to ease away the headache that had been pounding away for the past couple of hours. The fierce jets of cold water struck his skull with enough force to make him gasp. In the background he could hear the tinny jangle of the telephone ringing in the bedroom. Only French phones rang with such a noisy jangle. He ignored the sound. It would be James or one of the others trying to get him to hurry up and join them. They could wait.

Some time later McCarter emerged from the bathroom, wearing the clean slacks and shirt he'd taken in with him.

He was giving his hair a final toweling as he wandered into the bedroom, so he didn't see the two men who were searching the room until he was almost on them.

The unwelcome visitors were dressed identically in dark pants and sweaters, and each man wore a ski mask.

As McCarter became aware of the interlopers and saw the open drawers and bags, he reacted with the instincts that had kept him alive so far.

The closest man threw a hurried glance in his partner's direction, as if to ask what he should do now.

McCarter didn't give him the chance to receive any instructions. Swinging the damp towel down from his head, McCarter spun it between his hands, then doubled it in his right fist. He swung the weighty towel clublike, slamming it directly into the face of the man before him.

The sodden cloth, made heavy by the twisting, caught the man across the bridge of the nose, breaking the delicate formation. Blood spurted from the nostrils, soaking through the ski mask, and the stunned man stepped back in pained surprise. Keeping up his attack, McCarter advanced on the intruder, slashing the towel back and forth across his face. Dazed and losing his coordination, the man backpedaled furiously.

Seeing his chance, McCarter freed one end of the towel and coiled it around the man's neck, catching the loose end as it came round. He pulled on the towel, hauling the man toward him. Without hesitation he delivered a ferocious head butt that dropped the man in his tracks.

A scurry of movement to his right made McCarter spin in that direction. It was the second man, launching himself at McCarter. There was a gleam of steel in the man's right hand.

A knife.

McCarter held until the final moment, then dropped to one knee. The onrushing man was unable to reverse his direction. He ran directly into the clenched fist that slammed up between his thighs and hammered his testicles. The pain made him gasp. He stumbled by McCarter, tears filling his eyes as pain speared out from his groin. He fought to overcome the agony, turning in haste to confront the man who had attacked him.

McCarter was upright again, closing in. He caught the intruder's knife wrist in a two-handed grip, then twisted. The moment he had the knife clear of his body, McCarter loosened his right hand and delivered a brutal elbow smash that connected with his adversary's throat. Any cry of pain the man might have given was silenced by the crippling effect of the blow. The knife slipped from weakened fingers and the man slumped to the floor, clutching his throat and making terrible choking sounds.

McCarter picked up the knife and quickly searched the two men. They had nothing in their pockets. He crossed to the phone and dialed reception.

"Typical French reaction," he said to no one in particular. "You make a simple remark about their bloody television service and they send someone in to kill you."

The receptionist answered the phone.

"This is Mr. Browning in 204. Would you get a message to Mr. Greenburg and party in the restaurant. Ask them to come up here as soon as possible. Tell them it's important."

"NOBODY CALLED YOU," Manning said.

"Must have been this pair then," McCarter said. "Checking to see if the room was empty."

"Are we accepting this as nothing more than a hotel burglary, or do we assume that it has something to do with our mission?" Katz asked.

"I go for the second option," McCarter said without hesitation.

"Why?" Katz asked.

"Burglars in hotels are cautious. They're aware of the risks—a place full of people, security, guests coming and going all the time. They prefer to pick their victims and watch them for a while, get to know their routines. That takes time. Let's face it. We've been in the damn place for only a couple of hours. And I wouldn't put us down as likely marks for a hit. Burglars go for the obvious targets—couples on vacation, with jewelry, checkbooks, credit cards, cameras. Not a lot of that in my luggage."

"He's right," Manning said. "This happened too fast to be burglars. It's like they were waiting for us to arrive."

"I think they were," McCarter said. "I believe they knew we were coming here and who we are."

"I agree," Katz said. "That means we're being observed."

"It also suggests," Encizo said, "that there must be something to Hal's suspicions about a possible threat to the THAAD field trial."

"Not the way I like to have matters confirmed," Katz remarked. He glanced toward the two men sprawled on the floor. "What do we do about this pair?"

"Leave them to me," McCarter suggested.

"I think you've done enough to them already," Katz pointed out. "I believe this is something we should let our liaison sort out."

"Talpern?" Encizo asked.

"Yes. Don't you trust him, Rafael?"

Encizo shrugged. "I'm not sure. Maybe I'm being overly cautious after what happened here."

"Talpern is one of the few who know why we're here," James said.

"Hold on," Manning said. "If Talpern was in with these guys, he would have started to worry when only four of us joined him for dinner. Calvin said that David would be joining us later. If you had men breaking into someone's room and then realized they might still be in that room, wouldn't you start to get jittery?"

"Not if I was a good poker player," James replied. "But I see your point."

"Just sling the buggers out of the window," McCarter muttered, and stalked off to complete his dressing.

"Rafael, go and bring Talpern up here," Katz said. "Don't tell him what happened. We'll allow him the benefit of the doubt and watch how he handles the situation."

ERIC TALPERN REGISTERED shock, followed by outrage, when he entered the room and was informed of the incident. He immediately got on the telephone and contacted one of the French security men attending the French minister. Within a half hour a group of local gendarmes arrived and took the two men away.

"They will be held in the local station until some members of the Gendarmerie Nationale arrive to question them," Talpern explained, once they were alone again.

"They come under the jurisdiction of the defense ministry, don't they?" Katz asked.

"That's correct," Talpern said. "Since we're involved in something that's tied in with the French military establishment, they're anxious to learn who these men are. The French can be extremely sensitive when it comes to anything that might cause problems for the military."

"I'm feeling sensitive over something," McCarter announced as he rejoined the group.

"What?" Manning asked.

"My bloody dinner," he said. "I'm so hungry I could eat a horse. Then again, being in France, I might just have to."

CHAPTER FOUR

Heathrow Air Terminal, England

Mack Bolan's plane touched down in early morning. As it eased along the runway Bolan gazed out of the window with renewed interest in his surroundings, wondering what this particular visit to the U.K. would bring. He had been here on numerous previous occasions and he was sure this wouldn't be the last. Britain had its share of troubles, along with the rest of the world, and big-time crime had managed to gain a grip on the country.

This time Bolan's mission was tied in with a Stony Man initiative that had come down from the White House itself—sanctioned by the President and relayed by Hal Brognola. The big Fed had caught up with the Executioner at the tail end of a stormy few days in France, the culmination of a Bolan blitz that had wound its way from San Francisco to Hong Kong and ended in Paris.

The mission outline had been described to Bolan in a few short but explicit sentences. His brief had been to check out a North Korean named Han Nor. According to Brognola, Nor was the guiding hand behind North Korean missile sales to regimes on less than friendly terms with the U.S. and her NATO allies. There were also suspicions that a series of incidents, aimed at the THAAD antimissile system, might be connected. Stony Man's commando groups, Able Team and Phoenix Force, were being assigned to the mission. Brognola was arranging to have them attend a briefing at the Farm in Virginia. Because of the time factor, the Fed had decided to contact Bolan in France and initiate his part of the mission.

"Striker, this could be dirty," Brognola had said. "All we know for sure is Nor is in England. British sources tell us he's supposed to be having some kind of meeting with negotiators for the Libyans and the Iranians. It's also possible there could be others there we need to know about. The Koreans are selling those damned missiles like popcorn."

"And if the THAAD system was made to look vulnerable or even unreliable, its full-scale production could be in doubt," Bolan said. "That would encourage Korea's customers."

"Precisely what we don't need. This system is intended to be high priority for defense needs in the U.S. and Europe for a good number of years, Striker. It has to be seen to be working for everyone's sake. If the President wants to push through the proposed funding, there has to be full success with the development and the ongoing field trials.

"We have to determine whether Han Nor is part of the interference with the development program, or if it's just a coincidence that his sales push is running hand in hand."

"Coincidences like that don't sound too convincing to me, Hal," Bolan replied. "If Nor could guarantee that the THAAD system wouldn't be around, it would help his sales pitch and leave us and Europe open to nuclear blackmail."

"Just what I'm thinking, Striker," Brognola had agreed. "A courier will drop off all the documentation you'll need before you fly out. A contact will be waiting for you at Heathrow, a member of the British team that's been monitoring Nor's travels within the U.K."

"How much do you know about the possible THAAD link?"

"You'll have to wing that, Striker. If they mention it, you can take it on board. Maybe all they have are their suspicions about Nor. Handle it the way you want."

BOLAN'S CONTACT turned out to be Clair Tomkins, a blond, blue-eyed woman in her mid-twenties. She was waiting for Bolan inside the terminal at Heathrow. After a hurried introduction, she saw him straight through customs and out to a car waiting in a no-parking zone. The car was a standard Ford on the outside, but as it eased away from the terminal building, Bolan picked up the throaty growl of its powerful, supercharged motor.

Tomkins glanced across at him, a smile curving her lovely mouth.

"It will do the business, Mr. Belasko," she said. "We don't like to advertise our presence if we can avoid it. Not until the last moment. I never understand why they turn the sirens on in the movies when they're closing in on the bad guy. You can hear them coming for miles."

Bolan leaned back in his seat, watching the deft way she handled the car in the rush of traffic.

"I don't get many chances to go to the movies," he said. "And the name is Mike."

"You come across like a busy man, Mike." She easily handled the familiarity of using his first name.

So much for the legendary British reserve, Bolan thought.

"You could say that," he answered.

"And a pretty important one, too, according to your influence."

"Oh?"

"My boss said I have to give you every assistance. Get you clearance for wherever you need to go and not get in your way."

Bolan gave a low chuckle. "I'll bet he loves me for that."

"I don't think I'd put it like that."

"Look, Clair, can I level with you?"

"Yes."

"The way I operate, I need my freedom. It's the nature of my work. Believe me when I say I don't want to upset anyone. I'm in your country and I need your help. The last thing I want to do is have you against me.''

''I suppose we're in the same boat. Our orders came from the top, and the way we read it, the original request came from *your* top man. When the bosses agree, we have to play ball.'' She glanced at him. ''Something like that.''

Bolan nodded. ''Something like that. In the end we're all after the same thing. Finding out what Han Nor is up to.''

Tomkins indicated the glove compartment. ''In there you'll find a file with all we have on Nor since he showed up in England this trip.''

Bolan took out the papers and scanned the information contained.

''This isn't the first time Nor has been to England?''

''No. He's showed up a number of times over the past six months. Previously we've kept him under observation. Nothing too heavy, though, because we had no tangible evidence to say he was up to anything except his government assignment.''

''So what tipped you off this time?''

''We received a standard item from your people, general information passed between Washington and London. Included in it was a mention of Nor. It hinted that he was now being closely watched because there was strong evidence he was secretly brokering missile sales for North Korea. Our watch did link him to the Libyans, through their negotiator Victor Suliman, and to the Iranians. And we found evidence that he was mixing with certain undesirables from the fringes of the mercenary business."

"And you let my people in Washington know?"

"Yes. As you said, Nor is of interest to both our countries. We passed the Intel back to your people and the result . . ."

"Was me," Bolan finished.

She nodded. "Something tells me there's more to your visit than just Nor. I have a feeling he's linked to something heavier. Don't ask me why I feel that way because I couldn't tell you."

Bolan's silence gave her the only answer she needed.

"Look, Mike, I'm not going to pry. You have your orders the same as I do. Mine say I give you what you need and provide backup. I promise I won't compromise your efforts."

Her open honesty impressed Bolan.

"If the time comes, I'll give you what I have," he said.

"Fair enough. Oh, by the way, there's a holdall behind your seat. It came in by a special flight an hour before you arrived. It was handed directly to me with instructions to pass it over when you turned up."

The zippered bag contained Bolan's blacksuit and boots, plus his Beretta 93-R and the big Desert Eagle. Brognola had said he would arrange for it to be delivered into Bolan's hands. He grabbed the bag and took out the Beretta's shoulder rig, slipped off his coat and shrugged into the harness. When he had it adjusted, he took out the 93-R, checked it was fully loaded and engaged the safety. He slipped the pistol into the holster and pulled on his coat again. A couple of spare clips went in an inside pocket.

"Do you feel safer now?" Tomkins asked.

Bolan smiled across at her.

"It's no good in the bottom of the holdall if I need it in a hurry," he said evenly.

She pondered for a moment. "Does that mean you tend to attract the kind of people who go around shooting at other people? Or do you know something I don't?"

"I'd say a little of both."

"Great," she said.

She pressed her foot to the floor, the souped-up engine of the Ford pushing them along the highway with increasing speed.

"So tell me about it, Mike Belasko. I'm interested in hearing what makes you tick."

London, England

MACK BOLAN EASED out of the comfortable armchair and crossed the room to refill his coffee cup. He paused by the table, pot in hand, as someone entered the room.

It was Inspector Jeff Rawson, the man in charge of the special unit Clair Tomkins was part of.

Rawson, a tall, fair-haired man in his mid-thirties, did not look the part. His tanned good looks and casual dress might have suggested an actor rather than the head of a covert police unit. But Rawson was no novice. His grasp of the operation and his insight into the workings of the terrorist subculture earned the man Bolan's respect.

Within minutes of Bolan's arrival at the safehouse, located on a leafy suburban street in the outer suburbs of London, Rawson was outlining the unit's current status.

"Despite the fact that we have fresh, fairly conclusive evidence that Han Nor is meeting with representatives of terrorist groups who operate out of Libya, I can't take any decisive action."

"Not without obtaining legal warrants and the like?" Bolan said.

"Precisely," Rawson admitted. "You've probably heard all this before, from your own agencies. There isn't much difference between the U.S.A. and the U.K. when it comes down to it. If we moved on this group without getting permission, all hell would break loose. The unit would be slapped with so many legal writs, I'd spend the rest of my career filling in forms."

"They set us up to investigate these people, then tie our hands the minute we show signs of getting anywhere," Tomkins said bitterly.

"My hands aren't tied," Bolan said. "My brief is that I can make a move if I decide it needs to be made. And I don't have to carry any slips of paper with me.''

"I wish I had your pull," Rawson said, smiling at Bolan to show he held no bitterness. "Look, Mike, I personally don't give a bloody damn whether you haul Han Nor in instead of me or my team. Just as long as he doesn't get away with what he's been doing—which is abusing his position here in England by selling his country's missiles to anyone who comes up with the cash.''

"Can't you get any response from government departments?" Bolan asked.

Rawson shook his head. "Every time I try, all I get is the runaround. I get pushed from one department to another until my head aches.''

"Doesn't that make you suspicious?''

Rawson paused, and sensing his reluctance to speak, Tomkins jumped in.

"I'll risk having my head chewed off, but, yes, it does make us suspicious. Jeff is too much of a diplomat to say it. We believe there may be someone on the inside who's blocking our attempts to have the matter taken further.''

Bolan glanced at Rawson. The man nodded.

"Clair's right. The feeling is that we're being used. But how the hell do we prove it? We don't know who might be blocking us, or whether there are more than one.''

"In that case, I'm surprised I've been given such easy access to you," Bolan said.

"Your ticket has White House and Downing Street stamped on it. If there is an inside man, he's going to have to move carefully until he knows just how strong your clout is."

"I'd watch my back if I were you," Tomkins suggested. "Letting you in was easy. They could afford to be generous. Now you're in the country, they can deal with you at their leisure."

"Don't get the wrong idea," Rawson said. "It must sound as if I see an armed man behind every bush. I'm just concerned because things appear to be moving at Nor's end. Our inside man has passed us the word that the meeting set for later this week has been moved up to this evening. That was just before we pulled him out."

"Any reason for that?"

"He had a feeling he might have been spotted by someone from the past. Nothing concrete, but I saw no reason to put him at risk."

"Looks as if I arrived at the opportune moment," Bolan said. "Do you mind if I run a soft probe? See if I can latch on to anything?"

"Be my guest," Rawson said. "What about backup? Or do you prefer to work alone?"

"Alone," Bolan said. "If things get hot, I only have myself to worry about. I just need transportation to get there."

"Clair can drive for you. She knows the area well and she can describe the layout. While you go in she can wait and pick you up later."

Bolan accepted the compromise. He didn't doubt that part of Rawson's strategy was to have one of his own people on the scene to maintain involvement for his unit. The man was probably frustrated as hell because the strictures of his operational brief left him shackled. He'd been unable to mount anything substantial against the group he'd been monitoring because of legalities and a possible block being applied by some high-ranking, faceless official in the pay of the enemy.

It wasn't the first time Bolan had been presented with such a situation, and it was unlikely to be the last. International deals of the kind Han Nor was suspected of being involved in ran into millions of dollars. And when that kind of finance was being transacted, there were palms to be greased, doors to be opened—or closed.

When large handouts were being offered, loyalty went out the window. Big money could make traitors out of the most patriotic. The lure of riches and a safe, easy life in some pleasant corner of the world had long been the bait to catch those with inherent weaknesses.

The worldwide proliferation of civil wars, international terrorism and political maneuvering still demanded to be fed. Under whichever guise a particular scenario presented itself, there was a common need for weapons of every shape and size— from handguns right up to ICBMs, and everything in between. And the arms industry was only too happy to oblige, creating and selling their machines of destruction, even after the downswing in the Cold War.

Man's capacity for bringing pain and suffering to himself had not diminished. Death came daily, in a dozen hot spots around the globe, as faction fought faction, tribe slaughtered tribe. Whether under the banner of religion or the soapbox clamor of politics, somewhere, every day, someone died furthering a cause, or trying to resist it. Man could not rid himself of the specter of war. No matter how many times the clichéd "never again" was spouted by some optimistic official, the grim shadow would fall over some remote spot, and suddenly the familiar images and sounds would return.

Bolan's presence in England was not directly due to an actual conflict. His mission was to determine the involvement of Han Nor in the sale of missiles to regimes opposed to the United States. And there was the added question of whether the North Korean intended to sabotage the antimissile system known as THAAD. As it was soon supposed to be part of the American defense system, any threat to THAAD would be opposed with total force.

Bolan's translation of Rawson's words told him that the sooner he got his mission under way, the better. If the opposition had brought forward a planned meeting, it suggested there was something on the move. If Han Nor was having his meeting this evening, Mack Bolan wanted to be there, too.

CHAPTER FIVE

County of Buckinghamshire, England

The house was located in the leafy quiet of the Buckinghamshire countryside, some twenty miles out of London. Tomkins pulled the car to the side of the road, braked and cut the engine.

"This is where they've been meeting on and off over the past week," she explained.

"Who exactly?"

"Nor. His minder. Then there's Marcus Glastonbury. He's an arranger. He fixed the house here for the meetings. There's also Suliman, whom I mentioned before. We've spotted some others who have been on our books for some time. Roy Jerome and Ben Skyler—both ex-cops, now free-lancing, from what we've learned, under contract to a man named Jack Holder. He used to be a Royal Marine commando. Now he's part of a group who hire out to the likes of Glastonbury. From what we've been able to put together, Holder is running the U.K. section of a wider organization commanded by an ex-U.S. Marine named Jordan Delacourt."

"How close have you got?" Bolan asked.

"No further than observation at this stage," Tomkins admitted. "If we want to go further, we need a warrant to make it legal." She banged her fist on the rim of the wheel. "By the time we have the paperwork processed, our friends in there could have everything signed and sealed and be on their way."

"In that case we can't hold off," Bolan said. "I don't have the time to wait."

Tomkins glanced at him, realizing the intention behind the American's words. He meant exactly what he said. During her briefing, before she had even met the man named Mike Belasko, she had picked up the tone in her superior's rundown concerning the newcomer.

Belasko, it seemed, came with considerable clout. His clearance had come down from the highest authority within the British administration. No question there. The American involvement hinged on the presence of Han Nor. They had as much concern as the British over Nor's involvement. The man they were sending—Belasko—was more than just an observer. He was there to become actively involved. Up until this moment, Clair Tomkins didn't know just how involved he might become.

"How up-to-date is your intelligence?"

"The last report we had was four hours ago."

Bolan checked his watch. "It'll be dark in under a half hour. Good time for me to do some snooping."

"What do you want me to do?"

"Find somewhere to park, then you'll wait for me. And keep the engine running, in case."

"In case of what?"

Bolan smiled.

"If it happens, you'll know."

Tomkins drove for a quarter mile, then reversed the car off the road, pushing it deep into the cover of the thick shrubbery and trees that lined the road.

Bolan shed his outer clothing, revealing his blacksuit underneath. Tomkins watched in silence as he slipped into the shoulder rig that held the Beretta 93-R.

"Do you make all your house calls dressed like that?"

Bolan finished checking the 93-R and pushed it back into the holster.

"You only make fatal mistakes once," he said by way of explanation.

Tomkins nodded, her expression reflective, and Bolan picked up on the mood that had descended over her.

"Something that still hurts?" he asked.

"Hurts like hell," she replied, her fingers gripping the rim of the wheel tightly as she stared out through the windshield.

"Who?" Bolan asked. "A colleague? Someone closer?"

"My partner. For two years we followed a bunch of terrorists using London as their base. When the time came to close the net, Kenny got overanxious. He started to think we'd lose them if we held off until backup showed. He was convinced the terrorists were going to break out. So he went in on his own. But they were waiting for him. Cut him down with automatic fire. By the time we went in they'd gone. Kenny's murder was just a distraction, pulling us in one direction while they went out by another. We didn't even see them, Mike. All we got to do was bury Kenny. You see, there'd been a leak. Someone had tipped the terrorists off about our raid."

"That was rough," Bolan said. "No way it can be made easier."

"Every time I think about it I realize what a waste it was. A bloody awful waste. Kenny was so damn good at his job. He had so much ahead of him."

"For what good it might do, Clair, we have to make sure we don't let this bunch slip away. It won't bring Kenny back, but it could even the score a little."

She glanced across at him, recognizing the dedication he carried within him, and some of the dark memories surrounding her dead partner seemed to melt away.

"I'll be here when you get back," she said.

BY THE TIME Bolan made the return trip to the house, darkness was already casting its mantle across the countryside. He was able to approach the perimeter wall through the dense woods and shrubbery that lay around the place, moving silently and swiftly through the lengthening shadows.

Crouching at the base of the high stone wall, Bolan checked out the area. On his way in he'd seen nothing to cause him concern. If there was any form of security, it was inside the wall, which was fine by him. Containment was the watchword. Bolan didn't want his presence to become too widely broadcast this early in the game.

He checked out the wall. It was constructed from large blocks of hewn stone, with ample room between the blocks for hand- and toeholds. Once he had determined he could scale the wall, Bolan went up the sheer face with considerable speed. Reaching the top, he examined the top layer of blocks in case someone had placed sensors there. The only thing he saw was the deep moss growing between the blocks.

He pulled himself onto the wide top and stretched himself flat while he scouted the interior.

There were more trees and shrubs between the wall and the house. From where he lay Bolan could see the massive bulk of the ancient building. It was typical of its type. Towers jutted out from the main walls at intervals, giving the place the appearance of a fortified castle, a monolith of weathered stone and leaded windows. It was from a different age, a time when the masses were subjugated by a minority who held the wealth and the power of the nation in their hands. While the poor starved and wallowed in disease and misery, the ruling class took what they deemed theirs by right and birth.

Bolan considered that for a moment. When it came down to it, he thought, not a great deal had really changed. There was still a lot of that kind of thing around in the world—which was one of the reasons why the Executioner was still in business.

Dropping down to the ground beyond the wall, Bolan crouched behind some bushes and worked out his route to the house. The grounds would offer him cover almost up to the building. The combination of trees and shrubs, flower beds and fountains, was ideal for concealment.

Pausing between each move, Bolan moved from his point of entry to within twenty feet of the house. He knelt on soft grass behind an ornate fountain, the water tinkling gently across worn stone, and checked out the house. Floodlights had clicked on some time ago, bathing the structure in stark brilliance.

That brightness illuminated the hard-faced men patrolling the building. Bolan counted two of them at the front. They were plainly on watch. Their starting point was the ornate main entrance, with its massive doors. From there they walked the length of the house in both directions. Unhurried, almost leisurely, they were nonetheless guarding the place.

The patrolling guards didn't display a show of weapons, but Bolan didn't need physical proof to confirm his suspicions that they were carrying. The way they moved and carried themselves indicated these men were no ordinary servants of the house. Their very presence jarred with the faded gentility of the building. They wore the badge of their profession on their hard faces, in the cold gleam of their eyes and the arrogant step of their walk.

Bolan cut across the grass, intending to approach the house from the side, away from the hard glare of the lights. His progress was slow, dictated by his need to stay out of sight. His destination was the dark area at the side of the massive structure. No powerful lamps cast pools of light along there. Only the pale glow from the moon provided illumination, and that came and went as the clouds floated across the distant orb, plunging the area into deep shadow for long minutes.

It was during one of those dark periods that Bolan made his final dash across the grass and then pushed tight up against the cold granite blocks.

Easing the 93-R from its leather, Bolan put the selector to single shot.

He moved quickly along the outer wall, seeking a way inside the house. He found it in the shape of a narrow side door that opened into a room stacked with surplus furniture. Threading his way between the piles of chairs and tables, Bolan reached the far side, where another door showed a strip of subdued light along the bottom edge. He checked the handle and found the door was unsecured.

The warrior edged the door open a fraction so he could check out whatever lay beyond. It was a stone-flagged passage that ran in either direction. Only a dim bulb, dangling from a twisted cable, gave light. Slipping out of the storeroom, Bolan padded silently along the passage, the Beretta tracking ahead of him. The passage wound for a hundred feet or so until Bolan reached a flight of stone steps. The pervading chill of the place suggested he was below ground level.

Bolan climbed the steps and found his way barred by another door. He tried the heavy oak knob, turning it gently. It was stiff from little use, but it yielded to his firm grip and turned with a soft creak.

The door pushed back against Bolan's hand as it freed from the catch. He eased it open a little, giving himself enough space so he could see what lay beyond. What he saw was another room that was used to store items. These, however, were more suited to the everyday requirements of the house—cleaning equipment of every shape and size, ranged against the walls and stored on shelves. The room smelled of wax polish and soap.

The room allowed access to more stairs. Wooden this time and mellowed smooth with age and use, they led Bolan to a paneled corridor hung with oil paintings and heraldic coats of arms painted on replicas of medieval shields.

In the distance Bolan could hear voices. He cleared the door and hugged the wall, moving toward the speakers. Reaching the end of the corridor, he saw that he was looking out across the entrance hall. On the far side, to his right, were the huge oaken front doors. To his left a wide staircase rose to the upper floors. From the ceiling in the center of the hall, a great chandelier, glittering with fine spun glass and polished metal, cast its light across the area.

The conversation came from three men standing together at the foot of the stairs. They were neatly dressed in dark suits, white shirts and ties. At first they might have been mistaken for businessmen. The illusion was swiftly shattered as one turned slightly, hand brushing against his jacket to reveal a holstered autopistol on his left hip. Unconsciously the man eased the holster into a more comfortable position as he listened to the main speaker.

He was tall and lean, his face tanned, his brown hair cut short. He spoke quickly, his sentences short and clipped. His manner and bearing marked him as a military man. Still speaking, he glanced at his watch, then gestured brusquely to the others. It was a dismissive action, and the others turned and separated. They took up positions, one at the foot of the stairs, the other outside the double doors of a room across the hall.

Bolan checked back along the corridor. Though he was in a good position to monitor the comings and goings in the hall, his back was vulnerable. He could only stay and see who showed by putting himself at risk. But every probe he made into enemy territory was risky to a greater or lesser degree. There was no way to gain the information he'd come for without placing himself in a potential firing line. Not for the first time, he reminded himself. His life seemed to be a permanent cycle of risk-taking missions and life or death confrontations.

Movement at the top of the stairs caught his attention. Bolan picked out the figures moving in a loose group, beginning their descent.

He immediately picked out the squat, broad figure of Han Nor. The North Korean, though short in stature, compensated by having a forceful personality. His strong tones rose above the rest, his precise English almost drowning out the words of his companions.

Close to the Korean was his personal bodyguard. Another Korean, but this time of completely different stature. He wore dark slacks and a white short-sleeve shirt. Beneath the light cotton, his arms bulged with hard muscle and his powerful chest put the shirt under considerable strain. His head, set on a short neck, was completely shaven, adding to his air of menace.

Alongside Han Nor was a slight figure with black hair and dark skin. He was clad in an expensive suit that could only have come from one of London's exclusive tailoring establishments. Bolan knew him by name and reputation: Victor Suliman, negotiator for the Libyans. An international playboy on the surface, he was a shrewd businessman and had widespread connections within the global network of arms dealers. There was suspicion that Suliman also had contacts and protection within government circles and security agencies. It might have been why he seemed invulnerable. There was no doubt that he got away with a great deal, moving from country to country with impunity.

Bolan watched the group as they reached the bottom of the stairs and turned towards the guarded room. The doors were opened by the armed man. From his vantage point Bolan got only a quick impression of a softly lit, expensively furnished room.

A tall, fair-haired man stepped into view and ushered the group inside. The doors were closed, denying Bolan any further insight into whatever was going on. Despite that, Bolan accepted that he had enough to justify his presence.

Han Nor, in the company of Victor Suliman spoke volumes, confirming that the suspicions were no longer vague possibilities.

But did the partnership between the buyer and seller naturally involve them in the conspiracy directed at the THAAD project?

Bolan had his own opinion on that score, but he needed something harder than gut feeling.

Which meant a closer look at Nor and Suliman.

The creaking floorboard might have gone unnoticed by someone with less experience than Mack Bolan. Too many years surviving in the war zone had honed his senses to the limit. And part of him was on the alert for any distraction.

The creak was not repeated, but it made no difference. Already warned, Bolan reacted without thought. Turning and lowering his profile, he came around fast, the Beretta leading.

He registered the bulk of a figure towering above him. The man was partway through his move to strike Bolan with the barrel of the large autopistol in his right hand. Stretched up on his toes, the man was gathering himself for the downward strike when Bolan lunged forward, hammering the point of his shoulder into the guy's lower stomach. Bolan drove hard, putting all his energy into the blow, knowing that he might only have the chance for a single hit.

The target grunted as Bolan connected. He staggered back, sucking in breath through pursed lips. His right arm completed its strike, meeting only empty air as Bolan ducked low and crashed into the guy at knee level. The man fell back, trying to regain his balance. Bolan didn't give him the opportunity. He tensed his leg muscles and shoved upright, bringing up his left fist and slamming it under the hardman's exposed jaw.

The force of the blow snapped the guy's head back, teeth coming together with splintering impact. He leaned back against the wall, blood dribbling from his mouth, eyes out of focus. Bolan snatched the gun from his hand, then swept his legs from underneath him. He fell hard.

Bolan took a quick look around the edge of the wall and saw the armed guard by the stairs looking in the direction of the corridor. The man reached under his coat for his handgun, calling for his companion to stay at his post, before turning and heading directly for Bolan's position.

The soft probe was over.

If Bolan wanted to survive, his only course now was to backtrack and get out of the house as quickly as possible.

CHAPTER SIX

Bolan reached the door to the storeroom, his left hand reaching out to push it open.

He felt the door give and ducked through the opening. Behind him came the subdued chug of a suppressed gunshot. The slug took a large splinter out of the frame inches from his head. Something scraped across his left cheek, drawing blood. Then he was through the door and crossing the room, heading for the far door that would take him to comparative safety in the outer room.

Raised voices reached his ears, accompanied by the thump of running feet.

Bolan hit the door with his shoulder. It flew open and revealed a dark room in the subbasement.

A handgun fired out of the gloom. Bolan felt the slug cut the air and plow into the wall behind him.

He aimed the Beretta at the source of the sound, triggering twice, distancing his shots. A man drew a pained breath. Footsteps scraped across the floor as Bolan raced forward, clearing the steps in long strides.

He made out the swaying shape before him and swung at it with the heavy autopistol in his left hand.

It crunched against flesh, producing a grunt of pain. Bolan collided with the hurt man, sending him spinning. The dark figure bumped into a stack of furniture. Behind Bolan, unseen objects crashed to the floor.

He saw that the outside door was open. Black shapes filled it, light bouncing off the cold metal of weapons.

"It's Belasko," someone said. "Hc's been inside the house. Stop him."

The significance hit Bolan the moment the words registered.

They knew who he was, that he represented a threat to them.

And they were concerned that he had been inside and may have witnessed— What?

Noises behind him told him that pursuit still threatened from that quarter.

He kept moving forward. It was his only way out.

The figures were still crowding the open doorway. Bolan raised the borrowed handgun and began to trigger it, placing shot after shot into the dark figures. They fell back. At least one of them struck the floor, twisting and squirming.

Bolan went through the door at full tilt, taking the ones waiting completely by surprise. He wielded a gun in each hand, laying down a blistering volley that scattered the group. At least one more of his enemies went down, crying out that he had been hit.

Clearing the side of the house, the Executioner made for the lawn and shelter of the shrubbery and trees. The seconds were slipping away. The confusion he had created would last only a few seconds— long enough for him to reach cover, but certainly not enough to allow his escape.

As he pushed through the nearest growth of thick bushes, Bolan heard the soft sound of suppressed shots and the angry whip of the slugs as they chewed at the foliage.

Someone blundered into the deep shrubs off to Bolan's left. Turning, the Executioner watched the man as he pushed on, holding his SMG chest high.

Bringing up his borrowed autopistol, Bolan placed a single shot in the guy's head. The impact threw the target into the bushes, where he created enough noise for Bolan to break away in the opposite direction.

The autopistol's slide had locked open. Bolan tossed the empty weapon aside and kept on moving. His objective was the stone wall.

An armed man broke from the shadows ahead, lowered his autoweapon and opened fire. Bolan made a full-length dive across the grass, pushing the Beretta before him. His finger stroked the trigger, sending a 9 mm slug into the gunner's left upper thigh.

The impact made the gunner turn the SMG aside, and it stitched the trunk of a nearby tree. The cursing gunner felt his leg give way under him. As he sank awkwardly he saw Bolan's Beretta angle up to his chest. The single shot cored its way into his heart. The gunner toppled over on his back, wide eyes staring up into the night sky.

Rolling to his feet, Bolan dug in his heels and made his final dash for the perimeter wall. This time he reached it without being confronted by any other armed men.

Jamming the Beretta in its holster, he scaled the wall, ignoring the rough stone that scraped his skin. He hauled himself to the top and slid over the parapet, letting himself drop. He hit the soft grass and pushed to his feet. Without a backward glance Bolan set off along the dark country road, the 93-R in his fist.

He kept to the side of the road as much as possible, eyes and ears tuned for any pursuit. Even as Bolan paced himself for the return to Clair Tomkins and the waiting car, he picked up the sound of engines. He glanced over his shoulder and saw headlights probing the night. They were moving slowly, allowing the occupants to examine the sides of the road. He saw flashlights lancing into the dense thickets.

Ahead was only the soft black of night, paled by the moon and stars. The night was clear and fresh, a touch of moisture in the air, and Bolan anticipated rain before long.

He checked behind him again. The headlights were still there—motionless now as the flashlights deliberated over some dark spot.

He picked up the whooshing beat of rotors. The sound became louder, and Bolan spotted the heavy bulk of a helicopter following the course of the road just above treetop level. A navigation light pulsed on and off. The chopper paused, hovering some distance away, then cut off beyond the trees, heading away from the road.

Bolan checked his position. He was close now. The car, parked off the road, was no more than a couple hundred yards away.

Had Tomkins picked up the sound of the helicopter? If she had, would she have decided it was significant?

One of the prowling cars had moved closer, the sound of its engine becoming louder. Bolan pushed deeper into the shrubbery siding the road and stayed within the green shroud as he closed on the hidden car.

Tomkins was outside the vehicle, eyes cast skyward, searching. She became aware of his presence only as Bolan eased from the foliage and called her name.

"Let's go," he said, and the tone in his voice told her there was no time for asking questions. She slipped behind the wheel and started the car as Bolan climbed into the passenger seat.

She glanced at him, aware that he was concentrating. He opened his side window.

"Stop at the edge of the road," he instructed. "When I say go, you hit that gas pedal like there's no tomorrow. Don't bother about me. Just drive."

She nodded in understanding. Rolling the car gently forward, she braked when Bolan nodded.

"Leave the lights off."

He leaned out the passenger window, peering back the way he'd come. The pursuing car was still a distance away and had stopped again.

"Do it!" Bolan said.

Tomkins jammed her foot down and slipped the clutch. The Ford lurched forward, tires skidding for a few seconds, then gripping. The car shot forward and would have gone into the bushes on the opposite side of the road if it hadn't been for Tomkins's masterful handling. She slid the rear end around, bringing the vehicle on line, then let the souped-up engine really perform. The car built up speed with surprising swiftness, hurtling along the dark road at a reckless pace.

Twisting around in his seat, Bolan saw the prowl car accelerating.

"You know this area well?" Bolan asked.

"Oh, yes," Clair said. "Did a lot of my courting along these leafy lanes."

"Then lose that car behind us."

For the next ten minutes Bolan admired the lady's skill. She knew the narrow roads and back lanes of the Buckinghamshire countryside extremely well. She took the Ford along narrow tree-lined roads, back and forth until Bolan was totally lost. It was only when she finally brought them onto the main road, heading back to London, that she leaned forward and flicked on the lights.

"They're lost," she said, smiling at him from the shadows.

"Include me in that," Bolan said.

"Where to?" she asked.

"Back home."

She set the car along the open road, then leaned back.

"What happened, Mike?"

"For one thing, they knew I was coming."

"What?"

"Just as I was spotted, someone used my name. They'd been expecting me, but they hadn't anticipated my getting as far as I did."

"How far did you get?"

"Inside the house. Han Nor was there. And Suliman. That place has got armed guards coming out of the woodwork."

"Then we were right about it. Damn! We should have gone straight in and busted the whole bunch."

"And they would have been back on the streets within the hour," Bolan reminded her. "They would go straight undercover—stay out of your reach and carry on with whatever they were doing before you arrested them. You have to follow the book if you want to take these people off the register. Legal is the only way a police unit can go."

"You don't."

"I'm not a police officer. My rules are different. I see the problem and I go for it."

"But I can't, Mike. When I joined the force it was because I wanted to work for the law. To do that I had to take an oath to work within the boundaries set by the law. There are plenty of times I want to break out and go against the book, but I could never go against those rules."

"Police officers everywhere face that problem daily. The fact that they don't cut loose is to their credit, and I have respect for them all. But there's another level, where the people work beyond the law. They ignore every civilized rule, and the only way to handle them is on their terms. That's where I come in."

"Isn't there an American saying for that? 'Different strokes for different folks'?"

Bolan smiled at her. "You obviously had a wasted childhood, Officer Tomkins. Too much television and not enough fresh air."

BY THE TIME Tomkins slowed the car for the turn into the London street where the safehouse was situated, the rain had come. It sluiced down out of a clouded sky, glistening on rooftops and the black pavement of the streets.

As she straightened the Ford out of the turn, Bolan leaned forward to peer through the windshield, his face taut in the gloom.

"Mike, what is it?"

"Stop the car," Bolan said. "Pull over and kill the engine."

She did as he said, switching off the lights, too.

"What?"

"If they knew I was going to turn up at the house, maybe they know about this place, as well."

"But we've been here for over two months," she said. "Why haven't we been compromised before this?"

"Maybe it suited them to leave you alone."

"I don't understand."

"While your unit is operating, it keeps the opposition up-to-date on your progress. If there's someone watching your operation, they can counter any moves the police make. Shut you down and they might lose their pipeline. The next unit might be harder to keep watch on."

"Are you saying we have someone following every move we make? Passing information to the enemy?"

"It's happened before," Bolan said. "It can happen to any group. And I'm talking from experience now."

"But why the change now, tonight?"

"Maybe because their timetable has coincided with my appearance. They're close to a major deal and worried they're sailing too close to the edge. They heard that a loose cannon has been brought in, so they decide to strike first."

"So what do we do? If we can't go to the house, where can we go? Who do we trust?"

Tomkins realized that Bolan was not paying attention to her. He was watching the rearview mirror. He turned suddenly. She followed his gaze and saw a car edging into the street, slowly, lights dimmed.

"You might have lost them, but they still knew where we'd show up," Bolan said.

The young police officer reached for the ignition key. She brought the engine to life and dropped the Ford into gear. Spinning the wheel, she took the car away from the curb in a rubber-burning slide. The rear end rolled for a few seconds until she brought it back under control. Without hesitation she stamped on the gas pedal and the car leapt forward.

Bolan reached for the bag on the floor and pulled out the massive Desert Eagle. He worked the slide to lock in a round, checking the mirror again to estimate the distance of the pursuing car. It was closing fast.

They flashed by the safehouse, and another car joined the chase, rocking on its suspension as it shot out of a concealed driveway.

"Great," Tomkins muttered as she aimed the howling Ford between the rows of cars parked on either side of the street. Without warning she took a sharp right, the car skidding on the wet road. For once her skill was not quite enough to overcome the slide, and the Ford's rear clipped the side of a parked van. Without losing one second of composure, she eased through the gears, working the gas pedal to bring the car back on line. Then she hammered it to the floor again.

Ignoring the slanting rain, she pushed the car to the limit, cutting back and forth through side streets and intersections. Despite her excellent driving and maneuvering, the pursuit cars stayed on her tail. She angled across cross streets and brought them onto the Westway, barreling the Ford along the road in a spray of silver, passing every vehicle in sight.

"Why is there never a damn police car around when you need one?" she grumbled through taut lips. "And no radio in this thing!"

They swept down off the Westway, making their way to the Edgeware Road.

Behind them, one of the pursuit cars put on a burst of speed and closed on their rear. Moments later the Ford's rear window cracked and starred under the impact of a bullet.

Tomkins's shock swiftly changed to anger. Instead of accelerating away, she jammed on the brake. The Ford hung back and the pursuit car rammed the back end. She stamped down on the pedal, and the Ford drew away from the pursuit car, leaving it stalled in the middle of the road.

Bolan rolled in his seat as Tomkins once again took the Ford in a sweeping turn, cutting through side streets and at one point going through a red light.

For a while it seemed they might have ditched their pursuers, but as Tomkins eased the car into the light traffic along the Embankment, with the dark ribbon of the Thames on their right, Bolan picked up the familiar shape of the car that had originally followed them from the house in Buckinghamshire.

"I hate to say it, but that driver is bloody good," Tomkins said.

"I'm inclined to agree," Bolan said.

The continuing rain had emptied the streets of much of the traffic. That and the lateness of the hour gave Tomkins a fairly clear road ahead, as it did for the car chasing them.

They continued along, eventually coming to the dock road and the East End. A great deal of reclamation work had been carried out over the years in an attempt to clean up the deprived areas of the city. Tomkins coasted by the new structures, pushing deeper into the rougher areas, where she hoped to finally lose her pursuers, or at least give Bolan a chance to deal with them.

He had wanted to wait until they were away from the busy sections of the city, anxious to avoid any confrontations that might harm innocent civilians. Now, as the Ford rolled along narrow streets, where the lighting was dim and the buildings were largely deserted, he felt on home ground. Here, away from the noise and the activity of the city proper, he could face his pursuers.

"Priorities?" Tomkins asked.

"Staying alive," Bolan said. "And getting away from our shadows. Whatever it takes to do it," he added.

"I'm inclined to feel rather hostile toward them myself right now," she admitted.

"Ready to listen to a suggestion?"

"Yes."

"Somewhere along here you drop me off. You keep going and let me deal with our friends back there. Find a phone. Get in touch with someone you can trust and make them aware of what's going on."

"The only one I can trust right now is you, Belasko. Lord knows why I should. We only met a few hours ago. The crazy thing is I do."

"Let's do it, then."

Bolan checked the holstered Beretta. He kept the Desert Eagle in his right hand, his left on the door handle.

"Circle around, then slow down," he said. "Don't come to a stop, but keep moving. Don't pay any attention to anything going on back here."

She pushed on the pedal and the Ford surged forward. The lights of the following car faded briefly. She swung the car around the bend, hit the brake to slow it to a crawl and turned to wish Bolan good luck. All she saw was the passenger door swinging shut behind his dark figure. She put her foot down, and didn't look back.

BOLAN STRODE ACROSS the sidewalk and flattened against the wall as Tomkins gunned the Ford away. He saw its surviving taillight wink once, then fade.

His attention was caught by the approach of the pursuit car. It nosed around the bend, tires splashing through puddles at the curb.

The front passenger window was down. A man's head and shoulders leaned out. He was staring at the disappearing Ford. Bolan could see the autopistol clutched in one hand.

He leaned out from the wall and pumped a trio of .44-caliber slugs into the curbside tires. The car lurched and swerved away from him.

The gunner at the passenger window yelled something to his partners. Snapping up the handgun, he fired twice, the slugs plowing into the grimy brick wall above Bolan's head.

Bolan was already on the move. Crouching, his blacksuited figure blending in with the night shadows, he moved ahead of the slowing car, then turned and brought up the Desert Eagle two-fisted. He locked on to his target and stroked the big pistol's trigger. The slug caught one gunner between the eyes and whacked his head back against the doorframe. The stricken gunner flopped back, blood spraying from his shattered skull.

The car jerked to a full stop, doors bursting open to disgorge the other passengers. Bolan caught one of them as he emerged, pumping two slugs into his chest through the window of the rear door. The guy fell back, screaming, his chest shattered and bloody. He hung against the rear seat for a few frantic seconds, his fingers clutching the leather with as much desperation as he put into trying to stay alive. He failed on both counts, and as his fingers lost their grip, he slid facedown in the gutter, his lifeblood flowing away with the rainwater.

From the far side of the car someone opened up with a shotgun. It was a pump-action combat model, and the guy wielding it covered the whole area before him. His finger worked the trigger with frantic haste. Spent shell cases clattered and bounced on the ground around him.

It was only as the hammer fell on the last cartridge in the weapon that the guy realized he had been firing into thin air. His eyes had been caught by someone moving on his side of the car, almost on the other side of the street. He realized that the target had used the volley of shots to change his position.

The shotgunner swiveled his head and saw a spectral shape clad in deepest black. The tall, grim-faced man had a large pistol in his hands, and the shotgunner fancied he could see right down the muzzle in the split second before Bolan triggered the Desert Eagle and laid a bullet in his brain.

The shotgunner went over backward, almost like someone executing a back flip from a diving board. Only this time there was no water to break his fall, only the cold, wet, hard surface of the narrow street.

Bolan swept the Desert Eagle around in a tight arc, bringing the weapon to bear on the surviving member of the car's crew—the driver. He had been slower to react than his partners. Even so, Bolan didn't debate the point. The only thing that mattered was the stubby MAC-10 the driver brought into view from its hiding place under the dash. He leaned against the frame of the open door, the muzzle of the lethal subgun coming around to line up on Bolan.

As the Executioner registered the man's move, he snapped the Desert Eagle into position. The weapon bucked powerfully in his hand as he stroked the trigger. A single 240-grain projectile hammered into the driver's skull just above his left eye, burning its way through to emerge from the back of his head. The gunner's hand jerked the Ingram off to the side as he pitched over onto the wet street.

Bolan closed in on the stalled car and its lifeless passengers. He scanned the interior, with its blood-spattered seats. Leaning over the downed driver, he frisked the body, searching pockets for anything that might provide information. His fingers closed over a slim wallet and he pulled it out. He was about to repeat the operation on the others, but his ears picked up distant voices raised in alarm.

The gunfire had been heard. Bolan's eyes spotted a dark trench coat crumpled in the corner of the rear seat. He snatched it up and turned away from the death vehicle, slipping into the welcoming darkness of a narrow alley. He pulled on the coat as he moved, fastening the buttons and wrapping the belt around his waist, turning up the collar. He pushed the Desert Eagle into one of the spacious pockets, keeping his hand on the weapon.

The alley opened up on a dark square, with other narrow alleys leading off. Bolan cut through a gloomy arch, shoulders hunched against the cold rain.

Behind him he heard the distant sound of a police siren. From somewhere on the river a boat sounded its foghorn. The sounds only added to Bolan's isolation as he pushed into the maze of narrow streets, the empty buildings crowding in on him.

His mind was working overtime as he considered his next move.

Where could he go?

And who could he trust?

His only contact was separated from him. He didn't even know where to get hold of Clair Tomkins.

Bolan had knowledge, and the opposition would kill to contain it. At the present that information was doing little good, because while he was on the run he could not get it to the people who needed it most.

CHAPTER SEVEN

Palo Alto, California

"It's looking more and more like Hanson's family may have been kidnapped," Lyons said. "The only way to play this out is to leave him alone. The moment he realizes we know, he'll fall to pieces. That could come through when he talks to the people who have his family. If that happens, then they're no more use to the kidnappers and they get to be very dead, very quickly."

There was silence on the other end of the radio link. Lyons could visualize Hal Brognola chewing furiously on his cold cigar, pacing back and forth while he considered the options open to him and Able Team.

The team was back in the Stony Man aircraft in its parking slot at the airfield. In his mission update to Brognola, Lyons had spared no details and made no excuses. Surprisingly, Brognola made no adverse comments and even maintained his composure.

"How do you want to handle this?" Brognola asked.

"We should follow through with the information Bear gave us about the cash withdrawals in Carmel. I don't believe it was Stella Hanson who made those withdrawals."

"We have an update on that," Barbara Price said over the open link. "The Bear and his people have been chasing it down since we last spoke."

"Was I right?" Lyons asked impatiently, and showed no surprise when Price confirmed his earlier statement.

"There's a patient in the county hospital—name of Stanly Brock—the result of some back-alley fight. He took one hell of a beating. The local law thinks it was over some woman."

"How does it tie in with our investigation?" Lyons asked.

"I was coming to that," Brognola said. "When the cops checked his pockets they came across a couple of credit cards belonging to Stella Hanson."

Blancanales leaned forward. "What's this guy's background?"

"Small-time criminal. He's into burglary and stealing from cars. Picks pockets, as well. His speciality is using stolen credit cards to get hold of cash. Somewhere he'll have one of those electronic readers that can scan the user name from the strip on the back of the credit card. Once he has that he can go to any cash machine and milk it whenever he wants."

"But not kidnapping?" Lyons asked, picking up Blancanales's line of questioning.

"Way out of his league."

"Has anyone talked to him yet?"

"We're getting an update on his condition now. He was still under when the report reached us. Having a broken arm set."

"Looks like we get to make a hospital visit," Schwarz said. "Only this time, Pol, you get to carry the flowers."

"Be diplomatic, fellers," Brognola said.

"My middle name," Lyons said, unconvincingly.

County Hospital, Monterey Peninsula

THE SUPERVISOR on the ward was not happy with the visitors. Nor was she impressed with the ID that Carl Lyons flashed at her. She took her time scanning it.

"You realize this is not the place to carry out an interrogation," she warned frostily. "Federal agents or not, this is still a hospital."

"All we're going to do is talk to the guy," Blancanales said. "With luck we'll be gone in a half hour."

"Well, we can all hope, can't we," the supervisor remarked dryly.

They walked along the quiet corridor, making their way to the room where the patient was being kept under police supervision.

"We all going in, or what?" Blancanales asked.

"No," Lyons said. "Pol, you go talk to him. I want to check in with Stony Man."

Schwarz shrugged. "Maybe I'll go wash the damn car."

"I hate to see a grown man sulk," Lyons said.

Blancanales showed his ID to the uniformed cop at the door of Brock's room. Once the cop nodded, he entered.

Lyons, meanwhile, had spotted a pay phone farther along the corridor. He walked toward it, leaving Schwarz to hang around outside the room and chat with the cop.

Lyons punched in the number and waited for the connection. There was some whistling on the line that annoyed him, so he held the receiver away from his ear, turning to stare along the corridor.

Schwarz had his back to Lyons and was obviously involved in an animated discussion with the cop.

Beyond them the corridor was empty.

Turning in the opposite direction, Lyons saw two men approaching. They were talking together as they passed him, one of them glancing briefly in Lyons's direction before pulling his eyes away quickly.

As the pair moved away from him, Lyons eased around, studying the broad back of the guy who had avoided prolonged eye contact.

Something in the man's attitude bothered Lyons. He couldn't put his finger on it, but the guy's manner disturbed him. Maybe he was becoming paranoid, believing everyone was a possible threat. On the other hand, it wasn't a bad philosophy in his profession. As long as you didn't actually shoot the other guy before you were certain, there was no harm in being ultracautious.

Lyons slid his right hand inside his jacket, closing his fingers over the Python's butt, thumb touching the hammer as he eased it in the leather.

The two men were almost on Gadgets and the cop.

Lyons hung up the phone just as a voice on the other end asked his business.

Right now his business was here, in the hospital corridor, following his hunch that something was not quite right.

The shifty-eyed guy reached behind him with his right hand, slipping it under the flap of his sport coat. It reappeared a moment later, bringing with it a bulky autopistol. The guy's partner did exactly the same, each man moving in on a target.

The shifty guy homed in on Schwarz, the other on the cop, the pistols starting to come on target.

"Gadgets!"

Lyons's shouted warning filled the corridor.

Schwarz reacted instantly, dropping to a crouch and turning on his heel. His right elbow punched around with the impact of a piston, slamming into the shifty guy's side just over his ribs. Something cracked and the hardman gave a pained grunt. The pistol in his hand turned aside as he sagged away from Schwarz.

As the injured man stepped back, Schwarz rose to his full height, swiveling on his feet and delivering a crippling palm strike that came from below and connected with the underside of the target's jaw. The guy's teeth snapped together with enough impact to splinter some of them. His jawbone collapsed and his head was driven up and back. With blood spurting from his shattered jaw, the guy was shoved across the corridor and hit the far wall with stunning force. He slithered to the side and crashed facedown on the floor, the pistol bouncing from his hand. It spun across the shiny floor. The man on the floor was dead before the pistol stopped spinning.

During Schwarz's quick response, Carl Lyons tracked in on the second man. The Able Team leader saw that the guy had his gun leveled at the startled cop, who was desperately trying to free his own holstered weapon. Lyons realized instantly that he wasn't going to make it.

In the brief moment allowed for decision making, Lyons accepted that the only way to save the cop's life was to take out the attacker. His finger stroked the Python's trigger, and the weapon thundered loudly within the confines of the corridor. The heavy slug hammered into the gunman's skull, driving through and emerging from the far side in a burst of red. The dead man toppled sideways, colliding with the cop before he slumped to the floor.

Blancanales was now standing in the open door of the room, his pistol in his hand. He took in the dead man Lyons had shot and the motionless figure sprawled across the floor near the far wall.

"I can't leave you two on your own for a minute. What happened? They try to sell you hospital insurance?"

"They headed for the room, pulled guns and we handled them," Schwarz explained.

Raised voices were filling the corridor. Anxious faces peered at the men grouped around the bodies on the floor.

Above the general din, Lyons made out the strident voice of the supervisor they had clashed with earlier.

"I knew it!" she said when she reached them. "I allow you to visit in good faith and you start shooting up the patients."

Blancanales shook his head. "You got that wrong. They weren't patients."

"If it hadn't been for this pair, I'd be dead," the cop said.

The supervisor arched her brows and scowled at Able Team. "This isn't going to look good on paper."

Lyons turned to the cop. "Can you handle things out here for a while? We need to talk to Brock while this is still on his mind."

The cop nodded. "Go ahead."

Lyons pushed into the room, the others close behind.

On the room's single bed, bandaged and with a face every color of the rainbow, Stanly Brock surveyed Able Team with undisguised suspicion. Although he wasn't actually moving, it looked as if he was trying to back away from them and vanish through the wall.

"What the hell was all that about?" he demanded, eyes flickering back and forth between the three.

"The noise?" Lyons asked.

Brock stared at him as if Lyons was some kind of idiot. "Yeah, the noise!" he said through swollen lips. "Of course, the goddamn noise. And the shooting. What was it all about?"

"Seems a couple of buddies came by to discharge you," Blancanales explained.

"What buddies? I ain't got no buddies to bail me out. Who was out there? Huh?"

"When the cops get done we'll let you see their faces," Lyons said. "The way I see it, Stanly, you've upset someone bad enough that they want you dead. Those two out there had come looking for you. But they brought guns instead of flowers."

Brock was scared now. He stared around the room with the intensity of a caged monkey—frightened and angry all in one.

"I just don't get this," he wailed. "Why'd anyone want to kill me?"

Lyons, leaning against the wall, glanced at the man on the bed.

"You tell us."

"Stanly, I want to ask you a question," Blancanales said. "The answer could give us the reason why someone wants you dead."

"So ask."

"When the cops picked you up they found two credit cards in your pocket. You remember them?"

Brock thought for a moment. He was deciding whether answering was in his best interests. After a moment he looked at Blancanales.

"Yeah, I had the cards."

"Where did you get them?"

"This isn't my day," Brock said lightly. "First I get beat up on. Then someone tries to have me iced out. Now you guys want me to confess to stealing credit cards."

Lyons smiled. "Some guys have all the luck, Stanly."

"I believe whoever you took the cards from is the one who ordered you to be killed."

Brock's eyes widened. "Man, I heard of guys getting mad when they lose their cards. I never heard of one putting out a contract on that thief."

"Maybe it would be wise for you to talk to us, then, before they try again," Blancanales said.

Brock's eyes widened with alarm. "Look, guys, I'm no big-time player. I just deal in penny-ante stuff. I don't even carry a gun. That's out of my league."

"Well, it looks like you've stepped on the toes of some big-time honchos," Lyons stated. "Like it or not, you're in this up to your eyes."

Brock groaned. "So how do I get out of it?"

"You saying you took these cards from someone?"

"Yeah."

"Where?"

"Carmel. In the shopping center."

"Was he alone?"

"I...uh...no. He was with another guy. They were talking a streak. It was easy to do the lift. Then I was out of there."

"They must have made you," Lyons said, "then done some checking. Found out who you were. Getting yourself worked over and put in the hospital made it easy to trace you."

"Who are these guys?" Brock asked.

"Right now we'd like to know that ourselves,"
Schwarz told him. "Let's say we'd be happy if we
could ID them."

"You up to taking a walk?" Lyons asked.

Brock frowned. "Walk? Where to?"

"The corridor outside. Take a look at these two.
See if you recognize either of them."

"What if they . . . ?"

"They won't be bothering anyone ever again,"
Blancanales said.

They assisted Brock off the bed and escorted him
across the room. Lyons opened the door.

The bodies had already been covered with blan-
kets. Lyons had a quick word with the duty cop.
Then he turned and wagged a finger at Brock.

Pasty-faced and not too happy, Brock stared at
each face as it was uncovered. When the guy Schwarz
had taken out was exposed, the thief nodded quickly.

"He was with the guy I lifted the cards from.
Yeah, yeah, that's him."

His gaze traveled across the floor, picking up the
dark runnels of blood that had seeped out from beneath the blanket covering the man Lyons had shot.
Brock gave a low moan, his knees giving, and it took
the combined efforts of Blancanales and Schwarz to
keep him upright. They ushered him back inside the
room and onto the bed, just getting him settled when
the supervisor barged in.

"That's it," she stated. "I've had it with you people. Just get the hell out of here. There are two dead ones out there. You trying to make it three?"

"Thanks for your help, Stanly," Blancanales said. "Take it easy now."

In the corridor they were confronted by two plainclothes homicide detectives. Lyons went to meet them, producing his ID, and started to do some quick talking.

Blancanales turned to the uniformed cop.

"You okay?"

The cop nodded. "Thanks to you guys."

"Hey, no sweat. Glad we were here when it went down. They got any backup coming to help you?"

"Yeah, a few more uniforms. And we're going to move him as soon as we can."

A half hour and two telephone calls later, Able Team walked out of the hospital. They crossed the parking lot and climbed into the car. Lyons twisted around so he could see Blancanales who was in the back.

"One of the detectives I talked to is going to let me have copies of the morgue photos of those two when they're ready. They're going to see if they can ID them from the national computer files, as well."

"What do we do in the meantime?" Schwarz asked.

"Take a trip to Carmel. After the detective spoke to Hal, I got an update. The Bear came up with a possible location for us. He's been checking out recently rented property in the area. It seems likely our people might have taken a house off the beaten track, where they could hold Hanson's family. There are a fair number of houses around Carmel that are pretty isolated. Bear came up with five that have been rented out in the past three months. He's doing some more digging. But at least we have something to go on.''

Lyons started the car and took it out of the parking lot. He drove through town and picked up the coast highway that would take them to Carmel. He drove steadily, taking advantage of the bright weather and dry road. They reached the outskirts just before noon. Lyons pulled in at a gas station and went inside to buy a map of the area. He was in the office for ten minutes, and when he came out he was smiling.

''The guy inside marked all the places we want on the map,'' he said, passing it to Schwarz.

''The first one is about a mile along the highway, up a side road,'' Schwarz said.

The house was half-hidden by trees and bushes. Lyons parked on the side of the road. He took out the powerful binoculars stowed in the glove compartment and scanned the property.

''Anything?'' Blancanales asked.

''Only about a dozen kids, two dogs and a woman in shorts too small for her.''

"Not your average kidnappers."

"If they are, they're doing it in bulk," Lyons said as he started the car and swung it around.

During the next two hours they checked out three more of the houses, each time drawing a blank.

Just after two, they pulled into a roadside restaurant and took a coffee break. Lyons checked in with Stony Man. When he came back he shrugged as he sat down.

"Nothing yet," he said. "I checked with the detective, as well. He hasn't come up with anything, either."

Back on the road, they climbed the wooded hills above the town, looking for the fourth house on the map. It took them longer than expected. This one was pretty well hidden. It was accessible via a side road off the main side road. Before they reached the place Lyons rolled the car into the shadows and killed the engine.

"Something wrong?" Blancanales asked.

"I get the feeling this could be it," Lyons said. "All the others have been pretty accessible. Close to the main highway and easy to find. This one is well hidden. And a good distance from the highway."

"The man has a point," Schwarz said.

Lyons climbed out of the car and stood surveying the area.

"If I wanted somewhere isolated, this would be as good as anywhere," he said.

They checked their handguns, each man making certain he carried extra speed-loaders for the big Python revolvers.

"Let's check it out," Lyons said. "But take it easy. We've already seen how hard these guys play."

Before they exited the car, each man equipped himself with a small, neat transceiver. The compact communicators had a short range but would serve Able Team's immediate purpose.

They approached the house from three sides, moving in slowly and checking their surroundings with the caution of men who lived in a dangerous world and who respected how easy it was to make simple, fatal errors. Able Team had survived too many hazardous missions to allow a clumsy mistake to endanger them.

Carl Lyons reached the perimeter of the building first. He arrived just ahead of his partners by pure chance, not because he had hurried. Lyons might have been reckless sometimes, but he didn't carry a death wish. Crouching in the shadow of a thick stand of brush, he scanned the split-level house. Its design blended artfully with the landscape, so that from certain angles it was hard to see where house and foliage separated.

Taking his time, Lyons checked the house from end to end. He immediately picked up the front of a car poking out from behind the far corner. Closer examination showed movement behind a window at the rear of the house. There was a covered porch extending the width of the structure, and as Lyons watched, a figure stepped out through the door onto the porch. Lyons noticed the sleek Franchi SPAS combat shotgun cradled in the guy's arms as he lit a cigarette.

Lyons took out his transceiver and keyed the button.

"Ironman here," he said. "I'm at the far end of the house. Got a possible hostile spotted on the rear porch. He's carrying a Franchi SPAS shotgun. You don't hunt squirrels with one of those things."

"Thanks for the warning," Blancanales replied. "There's nothing at my end except a car parked close to the house."

"I'm clear here," Schwarz reported, then there was a pause, followed by a sudden eruption of movement, the sound carrying over the transceiver.

Lyons keyed his button.

"Gadgets?"

The only response was the sound of sharply drawn breath.

It was drowned out by the sudden and shocking crash of a shot, followed by two more.

Schwarz's transceiver fell silent, but the crackle of the shots could easily be heard as they broke the silence around the isolated house.

CHAPTER EIGHT

Lyons crashed through the lush shrubbery, ignoring the sting of branches slapping at his face. He tucked his head low on his shoulder, using his left hand to ward away obstructions. He heard more gunfire, the breaking of glass. His powerful legs pushed him on, covering the ground at an increasing pace, until he broke free and the house was before him, the parked car in view.

To his left he saw Schwarz down on one knee, his Python drooping in his right hand.

Yards away a sprawled and bloody figure testified to Hermann Schwarz's marksmanship. Close by the body was the SPAS shotgun.

"Gadgets?"

Lyons call broke the spell and Schwarz looked up. A furrow across his left temple was dripping blood, staining his shirt. He focused on Lyons.

"Second one went back in the house," he said. "Carrying a handgun. But he might have something bigger inside."

Blancanales appeared at the rear of the car.

Lyons held up his left hand, showing one finger.

"Inside the house," he said. "Cover the other side. We don't know how many more there might be, or what they're carrying."

Blancanales nodded and vanished.

"You okay?" Lyons asked.

"Just got the makings of one hell of a headache," Schwarz answered.

He pushed to his feet and crossed to the enemy he had downed. Picking up the shotgun, he waved Lyons on.

"I'll cover you from out here."

That was all Lyons needed to know. He ran for the corner of the house, away from the rear face, so that the building provided him with cover. Flat against the wall, he keyed his transceiver and called up Blancanales.

"I'm in position," Blancanales said. "Spotted movement at one window. That's all."

"Let's get this done," Lyons said. "I'm getting tired of being shot at so much lately."

"How's Gadgets?"

"Groggy but he'll survive. He's staying outside as backup."

"You call it, Ironman."

Lyons glanced back to where Schwarz was crouching with the big SPAS shotgun. As Lyons turned, Schwarz nodded in readiness.

"Go!" Lyons said into the transceiver.

He stayed low and ran for the porch. Going up the steps, he hit the door with his left shoulder and went into a shoulder roll across the kitchen floor. Crashing against the leg of a table, Lyons pulled himself to his feet as a shower of pots clattered to the floor. He made it upright, crossed the room and flattened against the wall to the left of the door.

Shots rang out and bullets tore large and ragged holes in the panels of the kitchen door. Splinters of wood flew across the kitchen.

From the far side of the house, glass shattered and a furious burst of shots sounded.

Carl Lyons braced himself, crouched and yanked open the kitchen door, hurling himself through.

He was met by a blast of gunfire that seemed to erupt no more than a few inches away, the noise deafening him.

BLANCANALES LAUNCHED a powerful kick at the front door, bursting it from the closed position. As the door swung inward the Able Team pro went through, ducking low and moving to the right.

The wide, low-ceilinged living room was occupied by two armed men, one of whom had his back to Blancanales as he pumped shots from an automatic pistol into the door leading to the kitchen.

The man closest to Blancanales was armed with an Ingram MAC-10, and the moment Blancanales appeared, the guy triggered the weapon. A stream of shots sizzled over Blancanales's head, shattering the window behind him.

Hitting the floor, Blancanales angled the Python's long barrel up at the autogunner and triggered the revolver twice, laying two .357 slugs in the guy's chest. The force knocked the dying man off his feet. He crashed to the floor, thrashing, blood pumping from the holes in his chest.

As Blancanales rose from the floor, the kitchen door burst open and Lyons came through, almost barreling into the guy stationed there. The man's gun went off almost in Lyons' face, and Blancanales swung up his Python and triggered a single shot into the back of the guy's skull. As the back of his head blew apart, the guy was slammed face first into wall. He slithered down, leaving a bloody smear, falling onto his stomach.

Pushing upright, Blancanales crossed the room to where Lyons was shaking his head. He glanced up as Blancanales appeared. Tears streamed from his eyes and he worked his jaw, trying to relieve the deafness brought about by the gunshots.

"A simple thanks would do," Blancanales remarked. "Don't get emotional on my behalf."

Lyons could still lip-read. He muttered something that even Blancanales could understand.

Blancanales called Schwarz in over his transceiver, then went to check out the rest of the house.

When he got back to the living room, Schwarz was sitting in a chair holding a wet towel to his head, and Lyons, who seemed to have recovered his hearing, was on the telephone. When Blancanales showed, he glanced at him.

"Nothing," Blancanales said. "The hostages were here, but they're not now. I'm guessing they moved them for security after the hospital shoot-out."

"You hear that?" Lyons asked into the phone. "We'll give the place a good going over before we move out, then give you a call so you can get the cleanup squad in."

He hung up.

"Find anything?" Lyons asked.

"All the bedrooms have been used. One looks like it could have been occupied by a couple of females. The others are definitely men's quarters."

"Anything left behind?" Schwarz asked.

"A few scraps. I haven't had time to go through them yet. First things first. You two okay?"

"Yeah," Lyons said. "Thanks, Pol, you pulled me out of a tight one there."

"No choice," Blancanales said. "Either that or break in a new partner."

Schwarz, despite his sore head, chuckled.

"Let's get this over with," Lyons said. "Pol, you head outside. Check out the car we saw parked by the house. And see if that guy Gadgets took down is carrying any ID. We'll take the inside."

Blancanales sighed. "Easy work for the walking wounded? Okay, I'll carry you guys, but just this once."

LYONS AND SCHWARZ were sorting through the collected debris when Blancanales reentered the living room.

"Area's clear," he announced. "There's been a couple of vehicles in and out. Tire tracks left behind, is all."

Lyons swept a hand across the objects laid out across the low table at which he and Schwarz were seated.

"Nothing here that's going to give us any help."

Blancanales gave a smug grin and produced a folded road map from his inside pocket.

"This was tucked behind one of the sun visors—an Oregon state map. There's a location ringed and some writing scribbled in the corner. I guess someone needed instructions to find the place."

He dropped the map on the table. Lyons took it and spread it out. Leaning over, Blancanales fingered the circled location.

"According to the note, it's a small ranch west of the Steens Mountains in Oregon. You have the Silvies River running between the ranch and the mountains."

"Sounds like cowboy country out there," Schwarz observed.

"Don't look at me," Lyons said.

"I've read a little about that part of the country," Blancanales said. "It's a big area, pretty empty. They run cattle and that's about all. Mountains and sage."

"A handy location to keep someone out of sight," Schwarz said.

"If this map belonged to the kidnappers, that is," Lyons pointed out.

"The car is a rental," Blancanales said. "The paperwork is in the glove compartment. It was rented a couple of weeks ago in Portland, Oregon. And every time a car is returned to a rental agency, they clean out anything left behind from the last person."

Lyons stood up, impatience showing on his face. He was becoming concerned because they didn't seem to be getting any closer to the kidnapped family of Walter Hanson, and with the recent events, the safety of the hostages could become a critical matter.

"Gadgets, bag up all the stuff we found. We'll get it shipped back to Stony Man. See if they can pick up anything. Same with the rental papers from the car."

"We going on another trip?" Blancanales asked.

Lyons nodded. "We'll call in Jack and he can fly us to Oregon. We'll give your ranch the once-over, Pol, just in case. We might get lucky and find something."

CHAPTER NINE

West of the Steens Mountains, Oregon

Jack Grimaldi set them down a mile from the ranch. He cut the power on the chopper and watched as Able Team pulled on their equipment, checking weapons and spare ammunition.

Lyons pulled out the transceiver and made sure it was fully functional before slipping it back in its pocket.

"Come in fast if you receive our signal, Jack," he said.

Grimaldi nodded. "I'll be there."

The trio moved away from the helicopter, cutting off slightly south. There was a ragged series of ridges breaking up the comparatively flat terrain, and Lyons had decided to use them for cover.

Grimaldi became aware of how quiet it was. He climbed out of the chopper and stood beside it. A faint breeze swept across the land, bringing the musky scent of sage. Grimaldi could feel the warmth of the sun on the back of his neck. He turned to stare at the hazy outline of the distant Steens Mountains, which crossed the horizon in a series of ragged peaks and troughs, vanishing in the far distance.

When Grimaldi scanned the direction in which Able Team had walked, he found he was unable to see them. They were already out of his sight. But they stayed on his mind.

"GIVE ME A CAR ANY DAY," Schwarz grumbled. He moved his Uzi, jerking the sling that hung it from his shoulder. "Who thought up this damn trek?"

"It was a group decision," Blancanales said lightly.

"Yeah? Well, next time we make a group decision, veto my opinion."

"Knock it off, you two," Lyons said. "It's like hiking with a pair of senior citizens."

"Who got out of bed on the wrong day?" Blancanales stage-whispered.

"I wonder," Schwarz said. "It's making him a little touchy, wouldn't you say?"

Lyons put on a burst of speed, his powerful legs carrying him away from Blancanales and Schwarz.

"Now you've done it," Schwarz accused.

Blancanales smiled.

They walked on, grateful that the sun was not too hot. Even so, the air held a cloying warmth that suggested the possibility of an imminent rainstorm. Heavy clouds were gathering over the distant high peaks.

When they had covered three quarters of a mile, Lyons waved them to a halt. Blancanales and Schwarz moved up behind him. Pulling a pair of powerful binoculars from his backpack, the Able Team commander bellied down on the ground and put the glasses to his eyes, scanning the terrain ahead.

"It's there," he said. "And it looks damn quiet. Not even a chicken running around in the yard."

"Any vehicles in sight?" Schwarz asked.

Lyons made another sweep.

"Nothing. If they are there, they'll most likely have any transportation in the barn."

He passed the binoculars across to Blancanales, who studied the place for a long time.

"There's nobody there," he said. "That place is deserted."

"You sound pretty sure," Lyons said.

"If our people were there, they'd be long gone by now."

"How do you figure?" Schwarz asked.

"Part feeling, part putting myself in their place. They've had a run of bad luck—they lose the computer copying setup, then their hit men are taken out when they try to ice the guy who picked up Stella Hanson's credit cards. If I was running the show, I would have done some quick thinking and quit the area fast. That's why the house at Carmel was clear. We just happened to run into the cleanup team."

Schwarz took the binoculars from Blancanales and had a look.

"I think he could be right," he said.

Lyons nodded. "Okay. But we still go in carefully, in case we're all wrong."

IT TOOK THEM OVER AN HOUR to reach the ranch. Up close the place looked even worse than from a distance. The main house and the outbuildings were all in need of repair. Weeds choked the yard, growing in abundance around the fence posts. Somewhere a loose door swung on dry hinges, making a soft, creaky sound that cut the warm air like a rusty saw blade. Occasional gusts of wind picked up dry dust and slapped it against the weathered boards of the buildings.

Able Team converged on the main house from three directions, closing in with silent precision.

Lyons covered the front, using every available piece of cover he could employ, and finally worked himself into a position where he could observe the entire front of the building.

At the rear Blancanales crouched behind an abandoned tractor and scanned the house. His keen eyes caught a flicker of movement in an upstairs window. He was steaming to full alert when he realized he was watching a curtain flapping from an open frame. He eased off, sinking back on his haunches, wondering how John Wayne had always made this kind of thing look so damned easy.

Hermann Schwarz was the last to reach his assigned position. Though his was the least tricky section to approach, he was forced to make a wide detour in order to reach it. Sweat trickled down his face as he wriggled the last few yards and sat with his back against the clapboard side of a small shed, a stack of worn tires hiding him from view.

Pulling his transceiver from his belt, he keyed the transmit button.

"In position," he said.

Lyons's response came through, followed by Blancanales's.

"I'm certain this place is deserted," Blancanales said.

"Let's do it by the book," Lyons said. "No point in anyone getting hurt."

They moved in on Lyons's command.

Entry to the house was made without resistance.

The interior, though showing signs of recent use, was silent and empty. Able Team made a thorough search from attic to basement.

Hot and dusty, they finally gathered in the kitchen.

Schwarz tossed a crumpled newspaper on the table. It was a week-old Los Angeles copy.

"Damn!" Lyons snapped. He snatched up the paper and stared at it. "All this way for nothing. We missed 'em again."

"I'll go call in Jack," Blancanales said, and left the kitchen.

"Time to make another sweep," Schwarz suggested. "We might find something."

Lyons shrugged, resignation on his taut face.

TWENTY MINUTES LATER Lyons and Schwarz were back in the kitchen. Their room-by-room search of the house had gained them nothing. They were preparing to leave when the door opened and Blancanales stepped inside.

His initial silence made them both look up, and the moment they saw the expression on his face they realized something serious had occurred.

"Pol?" Schwarz said.

"What's wrong?" Lyons asked.

"Outside," Blancanales said. "I found—"

He broke off and walked back outside, his partners following closely. Blancanales led them around to the back of the barn. Some distance from the building was an area that might once have been a vegetable garden. The rutted ground hadn't been touched for a long time and was sprinkled with weeds, except for a single patch that was clear.

Blancanales stood to one side so that Lyons and Schwarz could see what he had discovered. There was no need for words.

In the center of the plot was a wide oval of earth that had recently been created. Its surface was higher than the surrounding ground, and both Lyons and Schwarz saw why as soon as they focused their attention on it.

A human head lay exposed. The hair and skin was covered with clinging earth, and there was a dark, irregular hole in the back of the skull, the edges crusted with dark, dried blood.

Moving closer, Lyons circled the area and saw that Blancanales had scraped away more earth. He had partially unearthed three bodies.

All three had been killed in the same manner. A single gunshot to the back of the head. On one corpse the bullet had gone right through, emerging from the victim's face just below the right eye.

Lyons crouched near the bodies and saw where Blancanales had scraped away enough soil to reveal that all the victims had their arms pulled behind them and their wrists bound.

"The last time I saw anything like that was in Nam," Schwarz said, his voice tightening in his throat.

"The Vietcong used to do that to prisoners when they'd finished with them," Blancanales said. "And bury them in shallow graves so they wouldn't be hard to find. Serve as a warning to others."

"Who are they?" Schwarz asked. "The poor bastards."

Lyons glanced up as the sound of Grimaldi's chopper cut through the air.

"As soon as Jack touches down we'll get through to Stony Man and have Hal contact the local Feds and get some teams in here. They'll find out."

LATE AFTERNOON brought the rain that had been threatening all day. It swept down from the distant peaks, sheeting across the land in a silvery curtain, bouncing off the ranch buildings and drumming against the side of the helicopter.

Lyons was in contact with Stony Man again, and his impatience with the situation was wearing even thinner than earlier.

"I know the FBI has lost three field agents, Hal. We found them. Remember? Now these damned gray-suited assholes are jumping all over us."

"Cool down, Carl," Brognola soothed, understanding the man's impetuous nature. "I'm working it out as fast as I can. You know how these things go. It takes time."

"Sure, I know how it works. But these Ivy League graduates look at us like we're the bad guys. Hell, I'm even starting to feel guilty myself."

Blancanales nudged Lyons.

"Here comes Agent Croft," he said.

Lyons groaned.

The tall FBI man rapped on the hatch and Grimaldi slid it open. Croft, his suit protected by a waterproof coat, stared into the cabin from beneath the peak of his FBI cap.

"You going to make me stand out here in the rain, or what?"

"Call you back," Lyons said, and put down the handset. He turned to glare at Croft. "Depends what you want to say."

"How about thanks for what you did for our guys."

"I reckon that gets you an invite," Grimaldi said smoothly, reaching out a hand to haul the agent inside.

Croft sank into one of the side seats. He peeled off his cap and stroked a long hand across his balding head.

"I just got the word from my people in Washington. You check out just like you said."

Lyons might have made some comment if he hadn't caught Blancanales watching him very closely. He bit back.

"We lost contact with our guys about a week ago. They had been working this assignment for almost two months, trying to get the goods on a group of ex-military men who were suspected of hiring themselves out to clients looking for experienced people. We had a couple of tips, scattered information. This group was moving around a lot. Our intelligence was starting to gather background. Then we got the word that things were heating up. Whatever this group was into seemed to have moved up a notch.

"The last report we received suggested that the group might have some hostages. That was all we got. Our field agents were going to close in and try to pick up some hard information, then feed it back to us. They were somewhere in California then, around Fresno. Last thing we heard they were trailing the suspects upstate. Then they dropped out of sight. We heard nothing more until your call."

"We were working on the hostage angle," Lyons said. "Ours is part of a wider investigation. It involves national security so I can't—"

Croft held up his hand.

"I already got the word. It came down the wire like hot lead. I don't ask and you don't tell."

Lyons shrugged. "I don't make the rules, Croft, all I do is work by them."

"My department has been requested to furnish your people with whatever information we've gathered. It should be in your computer by now."

There was an awkward silence.

"The last thing we want is to upstage you guys," Schwarz said. "This isn't about scoring off each other. What happened to your agents, that was bad. They deserved better. A whole lot better."

Lyons cleared his throat. "When we catch up to this bunch..."

Croft nodded briefly. "Take them down," he said softly, then added, "You never heard that from me."

He then turned and slid open the hatch. Pulling on his cap, he stepped out into the rain. Schwarz slid the door shut and they watched the tall FBI agent tramping across the sodden ground, back to his own people and their continuing examination of the area.

"Let's go, flyboy," Lyons said.

Grimaldi started the chopper's engine.

"That was an okay guy," Schwarz said, settling in his seat.

Grimaldi increased the power.

"Yeah," Blancanales agreed, glancing across at Lyons.

"A nice guy," Lyons admitted, "for a Fed."

"Ironman, you're all heart." Schwarz grinned.

"Yeah," Blancanales said. "But only for a second."

Boosting the power, Grimaldi lifted off, and the ground dropped away under them. The Stony Man flier swung the chopper around, heading south. The ranch and the figures of the FBI team were lost in the rain mist, tiny specks on the vast Oregon prairie.

CHAPTER TEN

Stony Man Farm, Virginia

Aaron Kurtzman stared at the data on his screen and felt a swell of emotions—sorrow, anger, revulsion.

They all coursed through him, rising and falling as he read and reread the words filling his monitor screen.

Clenching his huge fists, he fought to control the churning in his stomach. Leaning forward, he rested his fingers on the edge of the keyboard.

"Listen up, people" he said, trying to keep his tone calm. "Clear your screens. I have to relay something for you to read. Then I want you to go back to what you were doing and get me the information I want. No excuses. No runarounds. I don't give a damn how you do it, but get me what we need."

When all the screens were clear, Kurtzman keyed in the instructions that would display the information on his monitor to each screen.

As the others read the data, a silence descended over the room. Only the subdued hum of the air conditioner intruded.

Kurtzman allowed his team a period of reflection before he broke the silence.

"We know who we're dealing with now. How they play. It's why we have to take them down."

"I knew Tom Barrymore," Carmen Delahunt said. The redhead was a former FBI agent, drafted by Hal Brognola onto the Stony Man team. "Right now the only thing I clearly recall is that we were always arguing over who should pay for meals when we were out on assignment. He used to say the man should pay. I insisted on fifty-fifty."

Kurtzman picked up a phone and spoke quietly to Brognola, then put down the receiver and keyed his machine to make a hard copy of the information. It was just coming off the printer as Brognola and Barbara Price entered the Computer Room.

"We've all read it," Kurtzman said, passing the sheet across.

The big Fed read the report and reread it. He took a deep breath and let it out softly. Handing the sheet to Price, he scrubbed a big hand across his face.

"The bastards," he said in a low but forceful voice.

"Why did they do that to them?" Akira Tokaido asked. For once the earphones to his portable CD player were dangling around his neck and his young face was serious. "I mean killing them is bad enough. But tying their hands behind them and shooting them in the back of the head. It was like an—"

"An execution," Barbara Price said. "That's exactly what it was, Akira. A ritual killing. It doesn't leave the victims any hope of escape. No chance to fight for their survival. Trussed up, shot, then buried in a shallow grave so they can be found. A warning to their adversaries: leave us alone or you could end up like this. It was done to shock, to deter pursuit."

"But it won't work," Brognola said. "Because we won't let it."

He turned and walked out.

"So let's do what the man says," Kurtzman concluded.

While the others settled to their particular tasks, Kurtzman looked back through what they had already done, trying to find the key that would provide a clear explanation. He sighed in frustration, annoyed at his own impatience. He should have learned that intelligence gathering was not an exact science. Nothing ever came easily. It was a hard grind, picking up snippets here and there, going over the material again and again until some small item, perhaps overlooked the first time around, dropped into place and the picture became whole.

It took almost two hours before Kurtzman heard the words he'd been listening for.

"I think this is it," Huntington Wethers announced.

Kurtzman wheeled across to look at his screen.

"I accessed the Interpol network and British SIS. Came up with this."

Kurtzman scanned the data as Hunt scrolled through the pages.

"Hold it," he said. "Go back to the bottom of the last page."

"What is it?"

"There," Kurtzman said, jabbing at the screen with a powerful finger. "That name has come up three times."

"Victor Suliman?"

"Suliman is a negotiator for the Libyans. One of the key men handling their weapons deals. Slippery son of a bitch, but not sharp enough to keep himself out of the headlines. He has an eye for the ladies and likes to gamble. Spends a lot of time hopping around Europe. Has contacts all over. London is almost his second home. He courts anyone who can help him get what he wants. And the scam is that lately he's been doing his best to work out deals for missiles."

"According to Interpol, Suliman was seen with Han Nor in Saint-Tropez, on the yacht he keeps moored there. That was less than a week ago."

"The file has some photographs. You want me to pull them up?"

"Yeah."

Wethers bent over his keyboard and interfaced with the Interpol file. Shortly the first image appeared on the screen. It was a shot taken with a telephoto lens and showed Suliman's yacht at its mooring in Saint-Tropez. Three figures could be seen on the sun deck at the stern of the vessel.

"Enhance that, Hunt. See if you can sharpen it up," Kurtzman said.

Wethers manipulated the image, sectioning off the three figures, and had the computer enlarge the isolated area. The three men were pulled into sharp focus.

"Han Nor. The other Korean is his bodyguard," Wethers said, tapping the screen.

"And the third guy is Suliman," Kurtzman said. "I've seen that face enough times before."

Wethers brought up more photographs. They all showed the moored yacht and Suliman entertaining different people over several days.

"There," Kurtzman said. "Han Nor again."

"Who's the dark-haired guy sitting at the far side of the table?" Wethers asked, indicating the stocky figure.

"Bring him up," Kurtzman said.

As the enhanced image came into prominence, Kurtzman gave a satisfied sigh.

"You know him?"

"I know about him," Kurtzman said. "We have him on file. Yuri Rostok, a Soviet. He was involved in the Russian nuclear-missile program. He was responsible for distributing warheads throughout the country. He even had a hand in distribution to Soviet Bloc countries. Talk had it he knew where every nuclear warhead was located."

"What does he do now?"

"Apart from show up on photographs with Han Nor and Victor Suliman? Good question," Kurtzman said. "I think we should try and find the answer."

"I'll see what I can dig up."

"You got anything else?"

Wethers retrieved a fresh set of images, still showing Suliman's yacht.

"This guy showed up a few times," he said, pointing at a slim blond man with a deep tan and expensive clothes.

"I know him," Kurtzman said. "Met him a few times years back, before he stepped across the line."

"Who is he?"

"Kurt Englemann, a brilliant computer programmer. He could have made a killing in the private sector. Problem is, he opted to work for the kind of people who believe hacking into other networks is the best way to get what you want."

"Looks like Englemann is on another gravy train," Wethers said.

Kurtzman grunted. "Make hard copies of all these photographs and the data. I'll let Hal know what we've found and see what he wants to do with it."

The moment the printout was complete, Huntington Wethers gathered the sheets and crossed to where Aaron Kurtzman sat hunched over his console.

Kurtzman glanced up as he sensed Wethers's presence.

"This should make interesting reading," the tall black man said, passing the sheets to Kurtzman.

"Give me a breakdown," Kurtzman said, running a hand across his weary eyes.

"I took the information we got from the people Able Team clashed with in Santa Clara, plus the make we got on the two who tried to kill the guy in the county hospital. Came up with some interesting connections.

"Doug Nolan and Lloyd Ray, the hit men at the hospital, served time together in an Army stockade before they were discharged from the service. They had been caught shaking down raw recruits for protection money. Since leaving the Army, they've both drifted through a number of jobs. Always ran close to the edge. Then they hired out as weapons instructors for a rebel group down in South America. Spent about three years all told. Had their hands into all kinds of things, including gunrunning. Dabbled in drugs. Then they signed up to work for a group run by an ex-Marine named Delacourt. Jake Hutchins, one of the hardguys in the Santa Clara firefight, was already on Delacourt's payroll."

"Should we know this Delacourt?"

"Not your ordinary merc for hire. Delacourt is into bigger things, so the story goes. Likes to move in high circles. Been known to make deals with the Libyans. Even the IRA. The guy has no scruples or loyalty to any state. Pay him and he's yours until the contract runs out."

"So he's the man behind our deceased hitters?" Kurtzman said.

"Yeah, but I think he's only providing the muscle and the action. There's someone else at the top."

"What about the guy Able Team took alive?"

"Archie Pemmel. No priors. He's a computer expert. Been out of work for a year. He says he was hired by Jennifer Sayato to set up the copying operation. I believe that's his only involvement."

"He's certainly involved now," Kurtzman said.

He snatched up one of the phones and punched in the number that connected him with Brognola. "We need to update everyone... Yeah, ten minutes it is."

Kurtzman rolled his wheelchair around.

"Listen up! Get your stuff together—everything we have. War Room in ten minutes. Don't be late, people."

BROGNOLA WAS SLUMPED in his seat at the head of the table. Beside him Barbara Price sat hunched over a notepad, scribbling furiously.

As Kurtzman and his team entered, Price glanced up, then went back to her writing.

"Tell me," Brognola said tersely, hardly bothering to look up.

Kurtzman made a play of clearing his throat.

"We have established a definite link between Nolan, Hutchins and Ray. They're all known to be on the payroll of Jordan Delacourt."

"Ex-Major Jordan Delacourt?" Brognola asked. "There are a number of agencies who have more than a passing interest in him."

"As far as I'm aware, the CIA still has a termination order out on him, since he turned rogue and sold out a couple of their deep-cover operatives," Price said, still writing. "The CIA guys turned up dead. Bound and shot in the back of the head."

"You want me to carry on?" Kurtzman asked.

"Just thinking out loud," Price said.

"Santa Clara and the hospital shoot-out are connected. The hitters are tied in with Delacourt," Kurtzman repeated. "It'll be interesting to see if any input we get from Phoenix Force and Striker links up."

"What about Sayato?" Price asked. "Any tie-in?"

"Nothing so far. We can't get anything on her. She appears to be a model citizen, but she met our main target, Hanson, then went directly to the factory site to pass along CyberPlus data disks for illegal copying."

"The possibility exists that she was only doing it for the money," Carmen Delahunt said. "Does she have to have sympathetic connections with Delacourt's group?"

"It isn't mandatory," Brognola said. "On the other hand, I can't see Delacourt bringing in a rank amateur. And don't forget that Sayato was the first to respond violently when Able Team challenged the group. She had an automatic weapon and she used it without hesitation. That isn't what I'd term civilian behavior."

"I'd hazard a guess and say she was in deeper than it appears now," Price said. "When did she join CyberPlus?"

Akira Tokaido thumbed through his printout. His input to the info check had been to make a list of CyberPlus employees and evaluate their backgrounds.

"Hey, I got it," he said. "She started there just over two months ago."

"Short and sweet," Brognola said. "Placed there to keep an eye on Hanson."

"Maybe I could talk to some of my FBI contacts," Delahunt suggested. "See if they have anything on her we haven't been able to pick up."

Kurtzman nodded. "Worth a try."

"Let's not forget the people identified as being on Suliman's yacht," Price reminded. "Especially this Russian, Rostok. And Englemann."

"We need a clearer picture of all these people," Brognola said. "Keep at it, Aaron. If I can help open any doors, give me a yell. All right, everybody thanks for your input."

Kurtzman lingered as his team left. He wheeled about and planted his chair in the center of the floor. Brognola looked up.

"Something on your mind?"

"You know damn well what's on my mind," Kurtzman said.

Price pushed aside her notepad, stroked back her hair and glanced sideways at Brognola. He stirred restlessly, quickly reaching out to pick up a fresh cigar and unwrap it.

"If I knew any more, I'd tell you," he said. "We might be jumping to conclusions. You know Mack as well as I do. Sometimes he just disappears off the map during a mission. He'll contact us when he decides it's time and he has something to tell."

Kurtzman sighed. He looked across at Price.

"I can see it, too, Barb."

"Yeah."

"What?" Brognola snapped. "See what?"

"That you're just as worried about him as we are," Price said.

Brognola refused to look her in the eye.

Because they were both right. Brognola was worried about Bolan. Damned worried.

CHAPTER ELEVEN

London, England

Standing in the shadows across the street from the safehouse, Mack Bolan watched for signs of movement. Lights showed in windows. There was a car parked in the drive. Bolan had been watching for almost a half hour. In that time he'd not seen a single movement from inside the house. The lighted rooms looked to be deserted. There could have been a perfectly reasonable explanation, but due to the evening's dramatic turn of events, Bolan took the cautious path.

It had taken him over two hours to return to the safehouse location. He had walked for a long time, distancing himself from the scene of the firefight. His lonely walk through London's backstreets had given him ample time to think matters over. Not that he had been able to reach any definite conclusions— apart from the fact that his mission was already compromised. Somewhere, someone was most likely congratulating himself on a job well done. That unknown person was fooling himself. The Executioner was alive and well, inconvenienced and on a slow burn. When that burn reached white heat, London was going to feel the hot wind of a Bolan blitz.

Shakespeare's Hamlet spoke of something being rotten in the state of Denmark. The same could be said for London at the moment. Bolan had picked up the suggestion from both Clair Tomkins and her superior, Inspector Rawson, that someone was blocking their progress. The night's events were bearing that out.

The wallet he had taken from the driver of the pursuit car had yielded over seventy pounds in cash, a couple of credit cards and a business card for a mail-order company in Southwest London. On the back of the card had been jotted a string of numbers that Bolan hadn't been able to decipher.

Finally hailing a taxi, Bolan had given the driver the location of the street where the safehouse was situated. As the vehicle wound its way through the late traffic, Bolan sat back in the darkness and tried to make sense out of the mission.

Apart from establishing a link between Han Nor and the Libyan negotiator Suliman, the Executioner had little to go on. In fact, the only other piece of information he had turned up was the business card from the dead driver's wallet, and as yet there was no definite proof it meant anything. The only way he would know for sure would be by visiting the mail-order company.

The taxi had dropped him at the end of the street, and Bolan paid the driver and climbed out.

The rain was still falling. It felt cold against his skin. He kept his hand on the Desert Eagle in the pocket of the trench coat as he moved along the street across from the safehouse.

Now he decided it was time to move.

There was little more to be gained by simply watching the place. He retraced his steps and crossed the street at a distance, then walked back down until he was close to the house. He slipped in through the open gates and pushed into the bushes that lined the short driveway, working his way up to the front of the house.

Pressed against the wall beside a window, Bolan peered in through the rain-streaked glass. He recognized the room where he had sat talking with Rawson and Tomkins earlier that evening, before he and the young policewoman had left for Han Nor's meeting place.

Now the room was empty. Lights still burned, but there was no movement. The door stood open, with light from the hall showing.

Bolan eased his way to the front entrance, up the three steps to the porch and its glass-paned double doors. The doors opened to his touch, and he stepped into the enclosed porch. The main door was unlocked. Bolan went inside and immediately became aware of the silence.

Taking the Desert Eagle from the coat pocket, Bolan held it two-handed, moving deeper into the house.

He found the first body by the foot of the stairs— a single shot to the back of the head. Blood had leaked out from under the shattered head and now dark and dried on the carpet. Bolan recognized the young police officer Inspector Rawson had pointed out to him during the swift tour of the house when he had first arrived. The man had been in charge of communications for the squad.

Two more bodies lay in the kitchen. They had both been shot in a similar fashion to the first victim. Their bodies lay on the tiled floor.

There were three more people to be accounted for, including Rawson himself.

Bolan found two of them upstairs. They had been killed in exactly the same way as the others.

Inspector Rawson was at the rear of the house in the room he had used as his office.

The filing cabinet, where he had kept the gathered information on the Han Nor surveillance, had been stripped of all of its contents. So had Rawson's desk, the drawers still hanging open.

Inspector Rawson was at his desk. He had been tightly bound to his swivel chair and shot at least three times in the back of the skull. One of the bullets had passed right through, tearing an ugly exit wound that had badly damaged his face. The front of his shirt was soaked in blood.

Bolan stood away and surveyed the ransacked office and its dead occupant. The wanton deaths in the house did not shock him. He was beyond being disturbed by the ugliness of sudden, violent death.

But the sheer cold-bloodedness of these executions horrified him. The victims had been refused the right to appeal their death warrant. It had been served with cold disdain for the basic right of a human being. Rawson and his people had been cut down like so much dead wood. Deprived of life without thought; by someone without a shred of feeling.

There was something more, an elusive element that Bolan couldn't put his finger on right away. It came to him a little later, as he searched through the house for his own luggage, which had been delivered on his arrival. He found it after a few minutes and changed into street clothing. He stowed the Desert Eagle away in the zippered bag, pulling on the Beretta's shoulder rig before donning the leather jacket.

It was then that he realized what was nagging him concerning the deaths in the house.

The ritualistic deaths of Rawson and his squad were intended as a warning to whoever was ranged against the killers and their organization: We know who you are and where you are, and we can kill you just like we killed these people—at our leisure and with impunity.

It was there in black and white, as clear as a headline. Rawson's squad of dedicated law officers, slaughtered for everyone to see.

Uppermost in Bolan's mind was Clair Tomkins. He had only been with the young policewoman for a short time. But in that time he had come to understand and respect her total dedication to the job. Her unremitting courage and honesty.

And now she was out there. Alone. Probably as friendless as Bolan himself. Being pursued by a largely unknown enemy—an enemy who had already shown his true hand. A hand dripping with blood.

Turning on his heel, Bolan picked up a telephone. He started to dial, then paused and replaced the receiver. More than likely, the phones were tapped.

He snatched up his bag and left the house as quietly as he had entered. With the collar of the leather jacket turned up and zippered tight, he crept through the bushes until he was able to observe the silent street. The only vehicles he saw were the ones parked along the curbs when he had arrived.

Bolan eased out the gate and walked steadily along the sidewalk, away from the house. At the end of the street, he saw a telephone booth. He went to it and dropped in the pound coins the taxi driver had given him in change, then punched in a number. He heard the phone clicking as it passed through the various satellite links and security screens on its way to Stony Man. When the number connected, Bolan asked to be put through to Brognola. When the big Fed came on, Bolan cut into his questions with a terse request to write down the number of the booth and call him back.

"Got it," Brognola said.

"I'll be waiting," Bolan said, and put down the receiver.

The pay phone rang within a minute. Bolan snatched up the receiver.

"Striker, where the hell have you been?" Brognola demanded. "Not a word for the past—"

"Chew me out later," Bolan said. "The mission has gone hard over here. Right now I'm on my own and out in the cold. The undercover people I was liaising with are all dead. I just found the safehouse full of corpses. All executed like some Mafia vendetta."

"Not more," Brognola muttered.

"What's that?"

"Able Team had a similar discovery in Oregon. Three FBI agents bound and shot in the back of the head. They were buried in a shallow grave. Left to be found as a warning, we figure."

"My thoughts here, too," Bolan said. "What's going on? This mission has jumped the rails."

"Have you made contact with your targets?"

"Yes. Han Nor is in bed with Victor Suliman, so that ties the Libyans in to whatever is going on."

"We may have a lock on that, Striker. There are some theories floating around we need to tie down."

"Anything I need to know about?"

"A possible link between a missing rogue computer expert named Englemann and Libya."

"Kurt Englemann?"

"The same."

Bolan checked the shadows around him. He was beginning to feel that his time was running out. He needed to move on.

"Hal, I'm out of here. I'll call you when I can. Right now I don't have any contacts over here. Check with your British opposite number, but tread lightly. There's a problem with security at this end. Someone is on the bad guys' payroll."

"Striker, where are you heading?"

"I'll be in touch when I arrive," Bolan said, and broke the connection.

He picked up his bag and melted into the darkness.

Moments later a black sedan rolled by the telephone booth. The headlights were dimmed, and it passed the empty booth and continued along the deserted street. From within the shadowed interior, blurred faces peered through the tinted glass, eyes searching the darkness. The soft glow from streetlights, penetrating the windows, struck briefly against the cold metal of weapons resting in ready hands.

The car reached the end of the street. It turned in a quiet circle and began to cruise the street again.

The occupants were not aware that Mack Bolan was watching *them*. They were too busy scanning the street, searching for the one man who might have evidence concerning their conspiracy.

Bolan followed the progress of the car along the street, saw it slow and stop just short of the house. Doors swung open and figures climbed out, pulling coats tight over concealed weapons. Three of them stood beside the car in deep conversation, then broke apart. They moved in different directions, patrolling the area on foot.

Easing his duffel bag to the ground, Bolan followed the progress of one man along the sidewalk. The guy was coming in Bolan's direction, shoulders hunched against the chill of the rain, head pulled down into his collar. He paused every few yards to check the area, eyes searching the shadows. Then he moved on again, each step bringing him closer to the Executioner's motionless form.

Only feet away, the hardguy came to a dead stop, head coming up, his face a wet blur in the light from the street lamp. His dark hair lay flat against his skull. Rain trickled down his face, dripped from the tip of his nose. He shook his head like some large shaggy dog, muttering something under his breath.

He took two more hesitant steps closer to Bolan's place of concealment.

And then awareness shined in his eyes and he stared directly at Bolan. His right hand slipped inside his coat, searching for the gun.

His wet mouth opened in the beginning of a shout.

Bolan came out of the dark, swinging the Beretta like a metallic club. The barrel whacked the man across the side of the skull, opening a gash that immediately spurted bright blood that spidered down his face and paled away into pink streaks as it was diluted by the rain. The blow twisted the hardman off-balance and he stumbled against the low wall fronting the garden of the house.

Not wanting to lose his advantage, Bolan struck again, the barrel slamming down across the back of the guy's head. The target grunted and tried to rise. Bolan reached out and laid his open left hand against the back of his enemy's neck and shoved down hard. The force of his maneuver slammed the man facedown against the top of the wall with a sodden thump. The man's arms and legs stiffened as he collapsed, moaning softly.

Leaning over the semiconscious form, Bolan felt inside the guy's coat and pulled out an autopistol. It was a Browning Hi-Power. Bolan pushed it into his coat pocket, turning as he heard a distant call.

On the other side of the street one of the downed man's partners had witnessed the tail end of Bolan's clash. He broke into a run across the wet street, un-limbering the gun he was carrying.

Bolan lifted the Beretta and tracked the moving figure.

At the last moment the running man realized he was already under Bolan's gun. He attempted to change direction, while still attempting to bring his weapon into play.

The 93-R fired a triple-burst, the three 9 mm parabellums chewing into flesh and bone. The moving figure faltered, legs losing coordination. He slithered on the glistening pavement and fell heavily, twisting over on his side, kicking for a few seconds before stillness crept over him.

Bolan had altered his position, angling along the street, keeping the parked car in the corner of one eye while he watched for the third gunman.

He showed suddenly, stepping out from behind a parked panel truck, loosing a single shot that caught Bolan in the left arm and tore out a bloody furrow in the flesh.

As he absorbed the pain, Bolan dropped to a crouch, fisting the Beretta in both hands and snapping off a 3-round burst that tore a bright scar along the roof of a parked car, causing the gunman to step back behind the truck. Bolan moved forward, closing on the truck, and peered through the rear window. He was able to see the hiding gunman through the windshield. The guy was waiting, his own weapon up and ready.

Bolan leveled the Beretta and triggered through the rear window. The triburst cored the rear and front windows, catching the gunman in the head. He fell from Bolan's view.

Across the street the idling car lurched forward as the driver stamped on the gas pedal. It clipped the wing of a car parked just ahead of it. The driver hurriedly reversed, then shot forward again. Tires squealed as the car was pushed at high speed. It fishtailed along the street and swung right at the end, vanishing from sight.

Bolan turned and went back to where he'd left his duffel bag. He grabbed it, then turned to the gunman who was still slumped against the low wall. The warrior nudged him with the barrel of the Beretta.

"You get one chance," Bolan said. "Unless you want to join your two deceased buddies. Make your choice, pal, but make it fast."

The man pushed unsteadily to his feet. He saw the gun in Bolan's fist and the look in his eyes, and he realized in that moment how close he was to losing his own life. Despite the pain of his injuries and the blood streaming from his nose, he nodded at Bolan.

"Let's get away from here," Bolan said.

Lights were coming on in houses along the street, and it wouldn't be long before people followed.

Using the muzzle of the Beretta, Bolan pushed his reluctant captive along the street, moving to the top end. He kept to the shadows offered by overhanging trees and shrubs, and when a narrow alley appeared he pushed the gunman into it.

"Where the hell are we going?" the man demanded. A degree of courage had returned, and with it came resistance.

"Don't make it too hard on yourself," Bolan said. "I don't have a thing to lose by killing you. You have plenty to lose. Maybe you want to die."

"You bastard."

"I've been called that before."

They continued on along the alley. It eventually opened onto another street, similar to the one they had left. Bolan took them right, and they walked briskly along the quiet residential street until they came to a main road.

Bolan's captive slumped against a wall. He fished out a handkerchief and pressed it to his bloody nose. His muffled voice cursed Bolan.

"My nose is broken, you son of a bitch."

"When you play with the men, you're going to get hurt."

"What the hell do you want with me? You can't walk me around London all bleedin' night."

"You're going back to your base," Bolan said. "So am I."

"Are you serious?" The man began to chuckle. "Take you back there? I can just see Holder's face—"

The man clammed up after his slip. Bolan didn't dwell on it, but he filed away the familiar name for future reference.

Jack Holder, the ex-Marine running the heavy squad for Han Nor.

"I don't like having to repeat myself," Bolan warned the man. "You don't have a choice."

"The hell I don't," the gunman said. "You going to kill me right here on the street?"

He turned suddenly, slamming his shoulder into Bolan's chest and knocking him aside. Before Bolan could reach out, the man had made a dash for the road, dodging the traffic. Brakes were jammed and tires squealed on the wet road. Horns blared noisily.

The running man crossed the center line, head down as he plowed through the swerving cars. He almost made it. He might have if his calculation of the speed of a massive red double-decker London Transport bus had been accurate. As it was, the vehicle caught him head on, slamming him to the ground before one of its heavy front wheels ground over his wriggling form. The bus skidded to a halt, traffic piling up around it. Doors slammed as drivers climbed out. A crowd began to gather.

Bolan stood watching for a few seconds, then eased into the shadows and walked away. He did not hurry. He simply walked into the dark wet night, his thoughts on what he was going to do next.

CHAPTER TWELVE

Aquitaine Region, France

Katz was awakened early the following morning by Eric Talpern. The liaison man stepped inside Katz's room the moment he opened the door, his face pale and his expression nervous.

"Just sit down and take a deep breath," the Israeli advised. "Whatever you have to say can wait a few seconds longer."

Katz closed the door and turned back to Talpern. Pulling the cord of his bathrobe tighter around his waist, Katz sat across from the man, watching him closely.

"I'm okay now," Talpern said. "I apologize, Mr. Greenburg. To be honest, I'm not used to this kind of thing happening around me."

"What kind of thing, Eric?" Katz inquired gently.

"You know the two men who broke into Browning's room last night?"

"Yes."

"They were being held at the local jail for the people from the Gendarmerie Nationale, as you know."

"Go on," Katz urged, sensing bad news was about to come.

"Apparently the Gendarmerie Nationale arrived very early this morning, produced the correct documentation and took the men away."

"I have a feeling I'm not going to like this," Katz said.

"Two hours later more of the Gendarmerie Nationale arrived with the same request. Of course, by then it was too late. The prisoners were gone."

"I don't believe this," Katz said.

"That isn't all," Talpern said. "An alert was broadcast. I have just been informed that the two prisoners have been located, only ten miles away, in a ditch. They had both been shot in the back of the head, doused in gas and burned."

Katz picked up the telephone. He dialed the rooms where the rest of Phoenix Force were housed and asked them to join him immediately.

Before they arrived Katz ordered a large pot of coffee from room service.

"This has to be bad news," McCarter said as he slouched into the room.

"By the look on your face," James aid to Katz, "I guess he has to be correct."

Katz nodded. He didn't say anything until Manning and Encizo had joined them. The Cuban closed the door and leaned against the wall, waiting for the Phoenix commander to speak.

Katz related what Talpern had told him.

"That's just dandy," James said. "There goes any chance of learning anything from them."

"Dandy?" McCarter snorted. "No, it's not bloody dandy. It's bloody well criminal. Somebody should go down to the cop shop and set light to the morons who let them go."

"Drastic even for you, Browning," Manning said.

"Yeah? Well, I'm feeling bloody drastic," the Brit complained. "You got any cans of Coke around this dump?"

Hearing a tap on the door, Katz ignored the remark. Encizo opened it to let a young maid in. She was staggering under the weight of a huge silver tray holding a huge coffeepot and large cups. Encizo took the tray from her with a wide smile. She took one look at the crowd of grim-faced men and retreated without a word.

"See what you did," James whispered to McCarter. "You scared her."

McCarter picked up a cup, filled it with hot black coffee and slumped into a chair.

"What about the genuine Gendarmerie Nationale?" he asked.

Talpern shrugged. "They went into conference with one of the French military people, then left. Refused even to speak to me."

"I just love the French and their charm," Manning said. "So what now? We're no further forward than we were last night. At least with those guys alive there might have been a chance of getting some information out of them."

"Dental records?" James suggested. "Maybe we can get a line on them through those."

"I don't think so," Eric Talpern said in a low tone. "Apparently whoever killed them must have had the same thought. Both the dead men had been battered around the mouth with an iron bar of some kind— with enough force to shatter every tooth in their heads."

"We do meet some charming people in our line of work," McCarter said. "Burning the bodies was so that we couldn't ID them from scars or bodily markings."

"And to destroy fingertips," Manning pointed out."

Katz, leaning back in his chair and sipping his coffee, glanced up at the Canadian's observation.

"Perhaps not," he said.

He put down his cup. Reaching for the telephone, he spoke to reception and asked for an outside line. Dialing a number, he waited for a response. When he spoke it was in fluent French. The conversation went on for a couple of minutes, during which Katz remained persuasive and calm. When he had completed his conversation, he thanked the person on the other end of the line and replaced the phone. Picking up his cup, he sat back, a satisfied smile on his face.

"He's done something bloody clever, and he wants us to suffer before he tells us," McCarter grumbled. "Well, I'm not asking."

Manning, able to understand French, caught the Israeli's eye.

"Smart move," he said.

"Let's hope it gives us something," Katz replied.

THIRTY MINUTES LATER Katz was alone. The others had returned to their own rooms. Talpern had gone to finalize arrangements for transportation to the test site.

Sitting quietly, smoking a cigarette and listening to a French radio station playing classical music, Katz allowed the strains of Beethoven's Fifth Symphony to relax him. He absorbed the music while he reflected on the events of the previous evening and the dramatic turn that had removed the captives from having to be questioned. Regardless of who they had been, Katz found the manner of their deaths repulsive in the extreme.

The enemy Phoenix Force was up against was proving to be thorough and extremely ruthless. If they dealt so severely with their own people, how would they behave toward a genuine opponent? The answer was not something Katz preferred to dwell on.

He concentrated on the matter at hand. If the officer in command of the local gendarmerie came through with his promise, there might yet be a way to salvage something useful.

A knock at his door brought Katz to his feet. He opened it to be confronted by a uniformed gendarme. The officer inclined his head.

"Monsieur Greenburg?"

"Oui," Katz replied. He gestured, inviting the officer into the room.

Closing the door, Katz turned, continuing to speak to the police officer in his own language.

"Thank you for coming so promptly, Captain Bouchett."

The policeman shrugged. "The least I could do, seeing it was one of your companions who suffered the invasion of his privacy. After he subdued the interlopers, I repay him by allowing imposters to spirit them away and kill them."

"From what we know about these people, they are extremely well organized," Katz sympathized. "Any credentials they would have shown you would have been excellent forgeries or..."

Bouchett glanced at him quickly.

"Or the real thing? Do you believe these people had official help?"

Katz raised his shoulders. "Who knows? We live in strange times, my friend."

Bouchett sighed. "Don't I know it."

"You are aware why my friends and I are here?"

"You are involved in the weapons testing at the training area." Bouchett nodded. "We were told to be very vigilant because there were going to be important people coming to the château for a few days. As the local civilian police, we are only told what is considered relevant."

"Did the Gendarmerie Nationale give you a hard time?"

Bouchett smiled. "They gave me hell. It was to be expected, of course. No doubt I will receive a further telling off from my superiors. Perhaps this time next week I will be demoted and riding a bicycle in my home village." Bouchett considered it for a moment. "Perhaps that would not be so bad after all."

"Did the Gendarmerie Nationale not ask if you had taken the prisoners' fingerprints?" Katz inquired.

"No. They were so busy trying to make me look small that they forgot to ask. I'm surprised. Such high fliers. You would expect them to remember the most basic of police procedures." Bouchett drew a manila envelope from inside his uniform. His face split into a wide grin. "And I was not going to remind them."

"They may remember later," Katz said.

"Don't worry. We took two sets as a precaution, in case the Gendarmerie Nationale asked for the arrest details."

Katz took the envelope. "If my people can identify them, I will let you have the information so you can keep it up your sleeve for future use."

Bouchett shook the Israeli's hand. *"Merci, Monsieur Greenburg."*

Katz opened the door.

"Au revoir."

"I'LL MAKE THIS BRIEF," Katz said.

"Go ahead," Brognola replied.

"I have some information I need checked—fingerprints from the two deceased burglars."

"How did you get hold of them?"

"Can't quite hear you," Katz said. "Line went fuzzy."

Brognola chuckled. "I get it. Listen, speak to Talpern. There's a secure fax unit installed in the THAAD control trailer. You can send the prints direct to home base. We'll do the rest."

"Be in touch," Katz said, and cut the connection.

"I NEED SOME SECURE TIME with the fax machine inside the THAAD control trailer," Katz said to Talpern. "As soon as we reach the test site, Eric."

Talpern shot him a puzzled glance. "I don't suppose it will do me any good to ask why?"

"He won't even tell us," James remarked, slumping back in the rear seat of the sturdy 4 × 4 that was taking them to the training area.

Encizo grinned. "You going to call a lady friend?"

"Maybe," Katz answered. "Who knows."

"Bloody silly games," McCarter snapped, staring out of the window at the passing trees. The problem was, he was certain he kept smelling tobacco smoke. But no one in the vehicle was smoking. The Brit hunched his shoulders. He was imagining things now. Next he'd be seeing tall cigarettes instead of trees.

"Tell us about Hanley," Manning said.

"Gil Hanley is a brilliant man. But he lives in his own world. He isn't interested in anything except his current project. That project is THAAD right now. Nothing else matters."

"Does that mean we won't be getting much of a welcome?" Manning asked.

Talpern couldn't help smiling. "Very understated. He knows you're coming, but that doesn't guarantee he'll like it. Don't get me wrong. He won't rant and rave at you. Probably he'll just ignore you."

"Sounds like a fun day ahead," Calvin James remarked.

"We're not here to have fun," Katz pointed out. "Or to socialize. We'll do our job and try to stay away from the personnel trying to do theirs. Eric, our job is to be on hand to prevent anything that might put THAAD at risk. If we do discover anything, I'll make a big noise about it. I don't care who is there from the French government, or the military. My priority is to protect THAAD, and if there is any sabotage, to try to dig out who is responsible for it, then to remove those people from the scene—by whatever means are deemed necessary."

Eric Talpern nodded. "I *do* understand what you're saying. But I'm only speaking for myself. What I'm trying to say is..."

"There are going to be some who resent us being present and who will do their best to ignore anything we want them to do," McCarter recited.

"Yes," Talpern said. "That is exactly what I believe will happen."

"Nothing beats being appreciated," Encizo remarked, putting into words what the other members of Phoenix Force were thinking.

Les Causses Training Area

GIL HANLEY BEHAVED exactly as Talpern had said he would. Following a cursory exchange of acknowledgments, the spare American adjusted his steel-rimmed glasses and returned to the discussion he was having with his French counterpart. Eric Talpern glanced covertly at Katz, making a faint gesture of apology for Hanley's attitude.

"Show me where the control trailer is," Katz said, having already dismissed Hanley from his mind.

Phoenix Force followed Talpern across the test site. The area was a vast expanse of wild grass and shrubs, with scattered stands of trees. The undulating landscape was composed of a series of flat areas, shallow hollows and low hills that stretched as far as the eye could see. There were no permanent buildings in evidence. From what Katz had learned, whenever the training area was being used, the unit in residence brought its own equipment, plus tents for the military personnel. Mobile units would also be towed in, then removed once the training sessions had been completed.

There were probably more vehicles and mobile units than usual on-site. Transport for the visiting government officials was parked well behind the control area. Close to Phoenix Force sat a mix of power generators, tracking units and control stations. Electric power cables snaked across the ground. A few hundred yards out from the main cluster of equipment were the mobile missile launchers, equipped with the rockets that would be used to take out the incoming missile, which would be launched by the U.S. Air Force for the actual demonstration of the THAAD system.

The site was a hive of activity. As well as the officials and the military observers, there were security teams and, most important of all, the technicians from the companies involved in the construction and development of the THAAD components. With the trail only hours away, they were carrying out final checks of equipment, aligning tracking and monitoring devices and attending to the endless routines involved in coordinating all the separate components that would be required to create a stable working environment for the THAAD system.

Talpern guided Phoenix Force through the confusion and frenzied activity, bringing them to the THAAD mobile control trailer. It stood on its own, slightly apart from the mass of equipment, a white-painted trailer, close to thirty feet in length. From its roof, sensors and electronic receiving and transmitting aerials pointed skyward. The only connection the trailer had with any other equipment was a thick power cable that hooked it up to a distant generator.

There were three armed U.S. Marines standing watch over the trailer. Talpern spoke with the one at the front of the trailer. The Marine checked his clipboard, then peered over it at the five men. He inspected the ID badges they wore. When he was satisfied that their credentials matched those he had on his authorization sheet, he turned to the trailer and went up the aluminum steps that allowed access to the entry platform. Keying in an access code, he opened the security door, then stepped aside.

Talpern led them inside. The first section they entered was the communications area. There were high-tech radio and telephone systems, plus a state-of-the-art fax machine.

"I'll leave you to your business," Talpern said. "I have a few matters to attend to. You'll find everything you need here. The power is on, so you'll be able to send your information."

Katz nodded. "While we're here I'd like to have a look around," he said. "No interference. Just a quick security check."

Talpern indicated a door in the far bulkhead.

"That will take you into the main control area. Once everything is set today, this trailer will be sealed and no one allowed inside until tomorrow. If you need to take a look, now is the time."

He turned to leave them.

Once they were alone Katz seated himself at the communications console and picked up one of the telephones. He punched in the number that would link him with Stony Man.

The others were busy having a look at all the sophisticated equipment.

"This is some setup," Calvin James remarked. "I'd hate to put a price on it all."

"I expect this is a special design for field trials and tests," Manning said. "If the system actually goes into production, I'd guess that the operational units will be less expensive and more functional."

Katz held up a hand as he was connected with Stony Man.

"Greenburg for the man," he said flatly, not wanting to use too many names. Despite the electronic scramblers and diversion devices, no open line was ever fully secure, and the Stony Man operatives were used to carrying out conversations in monosyllabic sentences.

"Go ahead," Brognola said gruffly.

"Stand by to receive a fax," Katz said. "Get back to me at the number I'm quoting as soon as you have a make." He gave the number that would enable Stony Man to return the information, then broke the connection. Turning to the fax machine, Katz placed the fingerprint cards on the feeder tray, punched in the number and keyed the transmit code. The machine dialed the number, made the connection and commenced its transmission. Once the cards had gone through, Katz picked them up and slipped them into his pocket.

"Let's go and check out the rest of the trailer," he said, and led the way to the main control area.

The interior was spotless and looked almost sterile. The equipment lining both walls was pristine.

"How do we find anything in a place like this?" James asked. "It's so tidy it's a crime."

"Makes me feel uncomfortable," McCarter commented.

"As a matter of interest, just what are we looking for?" Encizo asked.

He paced up and down the strip of pristine, light gray antistatic carpet, pausing every now and then to check an item at random.

"This is crazy," McCarter complained.

He had already given up and was leaning against the edge of one of the computer consoles, scowling down at his dusty shoes. "Admit it, Katz, we don't have a bloody prayer."

"David, stop moaning and at least pretend to look," the Israeli said.

"I could murder for a fag," the Brit muttered savagely.

"Not in here," James said. "Hanley wouldn't be happy if you dropped ash on his carpet."

McCarter's gaze trailed across the carpet. He felt inclined to agree with James. The floor was so clean, it hardly felt right even to look at it.

His wandering gaze was attracted at that precise moment by a few tiny fragments lying just below a recess of the console's cabinet. At any other time such small items might have gone unnoticed. But due to the overwhelming atmosphere of cleanliness within the control room, these fragments were noticeable by their very presence.

McCarter crouched and examined the fragments. He used the tip of the pen he had taken from his pocket to nudge them. The fragments were hard, curled and dark gray in color.

The same color, in fact, as the computer console.

McCarter scanned the side of the console. The smooth, dull gray paint was unmarked—until he spotted the recessed access panel set in the side of the cabinet. It was about a foot square and held in place by a screw at each corner. The gray paint on the heads of the screws was the same color as the console. McCarter could now see that there were flaked sections on each screw head where the base metal had been exposed. And the countersunk sections of the panel, where each screw was seated, also showed some flaked paint.

Someone had recently had the screws out.

"Katz!" McCarter said.

"What is it?" the Phoenix commander asked as he joined McCarter.

The Brit pointed to the fragments on the carpet, then the chipped paint.

Katz examined the evidence, then stood up. He looked the computer unit over, then turned to the other Phoenix members who had gathered around.

"It looks like David has uncovered something. What, we don't know. This unit has been tampered with. There may be an explosive device rigged inside that will detonate during the trial. Or..."

"Or what?" asked Encizo.

Katz glanced at him.

"I'm making a wild guess here. Perhaps instead of a bomb, someone has added or substituted a circuit board or a microchip that will affect the performance of the system."

"So how do we figure it out?" James asked. "We don't have enough experience to be able to tell. It's going to take a computer technician to do that."

"Agreed," said Katz. "But who do we ask? I don't particularly like the idea of asking anyone on-site to do it, because the person we invite in might be the one who planted the device."

McCarter, with a smug expression on his face, said, "Figure it out, guys. I already did my bit."

"I hate it when he has a success," James remarked.

"It still doesn't tell us how we handle this now," Manning said.

"I'll have a quiet talk with Eric," Katz said, "to see who might have worked in here recently. My guess is that the sabotage was done here on-site. The trailer would have been transported here under a security seal. If the interference had been done at the factory where the unit was constructed, the paint chips would have been spotted during the final clearing of the trailer before it was locked down for transportation.''

"Why don't we check with the Marine guard outside?" James asked. "If they've been on permanent watch over this unit since it arrived, it stands to reason they'll have a record of everyone who's been inside."

"Good thinking, Cal," Katz said. "Go and have a word with the sergeant."

As James passed through the bulkhead door, he heard the soft hum of the fax machine. Glancing down at it, he saw it was pushing out a sheet of paper. Turning back to the main control area, he called to Katz.

"Information coming through," he said.

Katz joined him and took the fax sheets as they slid from the machine. He checked them, a smile edging his lips as he read the data and scanned the photographs accompanying them.

"These are your intruders," he said.

McCarter took one of the sheets and studied the image printed there. He nodded thoughtfully to himself. Katz showed him the second sheet.

"According to the details," Katz said, "our boys are Klaus Deiter and Jurgen Wulf, both ex-East German cops. Since they left the ranks they've been mixed up in any number of criminal activities. Wanted by half a dozen European police forces. The

Bear pulled this information from the Interpol network."

Katz read on. "This is interesting. Over the last six months they appear to have moved on to higher things. Intelligence has linked them with an organization suspected of being involved with international arms dealing. Names listed include Han Nor and Victor Suliman."

"This is getting better all the time," McCarter said. "Why doesn't someone go and bust this pair?"

"International conspiracies tend to incorporate heavy names," Katz said. "We're already aware that this group has connections. It isn't going to be all that simple to deal with these people."

"I think I know the kind of 'bust' David means," Encizo said. "And legal doesn't enter into it."

"Bloody right it doesn't," McCarter said.

"You know we can't act in that way," Katz said firmly. "I also understand how you feel, and the way ordinary police forces and agencies feel because they have to follow rules and regulations the criminal fraternity doesn't."

"Yes, I know the script," McCarter grumbled. "But at least we get a chance at these people if they kick back at us."

"Hey, take a walk with me," James suggested. "You need some fresh air, David, my man."

McCarter followed James out of the trailer.

"He does have a point," Manning said. "Be honest, Katz. If we do tie all these names together and prove what they're up to, we'll have a conspiracy that is aimed at putting the security of the United States and even Europe at risk."

"Makes you wonder whether justice is being served, if these people are allowed to get away with it," Encizo added.

"Hold on," Katz said. "Who said they were going to be allowed to get away with anything?"

CHAPTER THIRTEEN

The Marine Sergeant's name was Ray Hogan. A sharp, highly trained professional, he was in the service for life. He examined James's ID, then McCarter's, taking a close look at the lean Brit.

"How can I help you, gentlemen?" he asked.

"We've just checked out the trailer," James explained. "Signs indicate someone has been tampering with the equipment, and not too long ago."

Hogan was silent for a few seconds.

"We've been on twenty-four-hour guard since the equipment came on-site. This trailer has never been left unattended for a single moment."

"No one is suggesting your people haven't done their job," James said.

"Has anyone been inside since the trailer arrived?" McCarter asked. "It would have needed checking over, connecting to the power generator."

"Sure," Hogan said.

"You have a list of who and when?"

"Damn right I do, mister," the Marine said.

"Mind if we have a look?" McCarter asked.

Hogan turned and crossed to the four-wheel-drive truck parked nearby. He returned with a clipboard that he pushed at McCarter.

"Thanks," the cockney rebel said.

James scanned the list.

"Only four people have been inside," he said. "Gil Hanley, Eric Talpern and two others we don't know—Saul Dexter and Phil Ketchum."

"Dexter and Ketchum are employed by the company developing the THAAD system—CyberPlus," Hogan said. "Trained technicians."

James ran a finger down the list. It detailed the times when each individual or team had entered the trailer, how long they had been inside and the time they left. There was nothing initially untoward about any of the visits—until James came to the last time Dexter and Ketchum had worked inside the trailer. He scanned the details, then read them again until he was certain of his facts.

"The last time anyone was inside was yesterday afternoon," he said. "The trailer has been closed up ever since."

"That's right," Hogan said.

"You spotted something?" McCarter asked.

"Maybe nothing," James said. "But look here. Dexter and Ketchum went inside the trailer just after three yesterday afternoon. They were inside for forty minutes, then came out. But Dexter came back five minutes later and was inside for another eight minutes."

Hogan took the clipboard and checked it. He frowned as he confirmed James's observation.

"That's correct. According to the note, he came back to replace a loose cable clip he'd found."

McCarter glanced at James. He didn't say anything, but the black warrior gave a slight nod.

"Thanks for your help, Sergeant Hogan."

"That last item mean anything?" the Marine asked.

"We don't know," McCarter said. "Could be all the bloke did was fit a new cable clip."

"We'll check it out," James said. "Be grateful if you kept this to yourself for now."

Hogan nodded. "Let me know if you need any help," he said.

"I'll keep it in mind," McCarter said.

"Do you have any ID on Dexter?" James asked.

Hogan brought a file from the truck. Inside were head-and-shoulder photographs of personnel on-site.

"There are matches to the ones on the lapel badges issued to all personnel," the Marine explained.

James and McCarter memorized Dexter's image.

They returned to the trailer, and James explained what they had found.

"Look into it," Katz said. "As David says, it might be totally innocent, but given the fact that there does appear to have been some kind of sabotage, we have to cover all the bases.''

Minutes later the Phoenix pair were standing outside the mobile trailer that served as the site office for the technicians working under Gil Hanley. The place looked to be empty. Never one to be put off by first impressions, McCarter pushed open the door and went inside.

A man was seated at one of the workstations, tapping information into the computer facing him. He glanced up as McCarter barged in. The Briton recognized him as Phil Ketchum from the photograph Sergeant Hogan had shown them.

Ketchum scowled up at McCarter.

''Who the hell asked you in? This is off-limits.''

McCarter cleared his dry throat, wishing he had a cigarette to ease his mood.

''Not to me, chum,'' he snapped. He took out his ID and waggled it in Ketchum's face. ''Read it and weep.''

''Okay, so you've got credentials. So what do you want in here?'' Ketchum asked, making it clear by his tone that he wasn't going to be very helpful.

''I need to talk to your chum Dexter,'' McCarter explained. ''Where is he?''

Ketchum considered McCarter's request. He leaned back in his swivel chair.

''Maybe I don't know.''

"Maybe you're a liar," McCarter countered. "Now we both have questions that need answers."

The shutters came down. Ketchum sat upright, his face taut.

"Now I remember. I don't know where he is. You want him, go look for yourself."

McCarter turned away and stepped outside, closing the door very quietly. He shrugged his shoulders at James's silent question and walked away until they were out of sight of the trailer.

"You upset him," James said. "I can tell. You're pretending to be calm and polite because you went and pissed somebody off."

"If I had a delicate personality, I'd be in a rubber room by now. You have an acid tongue, chum."

"You *did* upset somebody."

McCarter grabbed James by the arm and pulled him flat against the side of the truck they were standing by. He raised a silencing finger as James began to protest.

McCarter was watching as Phil Ketchum stepped out of the trailer. He took a quick look around, then hurried off across the site, wending his way between equipment and vehicles.

"Let's go," McCarter said. Without waiting for James, the Brit set off at a loping pace, staying well back but keeping Phil Ketchum in sight. Calvin James trailed after his Phoenix partner, knowing better than to ask any questions.

At the extreme eastern perimeter of the area, non-essential cars and trucks were parked, as well as supply trailers. Ketchum had already reached this section, and as McCarter watched, hidden by the tailgate of a standby truck, the technician vanished among the vehicles.

"He's up to something," the Brit muttered.

"Sherlock Holmes would have been proud of you," James remarked. "That guy is certainly acting weird. He's been in contact with you, though, which could explain a lot."

McCarter checked that his shoulder-holstered Browning Hi-Power was close to hand. Then he took off across the final open space, closing on the vehicle parking area and dropping to a crouch in the shadow of a large trailer wheel. He scanned the area, then waved James to join him.

The Phoenix pair waited a few seconds, using the time to check out their surroundings. Suddenly picking up a nearby sound, James turned and guided McCarter's attention toward it.

"Over there," he said.

McCarter stood upright and eased his lean form through the narrow gap between two semitrailers. As he approached the rear of the trailers, he caught the subdued murmur of voices.

Two men were talking in lowered tones.

He reached the rear corner of one trailer and peered around it.

Only yards away Phil Ketchum stood talking to another man, whom McCarter identified as Saul Dexter from the photograph that Ray Hogan had shown him.

"The boys are together," McCarter muttered. He eased the Hi-Power from its holster. "Wonder what they're talking about?"

"Let's ask them politely," James suggested.

McCarter smiled. "Up till now polite hasn't been getting us very far."

"Maybe, but Katz isn't going to be too happy with dead prisoners."

Before McCarter could make any response, he saw James's face harden. The black commando's eyes fixed on McCarter and he reached inside his jacket for his own weapon.

"Behind me," James mouthed silently.

McCarter had also heard the unmistakable click of a gun hammer being drawn back.

He didn't hesitate.

With a gathering of his powerful muscles, the Phoenix hardman threw himself forward, clearing the corner of the trailer. He landed on his left shoulder, tucked in his head and rolled.

Calvin James followed suit, his own leap for survival taking him to the right of McCarter. The lean warrior continued to pull his handgun from its holster. As he landed, arching over on his back, James had the Walther P-88 in his fist, the safety off, and he was seeking target acquisition.

That target turned out to be a heavyset man clad in blue coveralls and wielding a long-barreled revolver. Taken off guard by the swift reaction of the Phoenix pair, the would-be assassin hesitated between the two targets. The muzzle of the large revolver wavered between them, then lingered on McCarter.

The gunman's indecision did nothing to delay Calvin James's response. As he leveled his Walther at the man, and realized the other was holding back while he chose his target, the Phoenix commando triggered his autopistol, laying down a rapid 3-round volley. The 9 mm parabellums caught the assassin in the chest and throat, throwing him back, the revolver swinging sideways to discharge into the ground. The hit man fell awkwardly, choking violently as blood bubbled into his windpipe from the gaping wound in his throat.

David McCarter, taken off the firing line by his partner, rolled to his feet, the muzzle of his Browning settling on the retreating figures of Ketchum and Dexter. They had turned to leave the moment Ketchum recognized McCarter.

"Stay right there!" McCarter yelled.

Four long strides took him up to the pair. The Browning was held at arm's length and in plain sight, so there was no mistaking the Brit's intention as he closed in.

"Give me one good excuse and I'll gladly show you how this works," McCarter said. "I want you two facedown on the ground, with arms and legs spread! Now!"

Ketchum and Dexter did exactly as McCarter instructed. Once they were prone the Brit waited until James joined him. They each took a man and made a thorough search, checking for concealed weapons. Even when they were satisfied, Ketchum and Dexter were made to remain in the prone position.

The shooting had alerted the site. First on the scene was Sergeant Ray Hogan, pistol in hand.

"I might have guessed it would be you two," he said, eyeing the Phoenix commandos. "What the hell is going on here?"

"Try this pair," McCarter growled. "We came to ask them some questions. Next thing we know, the guy in blue coveralls turned up and drew down on us with a gun."

"Gun?"

Hogan turned on his heel and went to check out the man James had shot. He examined the bloody corpse, then leaned over to pick up the revolver the man had been carrying.

"That guy was only a damned mechanic. What's he doing carrying a gun?"

"Maybe he was insecure," McCarter suggested.

"Mister, he is not insecure any longer. He is dead."

"You went and did it again," McCarter chided Calvin James.

Katz appeared, followed by Manning and Encizo. The Israeli took in the scene, glancing at James and McCarter with an "it better be good" expression on his face.

"Now you're bloody well for it," McCarter whispered.

"Thanks for the support," James said.

"THAT'S THE WAY it went down," McCarter said as he completed his rundown on the shooting incident. "Cal had no choice. That big feller just came out of nowhere and drew down on us. It was him or us."

"Him or you," James corrected. "He decided to shoot you. And I went and stopped him."

"All right," Katz said. "Enough said. I'm glad you're both unhurt."

"Where are Dexter and Ketchum now?" Mc-Carter asked.

"Sergeant Hogan has them locked up in a secure trailer, under guard."

"Something I said spooked Dexter," McCarter said. "The minute I left him he went hotfoot to find his chum so they could have a chinwag."

"Us turning up and asking questions must have worried them," Encizo said.

"Only if they had something to be worried about," Gary Manning said.

"Precisely." Katz stood up. "It might be worthwhile checking out their lockers and toolboxes."

He led the way out of the trailer Eric Talpern had loaned them for their discussion. Talpern himself was in discussion with Sergeant Hogan. He glanced around as Katz called him.

"We need to check out where Dexter and Ketchum keep their equipment," Katz said.

Talpern nodded without speaking. The incident seemed to have genuinely shocked the man. He led Phoenix Force across the site and unlocked the trailer McCarter had visited before.

"Do you need me to wait?" he asked.

"No," Katz said. "We'll be fine."

"I have to go and talk to our guests. This whole unfortunate affair has caused them some concern."

"We'll let you know when we're finished," Katz said.

"Let's go over this place really carefully," Katz instructed. "Don't ask me what we're looking for. Just check the place out."

The interior of the trailer had been fitted out as an office cum workshop. Computers shared the space with electronic equipment and the tools of the technicians' trade.

"Who thought up this idea?" McCarter asked as he surveyed the mass of gadgetry.

"Come on, David," Katz said. "The sooner we start..."

"I know."

Each Phoenix member took a section of the trailer. They initiated a thorough search, checking drawers and lockers, folders holding documents, poking into every corner they found.

Almost a half hour passed.

Gary Manning slumped down in a swivel chair and stared around. The expression on his face mirrored the thoughts of the other Phoenix members.

"We could be staring right at something and not know it, Katz," he said.

"I can't recognize half this stuff," James commented.

"Half?" McCarter complained. "The only bloody thing I can recognize is this ashtray. And that's because it's got a fag end in it."

"It was worth a try," Katz said, almost ready to admit defeat.

"Hold on, guys, I think I've got something here," Rafael Encizo called from the rear of the trailer.

He was standing at a workbench that was bolted to the wall. As the others crowded around, Encizo showed them the small toolbox he'd emptied. He had a thin-bladed screwdriver he was using as a probe, gently inserting it into a slender gap between the bottom of the box and the front face.

"I wouldn't have noticed if the blade of the screwdriver hadn't been wedged there," he explained.

Encizo's gentle persuasion with the screwdriver blade suddenly bore fruit. The apparently solid base of the toolbox tilted slightly. A little more work with the blade enabled Encizo to reach inside and draw the false bottom out of the box.

A piece of foam padding covered the top of the secret compartment. When Encizo lifted it, there was another section of foam lining the base, and a computer circuit board nestling on it.

"I think this justifies our suspicions," Katz said. "It's time we brought Talpern in to take a look. Cal, go find him. It might also be a good idea to ask Gil Hanley along. Maybe he can identify this piece of hardware for us."

TALPERN WAS SHOCKED when he saw what Phoenix Force had discovered. He examined the toolbox, then the circuit board.

"You realize what this means," he said.

"It means someone has been buggering about with the THAAD control system," McCarter stated simply.

Gil Hanley didn't say a word. He simply reached over and took the circuit board from the box so he could examine it in detail. For a while he peered closely at the board, turning it over and over. Finally he handed it back to Katz.

"Can you identify it?" the Israeli asked.

"The layout is familiar," he said. "I'm pretty certain it does come from the control system. I can get you confirmation by checking the serial numbers printed on the board. The configuration looks like the one used by CyberPlus."

He turned and crossed to one of the computers. Logging in, he tapped in codes and brought up displays of complicated numbers. After juggling with the digits, he concentrated on one sequence, finally reducing the mass to a lesser display. He gave a satisfied grunt, nodding.

"Here," he said, gesturing for Katz to join him. Using the tip of a ballpoint pen, Hanley identified a number sequence.

"That's the one. Same as the circuit board. Now according to the analysis, that board is part of the system's IMRF—Identification Memory Recall Facility. In layman's terms it's the part of THAAD that recognizes an incoming missile as unfriendly and activates the seek-and-destroy sequence."

"So if someone laid in another board with false information, THAAD might scan an incoming missile, recognize it as a friendly and allow it to fly free?"

Hanley glanced at Calvin James as if the Phoenix warrior's words were a complete revelation to him.

"Well, yes, that could be done," he admitted. "My god, are you suggesting that's what may have been done to our trial unit?"

"Only one way to find out," Katz said. "Can you bring up the stored memory on screen?"

"It can be done," Hanley said.

"We'd better give it a try, then," Katz suggested.

Phoenix Force stood behind Gil Hanley as he booted up the main computer inside the control trailer. Eric Talpern's expression became distinctly grim as he recalled the incidents of the day. He seemed to be taking everything very personally.

The monitors in front of Hanley burst into life, each displaying a different set of images. Hanley ignored them all except the screen directly in front of him. As his fingers flew across the keyboard, the screen display altered constantly. He finished up with a screen asking him for security clearance. Hanley had to think about it for a few moments, then keyed in what must have been his personal access code. The screen digested the information, blipped, then changed.

"Got it!" Hanley said triumphantly.

He keyed in more instructions and was presented with yet another screen asking for information.

"It's asking for specifics now."

"What missile is being used tomorrow?" Katz asked.

Hanley stared at him, realization suddenly hitting him. "You don't mean . . ." He returned to his keyboard and tapped in data. The on-screen display changed, scrolling, then settled. Hanley was confronted with yet another demand for access codes. He worked on the keyboard for a few minutes, getting refusals at first.

"Someone has been tampering with the access codes," he said. "Everything has been changed around. The key is here somewhere. Even if this is a counterfeit program, it has to configure with the rest of the information or the main program won't accept it."

Hanley's fingers moved swiftly over the keyboard as he attempted to override the access denial. There was a sudden flurry of symbols across the monitor, then Access Granted appeared. This was followed by a simple text display.

"The incoming aircraft is due to launch an AG-86 cruise missile at a designated target five miles beyond the test-site location," Hanley said. "The test of THAAD's capability will be for it to track and lock on, then fire off its own ground-to-air missile, designated Rattler. If the first missiles miss, the Patriot-type missile system is held in reserve for close range.

"The original program for the test had been written so that the satellite detectors and the ground radar would recognize the AG-86 as unfriendly and take action. But the program now has the AG-86 as a friendly missile. The system would not acknowledge it as hostile and would ignore it.''

''Making the trial a slight disappointment,'' Manning observed.

''I can think of something stronger than that,'' James said.

''The project would be given the thumbs-down by a lot of people,'' Talpern said.

''I need a bloody smoke,'' McCarter muttered.

He wandered through the office and pushed the door open so he could step outside.

The first thing he saw was a brightly painted helicopter sweeping in over the site. Already low, it came in fast, and the moment he spotted it McCarter knew it wasn't in the area for a sight-seeing trip.

CHAPTER FOURTEEN

Stony Man Farm, Virginia

Fatigue crept up on Barbara Price during moments of inactivity. She was on her way to meet Hal Brognola in the Computer Room, following a summons from Kurtzman. She carried a clipboard in one hand and a mug of coffee in the other, and during the walk to the lab she allowed herself a few moments of relaxation. It was an indulgence she rarely allowed during mission time, but Price was aware of her own limitations. She also knew the toll that Stony Man placed on its operatives, so those few stolen moments were precious to her. Nevertheless she felt the heavy hand of tiredness steal across her, and determined to shake it off before she faced Brognola and Kurtzman.

"Miss Price, you okay?"

She blinked and glanced around at the voice.

Stony Man's chief of security stood regarding her with concern in his eyes

"I'm fine, Chief. Just taking five on my way to the lab."

He studied her for a moment.

"You take care now," he said. "Those boys out there need you."

He moved on, continuing his rounds. He shouldered the responsibility for the Farm's security, which was no easy task. Just one more of the dedicated team sharing the burden on the secret that was Stony Man.

Price reached the Computer Room and pushed through the door. Brognola was standing over Kurtzman's desk, staring at a monitor screen. The rest of Kurtzman's cybernetic team was in residence, and Price sensed a mood urgency. Crossing the room, she stood beside Brognola. He glanced up as she appeared. He looked almost haggard.

"Do we have a problem?" Price asked.

Kurtzman scrubbed a big hand through his hair, stretching his stiff body.

"Got some new information here," he said. "It took us a while to pull it all together, but once it gelled a lot of things started to make sense."

"Aaron's team has been scouring all their information sources on this one," Brognola explained. "Every scrap of information we've tagged has been followed to source, if possible—feedback from Able Team and Phoenix Force, and even the material Striker managed to let us have."

"We followed through on the background information the FBI gave us after Able Team found those dead agents," Kurtzman said. "We scanned CIA files, NSA—you name it, we checked it. We even accessed Interpol, Scotland Yard and the British SIS. Hell, we just threw out all the nets and trawled every network we could. Came up with a lot of garbage, but every now and then something clicked, so we started to put it all together.''

"This is starting to sound big," Price said.

"Maybe bigger than we first thought," Brognola said. "Akira, bring those print sheets over here."

Tokaido swept up a scattering of papers and carried them across to a table. He began to spread them out as Brognola, followed by Kurtzman and Price, joined him.

"We already know a number of the faces here," Brognola said. He pointed out the individuals they had dealt with earlier. "A connection has been established between Han Nor and Victor Suliman. The guy here is Marcus Glastonbury. We have him down as a fixer and arranger. He brings parties together for their mutual financial benefit and takes a nice cut for his troubles. The guy has worldwide connections and knows all the right people. Pretty handy around government circles, as well. The British government has used him on occasion. They might change their mind if he turns out to be dealing in illegal negotiating. *Maybe*. Now here we have Jordan Delacourt. He provides the frontline troops for this operation. Able Team tangled with a number of hardmen during their search for the missing Hanson family. All the deceased have been identified as being on Delacourt's payroll."

"My FBI contact threw in some more names for us to check on," Carmen Delahunt said, pointing out three of the photo images. "Harry Orchard, Mal Burton and Les Cribbins. They all work for Delacourt. The FBI has been keeping tabs on them for a while. They were seen in California recently, but they dropped out of sight around the time the Hanson family went missing."

"Do we have any starting point?" Price asked.

"Possibly," Delahunt said. "Cribbins, who's British, has an ongoing relationship with a girl in Las Vegas named Laura Francis. She works as a dancer in one of the casinos. Apparently he's pretty hot on her and doesn't like staying away for too long. She could be worth a visit to see if Cribbins has been in contact recently."

"I'll assign Able Team to that," Price said. "Give me all you have on this woman, Carmen."

Delahunt handed over a computer printout. "Thought you'd never ask."

"Now we come to the twister," Brognola said. "This one is Akira's. He can tell you."

"Remember we couldn't get anything on the Sayato woman," Tokaido said. "She seemed too clean to be true, especially when you look at what she was involved in. I did some more digging. There is a Jennifer Sayato, and she did go to UCLA. Her parents live in Hawaii. The problem starts with the body in the Santa Clara morgue. It's not Jennifer Sayato."

"Do we know who she was?" Price asked.

Tokaido nodded. "We do now. According to the coroner, the dead woman is Soon Tek Yun. He got this from her dental records. She's North Korean, but has been living in the U.S. for three years, ever since she defected from a trade mission over here from North Korea."

"They took Sayato's identity to plant their person at CyberPlus," Delahunt said. "But where is the real Sayato?"

"The way these people play, I'd hate to guess," Kurtzman said.

"Another connection with Korea," Price said. "It ties in with the sabotage theory." She paused as if there was more to say, but stayed silent.

Brognola glanced at her. "Something on your mind?"

"Probably nothing."

"Share it with us," Brognola said.

"I can't help thinking about the recent—and current—problems with the Koreans, all tied in with nuclear weapons and the spread of those weapons to certain regimes. If we look at who is involved in this present crisis, there are the Koreans and the Libyans. Some murmurs from Iran. Now we have Yuri Rostok, who was pretty high up in the Soviet missile program. I mean, what's his involvement? People of his expertise don't appear on photographs along with Nor, Suliman and Glastonbury just for the hell of it. Rostok is mixed up in this somewhere. I believe we need to know why, because I'm starting to get a bad feeling about it all."

Brognola watched Price as she spoke, listening carefully. He trusted her instincts as he would have trusted his own, and more than that, he respected her. She had proved her worth on more than one occasion. He saw no reason why he shouldn't go with her feelings this time, either. Because if she was right, Stony Man could be facing something much worse than a sabotage attempt on an antimissile system.

"All right, people, you heard the lady. Let's get those computers earning their keep. Dig and keep on digging. Every damn source you can think of, and then some. I need answers and I need them fast."

They left the Computer Room together, returning to the War Room. As the door closed behind them, Brognola made for the coffeepot and poured himself a cup. He took a gulp, then glanced at his watch.

"It's that late?" he asked.

Price nodded. That was the trouble with Stony Man—once they were inside, with no immediate contact with the outside world, time slipped by at an alarming rate. Night and day could pass unnoticed. Life and death played their eternal game, and friends could vanish alongside enemies.

"Anything come through from London?" Price asked, unable to hold back her curiosity.

"Yeah. I spoke to one of the prime minister's closest aides. Apparently Striker's report was accurate. The undercover unit has been wiped out. They're all dead. And the safehouse was compromised."

"And Mack?"

Brognola shook his head. "No word. He hasn't contacted anyone. Not surprising, since the undercover unit *was* his contact point. With it gone, Striker is on his own. He won't touch base until he knows it's rock solid."

Price dropped her clipboard on the big table and crossed to refill her own coffee cup.

One of the phones rang. Brognola picked it up.

Turning on her heel, Price caught the look of relief in his eyes even before he spoke.

"Striker! What's going on over there?"

Price leaned over and picked up on one of the other phones. She didn't speak, but simply listened in.

"I'm still in London. I'm going to check out this mail-order company. It trades under the name Variety Merchandising. One of the hardguys I took out earlier had their card in his pocket. It didn't seem like a business he would frequent, unless they're in his line of business. An outside chance, but I don't have anything else to go on. It's early morning over here.

The place looks pretty deserted, but I have a feeling something might be going down. I might get lucky and meet Han Nor and his business partners."

"Striker, I'm trying to set you up with a fresh contact, someone who can cover you if the need arises. Do your best to stay in touch."

"It's pretty hairy out here, Hal. Not always easy to find a phone when you need one. Any fresh Intel for me?"

"We've IDed a new face in the game," Price said, jumping in. "Yuri Rostok. He used to be in charge of Soviet missile deployment, including a fair number of the satellite states. He probably has the numbers on a lot of stashed hardware."

"That could step this mission up a notch or two," Bolan said. "From sabotage to high-stakes weapons dealing. Even nuclear blackmail. I can think of a few unfriendly regimes who'd give their annual wheat crop for a few tactical nuclear weapons they could use to wave at their enemies, the U.S. included."

"It's the route we were going, Striker," Brognola said. "Pretty scary when you think about it."

"So what is Han Nor doing for the deal?"

"I've been thinking about that since Rostok's name came up," Price said. "This comes off the top of my head, but it might be worth considering. North Korea can supply missiles but doesn't have the capability to produce a steady supply of nuclear warheads yet. Rostok could be the guy who can. Bring the two together and you have a going concern.''

"If I were you, Hal, I'd watch out for my job," Bolan said. "This is one clever lady."

"Damn right. And the way she lays it out is not far wrong, I'd guess. Korea can ship its missiles wherever it wants. Borders don't exist for the countries it deals with. In fact, they'll do everything they can to ensure they receive their missiles without any hitches. Rostok probably has the backdoor connections to ship his warheads the same way."

"Striker, what's your next move?" Price asked.

"You've given it to me. I go after Nor, Suliman and Rostok. See just how they're tied together."

"Hey!" Price said. "Take care now."

"Yeah. And you."

The phone went dead in Price's hand. She glanced across at Brognola. His expression matched her own.

They had briefly made contact with Mack Bolan, only to immediately consign him back to the hellgrounds.

CHAPTER FIFTEEN

Les Causses Training Area, France

The helicopter dropped low, skimming the ground as it headed directly for the site.

McCarter yelled a warning over his shoulder, yanking out his Browning and gripping it two-handed. He moved away from the chopper's line of travel, dropping to one knee, and tracked the moving aircraft as it sank to ground level. He could see a black-clad figure in the open hatch, wielding a Heckler & Koch MP-5. The guy opened fire, laying down a volley that drove the closest people into cover. Two didn't make it and went down under the spray of bullets.

Behind McCarter, the rest of Phoenix Force came piling out the door, weapons up and ready.

"What's going on?" Encizo asked as he came alongside McCarter. "Who are these guys?"

McCarter shrugged. "All I know is they're not selling health insurance."

The helicopter touched the ground and four armed figures sprang from the open hatch, fanning out across the site. They were all armed with H&K autoweapons, and it was obvious from the start that they meant business.

Katz tapped Manning on the shoulder.

"Let's try to cut them off," he said. "We can use the vehicles for cover. Cal, you circle around the other side."

"Rafael, with me," McCarter said. "Let's take out that bloody guy in the chopper before he hits anyone else."

Encizo nodded. He followed McCarter as the Brit cut off at an angle, closing in on the chopper and its armed guard.

They were still a distance away when another black-clad man dropped from the open hatch. He ducked low and planted himself near the front of the chopper. As he scanned the surrounding area, the H&K in his hands crackled suddenly and a uniformed figure slumped to the ground, clutching a bloody, shattered hip. It was one of Hogan's Marines.

McCarter spotted suited figures, guns in their hands, working their way through the parked vehicles and trailers. They were some of the assorted security men who accompanied the attending government ministers and military personnel.

Bloody idiots, the Brit thought. They should be taking care of their charges, not playing heroes.

He didn't give the agents any further thought.

The armed men near the front of the chopper had seen something that had drawn his attention. He swung around and triggered his weapon. Bullets clanged against metal, shattered windows and rocked the car that was the target. Bullets also found human flesh, and a man who had been using the vehicle as cover fell into view. The man's face glistened with red. He slumped forward across the trunk of the car, a handgun slipping from his fingers.

McCarter had seen enough.

"Cover me," he said to Encizo, and before his companion could protest, McCarter had broken cover and was heading directly for the helicopter.

KATZ AND MANNING had circled the vehicle that lay between them and the temporary guard hut. Calvin James had moved out on his own to make his approach from the other side.

They were still working their way toward the trailer when a burst of autofire alerted them. It came from the direction of the trailer.

"Go," Katz yelled, and broke into a trot, flicking off his P-88's safety.

Manning moved a few feet to one side, his own weapon held ready.

More autofire rattled out, followed by the single crack from a handgun.

As Katz rounded the corner of a portable outhouse, he saw the Marine who had been guarding the hut down on one knee, his right arm hanging limply at his side. He had transferred his pistol to his left hand, and as Katz took in the scene, the Marine triggered his weapon twice, punching 9 mm slugs into the upper chest of one of the attackers. The black-clad man went down hard and didn't move.

Turning abruptly, one of the remaining hardmen pointed his subgun at the lone Marine, his finger curling back against the trigger.

Katz brought up the P-88 and fired, his bullet driving into the side of the attacker's skull. It plowed through and blew out the other side, spinning the fatally hit man off his feet.

Manning and James appeared then, in different positions, and they joined the firefight without hesitation.

There was a rapid exchange of fire.

Calvin James, dropping to one knee, braced his autopistol in a two-handed grip. He aimed and fired in a split second, laying a bullet in the chest of one attacker. The guy stumbled, badly hit, but made a last-ditch attempt at firing. He was caught by another slug from James and a follow-up from the wounded Marine. The guy sank to the ground, releasing a deep, withering sigh as he expired.

Gary Manning fired on the move, catching his target in the right shoulder. The Canadian's bullet chewed a bloody chunk from the target's body. He cursed, spinning around to face the man who had shot him and began to spray the area with autofire. Manning felt something clip his left side, and moments later blood began to stream from the shallow wound. Forcing back the sickness that followed the trauma of the hit, Manning triggered his pistol, loosing off a steady burst of four shots. They caught the attacker in the upper chest and throat, knocking him to the ground, where he died in a welter of bloody froth that erupted from his gaping mouth.

"Check," Katz yelled to James, indicating the wounded Marine. Then he turned and went to where Manning had dropped to his knees, clamping a big hand over the soggy wound that seemed to be spilling enough blood to swim in.

"Jesus," Manning said, grimacing. "As David would say, it bloody well hurts."

"Sit down and don't move," Katz said. "I'll get medical help for you."

His words were almost lost in the sudden eruption of an explosion. Back where they had left McCarter and Encizo, a pall of smoke coiled into the air, staining the blue sky with oily tendrils.

"At least David appears to be enjoying himself," Manning said.

THE MOMENT MCCARTER SAW the second man, he nudged Encizo.

"Which one do you want?" he asked.

"No time for games, David," the Cuban said with a quick smile. "Let's go."

He broke to the right, indicating he was going to deal with the man crouched in the open hatch.

"Well, okay, I'll take the other bloke," McCarter said to himself, moving to the left.

The SMG in the guy's hands moved around as McCarter briefly showed himself. The muzzle crackled and a stream of slugs whacked into the side of the truck beside McCarter. He ducked back as metal fragments filled the air. Dropping to the ground, McCarter wriggled under the truck, beneath the rear axle, and gauged the distance between himself and the armed man. He leveled the Browning, aimed and fired in a fluid movement.

The single 9 mm slug caught the enemy just above the left ear, coring deep into his skull. He toppled over backward, his finger jerking the H&K's trigger, sending a stream of slugs into the chopper's canopy. The canopy starred and shattered, showering the waiting pilot with fragments, and a split second later he was hit by a number of the wayward slugs. The pilot jerked backward, hands and feet twitching in his agony. The idling chopper lurched violently, lifting a few feet, then dropped again with a solid crash.

The moment the helicopter moved, the guy in the hatch threw out a hand to steady himself. Rafael Encizo broke out into the open, his pistol up and firing. He emptied the magazine into the armed guy in the hatch, driving him back inside the chopper's cabin. The stricken man, lost in sudden pain, tried to return fire, but didn't realize that he was firing blind. His slugs tore through the thin fuselage and ripped into the fuel tank.

As the aviation fluid burst free, spraying in all directions, some fell into the shower of sparks caused by ricocheting bullets. The vapor ignited and the subsequent gush of flame raced back to the ruptured, spurting fuel tank. There was a swell of flame, followed by a heavy explosion that ripped the chopper apart and consumed it in a ball of fire. The aircraft vanished, burning fiercely, its alloy construction engulfed along with the men who had arrived in it only minutes before.

"Bugger it," McCarter muttered as he scrambled to his feet. "I know who'll get the bloody telling off for that little lot."

THE STRIKE TEAM had killed two and wounded two more, not counting Gary Manning. None of the attackers remained alive. As much as he would have liked to have kept at least one man alive for questioning, Katz comforted himself with the knowledge that Phoenix Force had responded as swiftly as possible and had prevented the strike team from inflicting even more damage. He regretted the deaths and wounding of the innocent parties, but it happened, and no amount of self-recrimination would alter the

statistics. Instead Katz concentrated on the living—
especially the two prisoners.

Once peace had been regained and the test site
brought under control, Katz decided it was time to
question Dexter and Ketchum. He had the pair
brought into the command trailer, where the rest of
Phoenix Force was assembled.

The prisoners were cuffed. Katz had them seated.

"We'll never know," he began, "whether your
friends had actually come to free you or silence you."

"Like they did to Deiter and Wulf," McCarter
suggested.

"We all know how that turned out," James added.
"Must save your bosses a hell of a lot on bonus pay-
ments."

Ketchum leaned back in his seat, a smirk on his
face.

"Don't waste your breath," he said. "You won't
get anything from us."

"Tut-tut," McCarter chided. "Who said we
wanted anything from you, fellers?"

"Maybe we just wanted to chat," Manning said
from where he was sitting. He wore a snug bandage
over the bullet wound. The painkillers the medic had
given him were starting to fade, and a nagging ache
was starting to burn. "And a chance to tell you we
found your little surprise."

"What's he talking about?" Dexter asked.

"The new circuit board you fitted to the control computer," Katz said. "The one that would have fed false information to the defense system and caused THAAD to fail its trail."

"To put it another way," James said, "you screwed up, guys."

"I think you knew it when I came to see you," McCarter said, glancing at Ketchum. "Which was why you must have called home base and told them to lift you and Dexter out. That's what you were discussing when we smoked you out and your pet mountain tried to pop us."

"All in all, you two are pretty inefficient," Manning said. "If I was employing you, I'd cut my losses and have you iced."

"Like Greenburg said, maybe that's what the hit team were on their way to do," Encizo said. "Making sure you couldn't talk. Dead men don't spill the beans."

He let the words hang in the silence that followed.

Ketchum's arrogant smirk remained in place. He was in control of himself. If Encizo's words had a ring of truth, Ketchum wasn't allowing any emotions to show.

His partner was another matter. Dexter had a sheen of sweat across his upper lip. His eyes moved constantly, flicking back and forth between the members of Phoenix Force. He fidgeted restlessly in his seat.

Katz took out a pack of cigarettes and used his steel prosthesis to extract one and light up. He took a long draw, inhaling the smoke. Out of the corner of his eye he could see Dexter watching the tobacco smoke curling up from the end of the cigarette.

Leaning across to Manning, Katz said quietly, "Take Ketchum out. I want Dexter on his own."

Manning nodded and moved behind Ketchum. He prodded him with the barrel of his autopistol. Ketchum looked up, startled for an instant. He opened his mouth to speak, but Manning jabbed him even harder with the muzzle of the gun, forcing Ketchum to his feet and turning him away from Dexter.

Encizo realized the ploy and stepped into join Manning. The Cuban didn't speak. He simply took out his Tanto dagger and laid the keen edge of the blade against Ketchum's throat. Ketchum felt the chill caress of the blade pressing against his flesh. He stayed silent, realizing that if he made any outcry, the blade would cut into his flesh through his own actions. He allowed Manning and Encizo to take him out.

Dexter, aware of something happening, tried to turn, but Calvin James stepped in beside him and cut off his view.

The door closed behind Ketchum. Placing the pack of cigarettes on the desk beside him, Katz waited. The aroma of tobacco filled the room. David McCarter tried to ignore the smell, but his longing for a cigarette was increased by the drifting smoke. He scowled at Katz across the top of Ketchum's head.

"We might be able to arrange some tight security for you," Katz said. "Releasing you to the local cops won't guarantee it."

"Not after what happened to Deiter and Wulf," James said. "Your people are well informed and organized. Two dead men prove that."

"It's not like that," Dexter said, too quickly and with little conviction in his voice. He slumped back in his seat, uncertainty showing in his eyes.

"Played you for suckers," McCarter said from behind the man. The Brit's words echoed around the room. "Hire you to do their dirty work, then have you wiped out when things start to backfire. Nice bunch to work for. Hope they paid you well. You're going to be an old man by the time you get out of prison."

"*If* he gets out," James said. "French jails aren't like those back home."

Dexter's head snapped around and he stared at the Phoenix commando. "A French jail? That won't happen. I'm an American."

"Trouble is, old chum, you committed your nasty little crimes on French soil. As far as they're concerned, that's all that matters. Once we turn you over to the French authorities, it's out of our hands."

"You can't do that," Dexter said. "I'm no professional criminal. I just..."

"Helped in an attempt to sabotage equipment being tested on French soil, courtesy of the French government," Katz said. "We are guests here. The French get very touchy about this kind of thing. They become extremely territorial in these matters. Of course the U.S. will probably protest over your being kept in a French jail, but they will have to tread very lightly because of the delicacy of the situation. Could take years to get you back home to stand trial. If you live that long."

"And in the meantime you'll be stuck in one of the French jails. You speak French?" James asked.

Dexter shook his head. He stared from man to man, seeking a sympathetic eye. Only Katz seemed to show any degree of concern.

"I'm not saying we could do anything, but we might try and get you on board a plane for the States. It would depend on certain things."

"Such as?" Dexter asked, seeing a glimmer of light at the end of an increasingly dark tunnel.

"You have to decide whether staying silent and remaining here in France is in your best interests," Katz said. "In the end, Dexter, it's up to you."

Dexter sank back in his seat, aware of what Katz meant. His salvation lay in his own hands. He could remain silent concerning his involvement with the sabotage conspiracy and these men would turn him over to the French authorities. If the people he worked for didn't get to him, as they had to Deiter and Wulf, then he would find himself locked up in a foreign country where he didn't even speak the language. He would be away from anyone he knew, out of touch with his own kind, abandoned and forgotten.

Dexter realized he had little choice. His best option rested with his own people. And no one else was going to do anything to help him.

So he helped himself, and he began by doing a lot of talking.

CHAPTER SIXTEEN

Las Vegas, Nevada

Jack Grimaldi had flown Able Team to McCarran International Airport and put the helicopter down in a quiet corner. As he shut off the power, the three Stony Man commandos disembarked, each man carrying a duffel bag.

"If this goes easy, we should be back in a couple of hours," Lyons said.

Grimaldi had to smile. He was used to the phrase. And knowing Able Team's propensity for attracting less than peaceful types, he would not have been surprised if they returned fresh from a confrontation.

"I made a joke or something?" Lyons asked.

Rosario Blancanales nudged the blond man's arm. "Remember, Jack has been out with us before on *peaceful* missions."

Lyons shrugged. "Not our fault if we bring out the worst in people."

"Take it easy, guys," Grimaldi said.

Crossing to the main terminal building, Lyons sought out the nearest car-rental company and rented some transportation. When the paperwork was completed he picked up the keys and led Schwarz and Blancanales out into the hot Nevada morning. The car, a dark blue Chrysler, was parked at the end of the row. As soon as they were inside, Lyons switched on the air-conditioning, working the control until the vents were blasting out ice-cold air.

"Go easy," Blancanales said. "I don't want to be the only guy to catch frostbite in Nevada."

"Never satisfied," Lyons muttered, gunning the engine and swinging the car out of the parking lot.

A little later, as they cruised along the Strip, with world-famous casino names on both sides, Carl Lyons took yet another glance in the rearview mirror and grunted.

"What?" Blancanales asked.

"We're being followed," Lyons said.

Neither Blancanales nor Schwarz turned his head to look behind. Instead they both turned their gaze on the rearview mirror.

"The Blazer or the Ford?" Schwarz asked.

"It's the Blazer," Blancanales said.

"How do you know?" Schwarz asked.

"Because it was parked up on the street when we left the airport."

"Maybe the Ford is part of the tail, as well," Lyons said. "A backup car in case they figure they've overdone it with the Blazer."

"Could be," Blancanales said. "But my money is on the Blazer."

"Okay, let's check him out," Lyons suggested.

He touched the gas pedal and accelerated, then made a left onto West Sahara Avenue. He drove a couple of blocks, then made a right. The Ford had gone, but the Blazer stayed with them—at a discreet distance.

"I've had enough of this," Lyons muttered. "You guys ready?"

Blancanales and Schwarz nodded, knowing better than to argue with Carl Lyons once he'd made up his mind to do something.

Lyons kept going for another few hundred yards, then stood on the brakes, bringing the rental car to a shuddering halt. He was out of the car, Python in his hand, running back along the street to where the Blazer had also come to a halt. Blancanales and Schwarz followed, spreading so they could cover the Blazer on all sides.

His weapon leveled at the two men in the front of the Blazer, Lyons ordered them out, with hands showing.

By this time Lyons's partners had joined him. They moved in to cover the Blazer's two occupants.

"Hold it! Hold it!" the Blazer's driver said as he stepped out of the vehicle. "FBI!"

"Oh, great," Schwarz said. "You hear that, Randall? Now we're being trailed by the Feds."

"Agent Marcus," the driver said. "This is Agent Kilkenny. You mind if I show you my ID?"

Lyons, scowling darkly, lowered his revolver. He stared in disgust at the pair of FBI men, and pointedly ignored the ID wallet that Marcus produced.

"I hate to ask this, but what in hell are you guys doing following us?" Blancanales asked, losing his usual cool in moments of stress.

"Our orders came via Washington. We were told to oversee you through any investigations if you turned up in Vegas."

"What do you mean oversee?" Lyons yelled. "This is our investigation. We didn't ask for and we don't want a pair of Quantico nursemaids."

"Mr. Randall, we didn't request this assignment," Kilkenny said. He was young, earnest and clean-cut, and didn't look as if he'd ever had a pimple in his life. "If we get orders from the top, we follow them, same as you would."

Blancanales stepped forward, replacing his Python in its holster.

"We've had a pretty rough few days," he said. "Most of the people we've met have done their best to kill us, so we're a little edgy. Cut us some slack, guys."

Agent Marcus held up his hands. "The last thing we want to do is get in your way. How about if we take a ride back to the airport and see if we can spot you guys coming in?"

"Okay," Blancanales said. "Hey, thanks for the thought. If we pick anything up that might help nail the people who shot your buddies in Oregon, we'll pass it along."

"Appreciate that," Marcus said. He glanced at Lyons, who was still simmering. "No hard feelings?"

Lyons smoldered for a few more seconds, then nodded slowly. He turned and made his way back toward the car. Blancanales and Schwarz followed. No one said a word until they were moving again and the Blazer had turned around and vanished.

"Nice of the FBI to worry about us," Schwarz said lightly.

Before Blancanales could add his flippant comments, Lyons's voice rose from the front of the car.

"Enough," he said. "No more FBI cracks or I'll shoot the pair of you myself."

LAURA FRANCIS LIVED in a rented house on the outskirts of Las Vegas. The house had a rear view of the open desert. Inside its fenced area, there was a wide patio and a medium-size swimming pool. There was a gleaming Mustang parked in the driveway.

Sitting in the chilled interior of the rental car, Able Team scanned the area. The quiet street they were parked on baked slowly in the heat.

"I didn't know dancers in Vegas were paid that much," Schwarz commented. "That's a nice place for a working girl."

"Maybe she supplements her income with some horizontal choreography," Blancanales said.

"Say what?"

"He means perhaps she turns a few tricks on the side," Lyons said.

"Oh," Schwarz said. "I thought they turned tricks on their backs."

"The heat's getting to him," Blancanales said.

"Could be her boyfriend Cribbins shares the rent with her," Lyons said.

"Why don't we go ask," Blancanales suggested.

They left the car and crossed the road to the house.

"I'll take the door," Blancanales said. "Talk to her politely and ask if she'll let me in."

Lyons nodded. "I'll go around back, just in case. Gadgets, you go with Pol."

As they reached the house, Lyons broke away from the others. He moved by the Mustang, running his hand along the smooth hood as he passed. The metal was warm, but that could just as easily have been from the hot sun. It didn't mean that the car had been out recently. Reaching the side gate, he let himself through and walked quickly down the length of the house, pausing as he came to the patio. Peering around the corner, he saw that the pool was empty, the paved patio area deserted. He slipped the

Python from his holster and held it down at his side as he moved around the corner of the house.

Flowering plants stood in brightly decorated clay pots, lining the rear wall on either side of glass patio doors. Lyons imagined he could see rapid movement on the other side of the glass doors. Despite the doors being closed, he picked up the sound of raised voices.

A shot followed. Then a woman's screaming voice.

Lyons lunged around the corner, the Python in his hand, thumb against the hammer.

The glass patio doors shattered as a heavy object was hurled through. As the sparkling shards of glass fanned out across the patio, a man leapt through the gap. He held a large chrome-plated pistol in his right hand. Long blond hair streamed out behind him. He hit the patio and would have kept right on running if Lyons hadn't slammed into him.

There was little time for using weapons. Lyons's full force drove the man across the paved area. He swung the heavy pistol up and clouted Lyons across the side of the head. The burst of pain angered Lyons and he hit back, slamming the barrel of the Python across the man's gun arm.

The pistol flew from the man's fingers. He compensated for the loss of his weapon by launching a looping kick that caught Lyons in the ribs, sending him stumbling across the patio. The man gave a wild scream and launched a second kick.

This time Lyons was ready and he dropped to his knees, then lunged up as the leg flew harmlessly overhead. The point of Lyons's broad shoulder slammed into the man's groin and drew a howl of agony. Keeping up his momentum, Lyons rose to his full height, laying his clenched left fist alongside his enemy's jaw. Blood spurted from a split lip. The guy spit, then threw himself at Lyons and caught him in a bear hug.

For a moment the pair teetered, then they toppled over the edge and into the swimming pool. Lyons lost his grip on the pistol as he felt himself being shoved deeper in the water.

Lyons had barely had time to grab a decent lungful of air, so he arched his body and twisted violently, turning the other man so he was beneath him. With a powerful thrust Lyons got his head above water, took a deep breath, then went under again and came into contact with the other man as he started to rise to the surface. Curving his body, Lyons got behind the guy, locked his arms around his throat and began to squeeze the air out of his lungs.

Bright bubbles shot to the surface and the guy began to panic. He thrashed around, arms and legs windmilling, but all he did was use up his dwindling air supply that much faster. Lyons hung on until the guy began to weaken, his movements becoming sluggish. Locking his legs around the man's lower body, Lyons held him underwater until he felt certain the guy had no resistance left. Then he pushed to the surface and allowed Blancanales and Schwarz to drag the man out onto the patio.

Lyons swam to the bottom of the pool to retrieve his Python before hauling himself out. He sat on the edge of the pool, sucking in air and dabbing at the bleeding gash in the side of his head.

"Were you going to drown him?" Blancanales asked.

Schwarz was looping riot cuffs around the prisoner's wrists, pulling them tight.

"We didn't discuss tactics at the time," Lyons said.

"He'll be okay," Schwarz said. "You must have scared the hell out of him."

"He's a scary guy," Lyons said. "What happened in there?"

"The girl answered the door," Blancanales said. Everything was all right until I mentioned the guy's name. Next thing, he comes out of the blue, hollering, and then he took a shot. Missed us and the girl, but she just went to pieces. We went in after him, and he took off. Threw a big bronze ornament through the patio doors. After that we sort of let you take over."

Lyons shrugged out of his waterlogged jacket. He draped it over the back of a patio chair, then stood back, dripping water onto the patio.

He noticed movement just inside the patio doors. A tall, lithe young woman, clad in shorts and a thin sweatshirt stepped outside. She was blond and blue-eyed, attractive. She moved gracefully, with the practiced control of a trained dancer. She had long, tanned legs, muscles firm and sleek beneath the flesh. She stared at the hunched figure of Les Cribbins, then at Able Team. Her eyes reflected the questions on her tongue, and there was doubt and confusion blending with fear.

"Who are you people?" she asked. "What do you want? And why has Les got a gun?"

Blancanales stepped forward, reaching out to take her arm and lead her to one of the patio chairs.

"Let's start from the beginning," he suggested.

Laura Francis sat down. Despite the heat, she was shivering, reaction setting in.

"I don't understand any of this."

"Don't listen to these blokes," Cribbins said, recovering from his session in the pool enough to speak. "They'll tell you—"

Lyons glared at the man. "You want to try another dive?" he asked quietly, eyes blazing with startling intensity.

Cribbins recognized the threat and fell silent.

Blancanales related the circumstances of their investigation to Laura Francis, giving her enough information so she could understand the complexities without becoming confused. She listened in silence, her disbelief slowly being eroded as Blancanales gave her fact on fact, leaving out few of the graphic details so that she might grasp the severity of Cribbins's involvement. When Blancanales had finished she glanced at Les Cribbins with a look of contempt.

"It's all true, isn't it, Les? Now I've heard what these people have to say, it all fits into place. All those times you disappeared for weeks on end, telling me you worked for a courier service that sent you all over the world. And those people you introduced me to—Harry Orchard, Mal Burton. It never meant anything to me then. But they were all the same. Like you. Hired guns—that's all you are. Paid killers."

Cribbins strained against the cuffs holding him, his face taut with anger.

"Never!" he yelled. "Never a hired gun, love. I'm a professional. A soldier. I don't sell myself cheap. Not like you."

The last remark brought her out of her chair. Her move was fluid and swift, and before anyone could intervene she lashed out and kicked Cribbins between the legs. He gave a moan and doubled over in agony.

"Son of a bitch," she said. "I wonder if he's a better shot with a pistol than he is with that. Because I rate him strictly amateur between the sheets."

She turned and went back inside the house.

Schwarz could barely keep a grin off his face. He hauled the gasping Cribbins to his feet.

"Looks to me like you lost out in every department today, pal. No girl. No job. And a possible kidnapping charge on the horizon."

"Easy come, easy go," Blancanales said. "What do we do with this guy, Randall?"

"Let's turn him over to the local FBI," Lyons suggested. "They're dying to get their hands on anyone connected with the murder of those three agents in Oregon."

Blancanales nodded. "I'll go make the call."

"Keep your eye on this creep," Lyons said to Schwarz. "I got something to do."

He went inside the house. Blancanales was already on the telephone, first contacting Stony Man. Lyons checked around and saw Laura Francis in the kitchen. She was spooning coffee grounds into a coffeemaker. As Lyons appeared she glanced up. Her eyes were moist.

"That wasn't very ladylike," she said.

Lyons smiled. "But it was a hell of a kick," he said.

She banged down the spoon and plugged in the coffeemaker. Her movements were abrupt and noisy. She turned suddenly and sat down at the breakfast bar, banging the surface with her clenched fist.

"Damn! He had me fooled, didn't he?"

"No way you could know what he was involved in."

She stared at him. "What about this family, the hostages? Do you have any idea where they might be?"

Lyons shook his head. "I don't see Cribbins telling us, either."

"Is there anything I can do?"

"When did he show up?" Lyons asked.

"Only a couple of hours ago."

"How did he arrive?"

"The car parked outside."

"Was his visit unannounced?"

"No. He called me an hour earlier to say he was in the area and he was going to drop by."

Lyons's interest peaked. "An hour before he arrived? You certain of that?"

She nodded. "Definitely. Does it help?"

"Maybe," Lyons said. He went to where Blancanales was still on the phone. "Get those FBI guys over here fast. We might have a lead."

Blancanales nodded.

Lyons went back outside. "Lester," he said to Schwarz, "check his pockets for keys to that car parked outside."

Moments later Lyons was making his way to the vehicle parked in the driveway. He unlocked it and began a thorough search. The interior was clean and tidy, with little to distinguish it. There were no personal effects.

Lyons slumped back against the seat, running his gaze back and forth across the windshield.

Come on, Carl, he told himself, find it. Find what's under your damn nose—something that's going to point the way to where Cribbins came from, and maybe take you right to where those bastards have Walter Hanson's family.

The answer had been inches from his face. Lyons reached out to flip down the driver's sun visor and expose the registration card. He felt like a rookie cop on his first day out. How many times had he bawled out fresh-faced cops himself for disregarding evidence right under their noises?

He scanned the details printed on the card. The car was registered in Nevada.

To a Thomas K. Brandy.

Who the hell was Thomas K. Brandy?

Lyons slid out of the car and went back inside the house. He made his way to the kitchen, where Laura Francis was pouring fresh coffee into mugs. She handed him one.

"Thomas K. Brandy?" Lyons asked her, waiting for a reaction.

The girl shrugged her slim shoulders. "Never heard the name before."

Taking his coffee, Lyons crossed to the kitchen telephone and dialed. He waited until the connection was made and asked for Barbara Price.

"I need a trace on a vehicle registration," he said. "Mustang. Registered to Thomas K. Brandy. Nevada plates. I'll hold."

Brognola's gruff tones interrupted the silence.

"How goes it?"

"We picked up Cribbins at his girlfriend's," Lyons said. He saw Laura watching him, saw her lips moving in silent protest. "His ex-girlfriend. The lady had her eyes opened by recent events."

"Did Cribbins say anything?"

"Nothing you'd find helpful or amusing. But we might hit pay dirt with the car he was using. That's what I called about. The Bear is running it down now."

Kurtzman broke into the conversation.

"He has run it down, hotshot."

"I'm all ears."

"Thomas Kirk Brandy. Age forty-eight. His location, according to Nevada records, is a place called Roaring Fork, which used to be a railhead back in the early part of the century, but now it's more or less a ghost town. Nothing there but derelict buildings and tumbleweed. Brandy did a hitch in the armed forces. Had his day of glory in Nam, where he was once attached to a special unit. Guess who was his commanding officer?"

"Delacourt?"

"You got it, buddy. No one could prove it, but Brandy was suspected of supplying Delacourt with black-market goods. Since he left the forces he's dabbled in various dubious operations. The guy is slippery. He always manages to stay ahead of the law. Never been caught with the goods. Always seems to have plenty of money, but he dresses and acts like a bum."

"Where did all that come from?" Lyons asked.

"Various sources. His sheet rolled out like a red carpet."

"Let's keep our fingers crossed that he still does favors for Delacourt," Lyons said. "Thanks for the information."

"Anything else?" Brognola asked.

"We're turning Cribbins over to the local FBI. We met them on the way in. They stood off while we followed our lead. I get the feeling they can make good use of Cribbins."

"Okay by me. I take it you'll be following up on the information Bear gave you?"

"It's our only solid piece of information. We might get lucky. If we do, we'll try to pull Hanson's family out alive."

"Watch your backs, you guys," Price said. *"¡Vaya con Dios!"*

"If he'll have us," Lyons replied, and hung up.

CHAPTER SEVENTEEN

Hertfordshire, England

Bolan had removed the big Desert Eagle from the duffel bag and strapped on the high-ride holster. He had dropped spare clips for the Magnum and the Beretta into the inner pocket of the leather jacket. The Browning Hi-Power he had acquired went under his belt in the small of his back, covered by the jacket. Then he had stashed the duffel bag out of sight beneath a low parapet.

He had breached the perimeter fence with little difficulty. Security around the establishment was low-key, but apparent to the Executioner. He spotted a couple of hard-looking guys wandering around at a distance, but they didn't pose any serious threat to him immediately, so Bolan bypassed them and headed for the main building.

His entry to the site had been easy. Maybe too easy, he decided. Based on the earlier realization that his presence in England was known to the opposition, Bolan wondered if they were allowing him to get in without problems, so that he would be on their ground, within the confines of the site and under their jurisdiction. If that was the way they were planning things, the Executioner was going to show them it didn't always pay to cage the tiger.

Light was just beginning to penetrate the misty dawn. The air was chill and damp. The overcast sky threatened more rain, clouds bunching together in swollen formations.

Some of the chill seeped through his clothing. He concentrated on the matter at hand, pushing his personal discomfort to the back of his thoughts.

As he moved deeper into the maze of buildings, the size and shape of them made him wonder what their original purpose might have been. The site itself was massive, rolling back for a number of acres behind the clutter of buildings.

It suddenly came to Bolan where he was. This was the site of a former film studio—one of the many production companies that had flourished on the outskirts of London from the twenties until the late seventies, when the British film industry began to go under. This particular studio had hung on for a little longer, turning to productions for television, but even that failed to provide enough revenue to maintain the organization. Now the sprawling complex had been rented out and was being used by Variety Merchandising to store its goods and house its administration offices.

And what else? Bolan hoped he might find out. Nearing the main block, Bolan spotted a car. It was parked close to a brick outbuilding, and had remained hidden from his view until now.

Bolan recognized it immediately.

It was Clair Tomkins's Ford.

Bolan pulled the Beretta, flicking the selector to 3-round burst.

He circled the building, using the cover provided by the overgrown shrubbery that had been planted long ago, now left to grow wild. Grass sprouted in between the bushes, knee high in places and wet with dew at this early hour. Minutes later Bolan was closing in on the east side of the office block, searching for access.

He almost walked into the first of the roving guards.

They came face-to-face, having missed sight of each other until the final moment.

The guard reacted swiftly, one hand moving to the compact transceiver clipped to his belt, while the other swung up the H&K MP-5 he carried, using it clublike.

Bolan ducked beneath the wild swing, hearing the weapon whistle over his head. His left fist slammed into the guard's right side, striking his ribs with enough force to draw a strangled grunt from the guy. Bolan forced the attack, punching the same spot hard and fast, until the injured guard sagged at the knees. As his head drooped, breath gusting raggedly, Bolan slammed his right knee into the exposed face.

The impact threw the guy off his feet and dropped him on his back with a solid thud. The SMG bounced from his fingers. He twisted over, clawing for the weapon. Bolan leaned in close and encircled the guy's head and neck with his hands and arms. A hard twist and the guy's neck snapped. The guard stiffened, legs kicking straight out, then he became limp and still.

Bolan snatched up the MP-5, checking the mag, then frisked the dead guard for a spare clip that went into his pocket. He cradled the weapon under his arm as he reholstered the 93-R.

This was no time, he decided, for too much pussyfooting around. The only way to handle this situation was with an out-and-out blitz that would take the enemy by surprise.

Following the wall, Bolan searched for a way in. The first door he saw caved in under his powerful kick, and Bolan barreled into the silent passage, the SMG tracking ahead of him. He was no more than a few yards in when an armed figure stepped out of a door. The guy, in shirtsleeves, with an autopistol in one hand a cup of coffee in the other, scanned the passage in both directions before catching sight of Bolan.

"It's fuckin' Bel—" he yelled.

Bolan silenced him with a short blast from the SMG, the stream of slugs shredding the guy's throat and driving him back against the wall where he stood, cold shock in his eyes and hot blood pumping from his ravaged flesh. He was still sliding to the ground as Bolan stepped by him, peering into the room the guy had come from.

A pistol cracked from the far side of the room. The gunner was reaching for a telephone as he triggered the weapon, the bullet plowing into the wall inches from Bolan. The Executioner dropped to one knee, swinging the SMG up in a deadly arc, triggering a burst that tore open the hardman's lower torso and kicked him back over the desk holding the phone.

As the guy crashed to the floor, Bolan turned and left the room, continuing along the passage. He reached the far end without seeing or hearing anyone else. But when he kicked open the door at the far end, stepping to the side as it crashed wide, a sustained burst of fire stitched the passage wall with slugs. Plaster and wood splinters showered across his back.

Bolan, hearing running footsteps approaching, leaned around the doorway, catching a glimpse of the trio heading his way. He opened up with the SMG, his raking burst taking out one man immediately, cutting his legs from under him in a bloody mist. The guy crashed to the floor, screaming, and his companions hesitated for an instant, realizing that they had left themselves without any close cover.

It was too late for them to rectify that mistake. The two gunners caught a brief glimpse of a tall, dark-haired man framed in the open doorway. The subgun in his steady hands was already lined up on them, and before either could bring his own weapon on line, the SMG began to crackle. The pair went down in a hail of slugs that cleaved flesh and shattered bones. Internal organs were reduced to traumatized jelly, and the stricken men were reduced to squirming bloody objects.

Ducking low, Bolan entered the blood-spattered room. It looked as if it was being used as some kind of communications center. There were computers, fax machines, and telephones. The walls were dotted with charts, maps, lists. At this time of day, there did not appear to be too much taking place. The gunners who had attacked Bolan appeared to be nothing more than internal security for the operation, whatever it was.

Bolan closed the door and moved to check out the three gunners. Two were dead. The guy he had dropped first had stopped screaming and lay clutching his shattered limbs, moaning softly to himself. He looked up in alarm as Bolan crouched beside him.

"Where's Clair Tomkins?" Bolan asked.

"I never heard—" the wounded man began to say. He stopped the moment Bolan pressed the warm muzzle of the SMG against his mouth. "Don't!" he pleaded.

"Then answer the question and stop wasting my time."

"They've got her over in one of the old soundstages. Number three. You can't miss it. Out the back."

"How many guns around here?"

The man managed a thin smile. "More than you can handle, Belasko, so don't say I didn't warn you."

"Thanks for the advice," Bolan said. He took away the man's discarded SMG, slinging it across his shoulder by the webbing strap.

"What about me?" the man demanded.

"If you're still alive when I'm through, I'll call for help. If you're not, it won't matter."

With the man's soft curses ringing in his ears, Bolan moved to the far end of the room and went through the door, entering another passage, lined with doors to empty offices. He reached the far end. There was a door there, with a glass panel in its upper half. Bolan could see the wide expanse of the former studio stretching away, the massive soundstages that looked like huge aircraft hangars. There were eight of them, with numbers painted on the high sliding doors.

Bolan's interest focussed on number three.

He was about to open the door when a figure appeared—a guy dressed in casual clothing, brandishing a sawed-off shotgun. The man ran up to the door and shoved it open, still moving. In his haste he failed to see Bolan. The Executioner thrust out his right foot, jamming the opening door and pushing it shut again.

Unable to halt his forward progress, the shotgunner collided with the door, his head and shoulders impacting with the glass panel. The glass shattered, and the guy fell partway through, struggling to keep his balance. Bolan reached out with his left hand and caught hold of the guy's dark hair, yanking him through the broken frame. At the same time he rammed the SMG's muzzle into the guy's chest and pulled the trigger, burning a bloody hole through the man's body. Gouts of bloody flesh erupted from the guy's back. He let out a single stunned grunt as the lethal volley cut through his spinal cord, then he flopped to the ground.

Bolan yanked open the door, stepping over the gunner, and ran across the open space between the administration block and the gigantic soundstages. As he made his run Bolan ejected the near-exhausted magazine and replaced it with a fresh one, cocking the SMG. He reached the second soundstage and paused to check the area. Then he ran to number three.

Bolan heard the doors rattle. Someone inside was either going to open them or secure them from the inside.

He turned and made his way to the side of the building, where he found a small door. Bolan checked it. The door was locked. He remedied that by blowing out the lock with the SMG, then booted the door open and went inside fast, ducking low and to the side.

The interior was gloomy compared to the outside, which suited Bolan fine. He heard a commotion from somewhere within the vast building. Sound carried, echoing.

Someone was shouting orders in a high, cultivated voice that sounded out of place against the harsher, sharper tones that replied.

In the short time he had been inside the building Bolan saw that much of its floor area was taken up by stacked crates and boxes. Steel shelves held other piles of goods. He used the stacks to conceal his movement, working his way deeper into the building, searching for the source of the yelling.

He suddenly broke free and saw a cluster of prefabricated offices that were metal framed and paneled, with glass upper sections. Lights shined from behind the dusty glass, and Bolan made out figures moving around inside.

He scanned the surrounding area. There was an open area of flooring around the offices, twenty-five feet wide.

Off to his left Bolan saw movement. A lean figure wielding an SMG stepped out from the shadowed stacks of crates. The guy was moving slowly, methodically, from one block to another, searching. Bolan expected there to be others, doing the same thing.

He caught a soft whisper of sound behind him a moment later—the rustle of clothing brushing against stacked crates. The next sound was one Bolan would never mistake for anything other than what it was—the oiled click of a gun hammer being eased back.

He sagged, turning, stretching out full length, then heard the handcuffed curse. Then Bolan looked up at the guy's startled, shadow-etched face, and stroked the trigger on the MP-5. The short burst took off the front of the guy's face in a burst of bloody red, and he arched over on his back without a sound.

As Bolan gained his feet he heard footsteps closing in on his position. A split second later the lean guy he'd briefly seen before stood framed in the opening between the crates. Bolan turned sideways, pulling back on the trigger and emptying the SMG's mag into the lean form. The guy went backward as if he'd been yanked on the end of a rope, skidding across the floor.

Tossing aside the empty SMG, Bolan unlimbered the Desert Eagle, snapping off the safety, and broke clear of the crates. He went straight across the open space, his sole object the office block.

Three-quarters of the way across, he heard a yell. Autofire split the air, the shots sounding metallic as they rattled and vibrated within the massive building. Slugs chewed the floor in Bolan's wake, stinging the backs of his legs with concrete splinters. Sucking air into his lungs, Bolan increased his pace, seeing the office block looming before him. He tucked in his head, throwing up his arms to cover his face, and took a headlong, reckless dive through the closest window. Glass imploded as Bolan's hurtling form crossed the sill. He landed inside, half rolling as he skidded across the floor and crashed to a stop against a row of metal filing cabinets standing against the wall.

He came to his feet in a rush, broken glass spraying from his clothing, and as he turned to face the way he'd come, he saw a single armed figure racing across the floor toward the block. Bolan swung up the massive Desert Eagle and triggered two shots. The 240-grain bullets caught the target chest high, splintering bones and spinning the guy off his feet. He was slammed to the floor in a writhing heap.

Bolan turned and peered through the glass partitions that separated the individual offices.

He spotted movement two sections away.

A gun fired, the bullet shattering the partitions. The shot was wide. Bolan returned fire, driving the shooter to cover, and in the time the figure was out of sight Bolan went through one connecting door, then another, meeting the guy as he emerged from cover pawing at a bloody gash on his cheek.

The man was tall, with fair hair and pale, fine-boned features. He was dressed in an expensive suit, and even at this early hour of the day wore a crisp shirt and neatly knotted tie.

Whatever else he might have been, he was no gunman. The small-bore revolver he carried seemed to be giving him some problems, and his concentration was on that rather than keeping his intended target under observation.

Bolan had no reservations as to what his priority was. He slammed open the office door, took two long steps and swung the Desert Eagle in a backhanded strike that caught the suited man under his lean jaw. The man staggered back, blood flowing from the ragged gash. He collided with one of the chairs that dotted the office and crashed to the floor. The revolver bounced from his slim hand. Bolan snatched it up and dumped the cartridges on the floor.

Standing over the whimpering figure, Bolan lowered the Desert Eagle's muzzle until it was centered on the man's face.

"Where is she?" he asked.

The man stared up at him, not comprehending. He kept touching his jaw, gasping at the pain, seeming unable to comprehend where all the blood was coming from.

Bolan kicked against the man's legs.

"Last chance. Where's Clair Tomkins?"

Something in the Executioner's tone broke through. The man stared up at him and visibly shuddered.

"Next office."

Bolan reached down and yanked the man to his feet. He shoved the tall figure before him, following him through to the office beyond.

Tomkins was hunched against the office wall, hands and feet bound. Her clothing was wrinkled and dirty, torn in places. Dark, dried blood marked the front of her blouse. She raised her head as Bolan entered the office, and the first thing he saw were the heavy bruises darkening her skin. Her left eye was badly swollen, the flesh puffed and raw, and her lips were split and bloody.

"Took your time, Belasko," she said slowly. "What does a girl have to do to keep your interest?"

Bolan placed his hand between the tall man's shoulders and shoved him to his knees in front of Tomkins.

"Untie her, and don't waste time."

"Might not be the right place," she said, "but I'll do the introductions. Mike, this is Lawrence Pennell. The Right Honorable Lawrence Pennell, member of Her Majesty's government. A junior minister with special responsibilities. You want to know what those are? He works for the Ministry of Defense. He has also had extensive foreign experience. Worked in the Far East, Latin America, the Gulf States."

As Pennell finished freeing her, Tomkins pushed to her feet, using the wall to steady herself. She self-consciously brushed at her stained clothing.

"We need to get out of here," Bolan said.

"I heard about my squad," she said. "They couldn't wait to tell me how they murdered them all. Killed every last one."

Bolan reached out to take her arm.

"Later," he said gently.

"You know who betrayed them, Mike? He's standing right next to you. The Right Honorable Lawrence Pennell. He gave away our location. Set up my squad so they could be slaughtered. He was the one who gave your name to his people, too. That's why they were waiting for you at the Buckinghamshire house, how they kept on our tail. He's been feeding them information."

"For God's sake, woman, stop your infernal whining!" Pennell said, briefly forgetting his position. "Do you think I give a damn about this loutish Yank, or those back-street policemen? You seem to forget who I am. One phone call and I can have you dragged off and locked up until you're forgotten about. You obviously do not have any idea of the influence I command.''

Whatever Tomkins said was lost in the sudden burst of movement that propelled her at Pennell. Her supple form slammed into him, one knee driving up into his groin with such force that it ripped a howl of animal hurt from his lips. At the same time the heel of her right hand thrust up to connect with the underside of his jaw, driving it shut with crippling force. Blood burst from his mouth as he bit through his own tongue, teeth splintering under the impact. The upward momentum forced Pennell's head back and exposed his taut throat. The point of Tomkins's elbow pulled forward and then slammed back, driving into that naked area.

Pennell began to gag, his crushed windpipe denying him air. He stumbled away from Tomkins, hands clutching his damaged throat, choking violently. Falling to his knees, he bent over, retching, dribbling uncontrollably.

''Now we get out of here,'' Bolan snapped, taking hold of her arm and pulling her with him.

''All right,'' she said. ''Do you have a spare weapon for me?''

Bolan handed her the backup pistol from behind his belt.

''You know how to use it?''

Her look was scathing.

"Han Nor? Suliman? Where are they?" the warrior asked.

"They left late last night. I heard Pennell talking to Holder about it."

"Jack Holder?"

"You know him?"

"Picked up the name."

"He runs the goon squad for this end of the operation. His people carried out the hit on my squad."

"Did you hear where Nor and Suliman were going?"

"Pennell couldn't wait to tell me. He was enjoying every damned minute of it. They were on their way to Suliman's boat in Saint-Tropez. Then they were heading for somewhere called Camp Nine. Does it mean anything, Mike?"

"Maybe," Bolan said.

They were on the move now, crossing the huge expanse of the soundstage. Bolan caught Tomkins's hand and led her to the side door he had used to get inside. He reached the door and eased it open. Outside, the rain had come. It dropped cold and heavy, bouncing off the concrete.

"Your car is at the front," Bolan said.

"Just point me," she replied.

They ducked through the door, Tomkins hard on Bolan's heels as they moved. The downpour hammered at them, soaking them in seconds. The rain bounced off the concrete, misting the air.

Bolan was all set to make the dash across to the main building when he heard the growling roar of a car engine. He glanced around and saw three vehicles converging on their position, headlights bright even in the falling rain.

There was a moment of near inactivity—each side weighing its next move.

"Holder!"

Tomkins pointed at the hard-faced man with short-hair stepping out of one of the cars.

"Let's go," Bolan said, taking her arm and heading back between the two soundstage buildings.

They ran hard and fast, Bolan's only consolation the fact that there was no way Holder could bring his cars after them down the narrow alley between the buildings. Tomkins kept up with him, ignoring the ache in her body, the stinging soreness of the rain on her bruised face. The only thing that mattered right there and then was keeping out of Holder's hands and staying alive.

They reached the far end of the alley, chests heaving as they sucked air into their starved lungs. Before them lay the studio backlot, a warren of false-fronted buildings. The mock streets and squares, long since fallen into disrepair, were silent reminders of the studio's past, when make-believe and fantasy were the order of the day, long removed from the grim reality of the present situation.

"If they reach us," Bolan said, "don't hesitate to use that gun."

Tomkins's only answer was to give him a slow, lopsided smile.

The sound of approaching engines and the squeal of tires on wet concrete reached their ears. The first vehicle came into view, slithering off-line as it rounded a pile of debris. It lurched to a stop, doors opening to disgorge armed men.

"You want to try for the car?" Bolan asked.

"I don't expect we'll be able to pick up a cab."

The Desert Eagle tracked in on one of the gunners as he moved from the car to cover. He didn't reach his destination. The heavy slug from the big pistol slammed him to the ground with the power of a lightning bolt. He rolled, arms and legs spread wide. Bolan fired twice more, laying bullets close to the other gunners and scattering them to cover.

Bolan taped Tomkins on the shoulder.

"Go now," he said, "before the others have time to react."

He pointed to a jutting stack of concrete blocks, half-overgrown with grass, only yards from their position. Tomkins didn't hesitate. She ran directly for the stack, throwing herself down behind it, and she was up and ready by the time the gunners had raised their heads.

They ventured clear of the car's heavy bulk, SMGs probing the way ahead.

Tomkins fired from cover, her bullet taking one man in the leg. He twisted around, yelling in alarm, and then fell silent as Bolan's follow-up bullet caught him in the throat.

The other two gunners opened up, firing wildly, unsure where the hostile shots were coming from. Bolan leaned out and took a long aim before triggering the Magnum. He rode the recoil and saw his target go down hard.

The survivor turned his weapon in Bolan's direction, holding back on the trigger. Slugs tore away the edge of the brick wall, showering Bolan with splinters. One slug caught the barrel of the Desert Eagle, lifting the gun out of Bolan's tingling hand.

Without pause Bolan unlimbered his Beretta. He dropped to his knees, flipping the forward lever down and using it to steady his aim as he followed the sprinting gunner. A touch on the trigger sent a 3-round burst into the running man, stopping him in his tracks. He fell without a sound.

Bolan moved away from the alley, gesturing to Tomkins, and they both ran for the car, tumbling in across the seats. As Bolan turned the key, firing up the engine, Tomkins shouted. Bolan looked up and saw a vehicle lurching into view, accelerating. Armed figures leaned out of open windows.

"They've spotted us, Mike," she said.

Bolan stamped on the gas pedal and set the car into motion, fighting the tail slide as the tires fought for grip on the wet ground. The car picked up speed. Tomkins, glancing in the rearview mirror, yelled in alarm.

"Watch out!"

The pursuing car slammed into the rear of Bolan's vehicle. It bounced off, but before Bolan could regain control of his car, the front end hit the corner of a house set. The plaster-and-frame construction collapsed in a cloud of dust, showering across the car.

Bolan kicked open his door and rolled out. Prone on the wet ground, he brought the 93-R on track and caught the closest gunner on the run. The man, too eager for the kill, had not checked out his ground before closing in. Nor had he allowed for Mack Bolan, whose Beretta chugged, sending three fatal 9 mm tumblers into the advancing gunner.

Rolling to his feet, Bolan looked inside the car. The passenger door was open, but Tomkins was not in sight.

The rattle of autofire forced Bolan to cover. He took a long dive across the hood of the car, crashing down into the remains of the false-fronted building. He ducked beneath a slanting section of plaster, coming out in the mock tangle of alleys and arches of an old city set. He ran on, turning this way and that, realizing that if he was not careful he might easily trap himself.

Behind him he heard voices, the roar of car engines, the sudden crackle of gunfire that made him think of Tomkins. But right at that moment he was unable to help her if she was in trouble.

The sound of footsteps on the concrete alerted him, and he turned, ducking beneath a low arch. He felt his jacket snag on something. It held and no amount of pulling could free it. His pursuers were closing in. Bolan slipped his arms from the sleeves, leaving the jacket, and plunged on, turning and twisting as he tried to get himself out of the complex maze of alleys.

He broke through a boarded section into an open courtyard, rain sluicing down off the low roofs around him. Before he could cross the courtyard he heard the sudden roar of engines, and the exit was blocked, headlights blinding him.

CHAPTER EIGHTEEN

The Nevada Desert

Carl Lyons adjusted his Starlite night-vision goggles, then reached out to pick up his M-16. He checked the throat mike of the personal radio transceiver he was wearing, hearing the soft hiss in the headphones.

"Able One to Able Two and Three. You copy?"

In sequence Blancanales and Schwarz acknowledged.

"Get set to move in thirty seconds on my mark," Lyons instructed.

He watched the second hand on his watch as it counted down the numbers.

The desert lay velvet black and still around them. There was no moon and only a few stars, which suited Able Team. The heat of daylight had been exchanged for a chill in the air.

The deserted town of Roaring Fork squatted on the landscape without pretense to anything except practicality. There was no hint of Old West romance to the place. It was an unlovely scattering of weathered buildings, most of them open to the elements now. Once they might have served a purpose, but not anymore. Now they housed desert life, piles of drifted sand and choking weeds.

Except one structure—the abandoned service station, with its tilted gas pumps and creaking sign. The building itself had been repaired and added to. The living quarters had been extended with modern materials and a large, barnlike outbuilding tacked onto the north side.

Able Team had traveled to within three miles of the place by helicopter. Jack Grimaldi had dropped them off and now sat waiting, in radio contact, his machine idling.

Lyons, Blancanales and Schwarz, outfitted and wearing the headsets, had walked into Roaring Fork, arriving about a half hour back. They had split up, each man primed to move in from a different direction when they made their strike.

Each man wore black, with hands and faces darkened. As well as the standard Colt Python handguns, they carried M-16 rifles, plus Ithaca Model 37 12-gauge shotguns loaded with a selection of special rounds. The composite selection was made up of Shok Lok cartridges for blasting door locks and hinges, with the rest of the 8-shot magazines holding Stingbag rounds that ejected cloth bags filled with small lead shot designed to incapacitate rather than kill. The Stingbags were a precaution in case of hostage closeness to a known hostile.

Using the Starlite goggles, Able Team would be able to operate in the dark, seeing their targets without being seen themselves. Blancanales, during his circuitous route to his position at the rear of the building, had located the generator that provided power for the place. On the thirty-second mark he would disable the power source, leaving the house without light. It was standard practice, but not without risk. No forced entry to a possible hostile environment could be guaranteed one hundred percent.

Darkness worked for and against everyone, even those equipped with specialist equipment. Every man in Able Team knew that and accepted it. If they hadn't, they would have been earning a less hazardous living selling dry goods behind a counter.

The second hand touched base.

"Go," Lyons ordered.

He began his own assault, belly down in the dust, worming his way across the ground in front of the main building. Powerful floodlights illuminated a wide area around the building. Lyons paused on the edge of the lighted area and waited until Blancanales completed his initial task.

The lights were suddenly cut, plunging the house and surrounding terrain into darkness.

"Hit it now!" Lyons ordered, pushing to his feet. He ran toward the house, his eyes fixed on the front door. The image before his eyes was overcast with the green glare of the goggles. Lyons hit the porch steps and went up. He leveled the shotgun and triggered a round into each door hinge, tearing them free from the frame. He shouldered the damaged door and it swung inward, breaking free from the inner latch and crashing to the floor.

Lyons didn't hesitate. He dropped low and ducked inside, going to his knees.

The crackling roar of an autoweapon filled the room. Behind it Lyons could hear the relentless curses of the gunner. He moved his head, searching, and picked up the dark outline of the man firing the SMG. Lyons arced the Ithaca around, triggering a single round of Stingbag shot. The gunner stopped cursing, his breath slammed from his body by the force of the striking lead-filled bag. He tumbled over backward, smashing into furniture as he went down.

"One down. Front of the house," Lyons said into his mike.

ROSARIO BLANCANALES USED his shotgun to blast his way in through the rear door. Moments after his rounds tore away the hinges, an autoweapon began to fire from inside the house. Blancanales felt something skim across the back of his right hand. He turned aside, feeling splinters of wood lash his lower face, then felt a harder blow over his ribs on the left side. He felt himself go down to his knees, a rush of nausea washing over him. He cast aside the shotgun and unslung the dangling M-16, fingers fumbling as he tried to cock the weapon. He succeeded and turned it in the direction of the door as someone dragged it open.

Through his goggles Blancanales saw a green shape emerge from the shadows, wielding a stubby SMG. The muzzle turned in Blancanales's direction. He hauled up the M-16 and pulled the trigger, placing shot after shot in the bulky shape looming closer. The other man's SMG flickered briefly, and Blancanales felt his own body pull back as he took a second hit. He fell, landing on his back, still firing the M-16 at the green shape. He saw the man arc away from him, the SMG jerking skyward. Then he was gone and Blancanales was alone. In his earphones he could hear voices, a distant clamor, gunshots.

Then it all began to fade, and Blancanales realized that the green images in his goggles were turning gray, then black, then fading—and the sound was also going, leaving him alone and in utter silence.

THE SIDE WINDOW the provided entry for Hermann Schwarz caved in under the impact of the Ithaca's twin charges. Once he was over the sill Schwarz dropped to the floor and scanned the room. There was only furniture. No movement. He slung the shotgun from his shoulder and brought the M-16 into play. On his feet, Schwarz crossed the room, kicking aside any items in his way. He put his left hand on the doorknob and eased the door open.

He could hear shooting from both the front and the rear of the house, and picked up Lyons's message as he took out his first adversary.

Pulling the door wide, Schwarz leaned out, scanning the long passage that ran in either direction.

A figure appeared to his right, large and bulky, carrying a powerful-looking autorifle. The guy was feeling his way, one hand brushing the wall while he searched the dark passage with the muzzle of the weapon.

"Put the weapon down," Schwarz ordered. "You're covered."

"Go to hell, asshole!" the man yelled, and guided by Schwarz's voice, he opened up with the rifle.

Schwarz ducked as the volley peppered the wall over head. Dust and chunks of plaster rained down on his back and shoulders.

Turning the muzzle of the M-16, Schwarz laid two 5.56 mm slugs in the gunner's chest. The bullets slapped the guy back against the wall, then tumbled him to the floor. He made an attempt to gain his feet, triggering more shots from the autorifle, and Schwarz had to put two more shots into him. This time the figure flopped belly down and lay still.

Moving along the passage, Schwarz kicked open each door he came to. The rooms he examined were cluttered but clear of people.

"One target terminated. Moving through toward front of the house," Schwarz said into his mike. "No sign of hostages."

A wild roar filled his ears. It came from his left. Schwarz turned in time to see a heavy, barrel-chested, green-tinted figure lurching at him. He held a long machete in his right hand and he swung the weapon at Schwarz's head. Schwarz pulled himself away from the deadly blade, his action raising the M-16. The machete struck the autorifle, almost tearing it from Schwarz's fingers.

He reacted swiftly, reversing the rifle and slamming the butt into his attacker's sagging gut. Hot breath gusted from the guy's mouth, and he sagged away from Schwarz, giving the Stony Man commando time to slash the stock of the M-16 upward. It crunched under the big man's flabby jaw, knocking his head back, and allowed Schwarz the opportunity to hit him again with a flat crack across the side of the head with the M-16.

The big man spun around, falling heavily against a door that gave way under his considerable bulk. As the guy fell facedown into the room, the door beneath him, Schwarz heard a shocked gasp from inside. He poked the M-16 ahead of him and peered into the darkened room.

Pressed into the farthest corner, unable to see Schwarz, were three figures—a woman, a teenage girl and a young boy.

Schwarz keyed his throat mike.

"Able One from Able Three. Have located hostages. They appear unhurt."

There was no immediate response from Lyons or Blancanales. Then Lyons's voice came over the air, urgency in his tone.

"I've found Pol," he said. "He's down. And I think he's badly hit."

BY THE TIME GRIMALDI put the chopper down, Lyons and Schwarz had the hostages outside and the surviving kidnappers cuffed and ready. They were also attending to Rosario Blancanales. He had been hit by a couple of 9 mm slugs—one over the ribs on his left side, the second just above his left hipbone. He had been losing blood heavily until Schwarz applied a pressure pad from his first-aid kit.

Grimaldi had already called in for help and had arranged to fly Blancanales to the closest emergency room. While Lyons used the radio to contact Stony Man, Grimaldi crossed to where Schwarz was tending Blancanales.

"How is he?" the Stony Man pilot asked.

"How the hell do you think?" Blancanales asked weakly.

Grimaldi smiled. "He's going to be all right," he said. "Still a mean son of a bitch."

Then Lyons came over and touched Blancanales on the shoulder.

"Hang in, Pol, we're moving you out right away."

They carried Blancanales to the helicopter and secured him in the rear of the cabin.

"Get out of here," Lyons said.

"You can reach me at this number," Grimaldi said, thrusting a card into Lyons's hand.

Schwarz moved the Hansons to a safe area while Grimaldi wound the chopper's engine up, lifting off in a cloud of choking sand and dust. Lyons joined them after he'd watched the aircraft vanish in the dawn sky.

Stella Hanson, looking slightly gaunt after her ordeal, said, "I hope he'll be all right."

Lyons nodded, his mind elsewhere.

"He'll make it," Schwarz said. "How are you and the kids, Mrs. Hanson?"

"We're fine now, thanks to you people. What about Walter?"

"We already have someone on their way to give him the good news."

Stella Hanson sighed, drawing her children close.

"So it's all over then?" she said.

Lyons caught her words and glanced at Schwarz. Able Team's assignment appeared to have been completed. But from what Hal Brognola had told him during their quick talk over the helicopter's radio, there was still no respite for Phoenix Force or Mack Bolan.

CHAPTER NINETEEN

Hertfordshire, England

Things might have been different if Jack Holder hadn't been a talker. But he couldn't resist bragging about killing Clair Tomkins. So he revealed his position—and unleashed the Executioner's fury.

Bolan's first shot hammered a bloody hole through Holder's upper chest. The hardman spun around, gasping against the pain that blossomed in his chest. The effect of the 9 mm slug left him almost powerless to react. He stumbled, slipping to his knees, the SMG dropping from his hands. A stifled groan bubbled through clenched teeth, and despite his desire to remain indifferent to the wound, he was unable to stop the spreading numbness from hampering his movements.

Holder's agony was punctuated by a second shot, which he took in the head. He lost consciousness in an instant. He was not aware of toppling over backward, eyes turned to the sky so that the falling rain struck his exposed face.

Had he remained alive, he might have been witness to the brief but bloody conclusion to the hunt he had led.

Holder had barely begun to fall when Bolan turned the Beretta on the two gunners who had accompanied him.

The taunt thrown by Holder had pushed Mack Bolan over the redline, and he turned his weapon on the surviving pair with a vengeance. His speed and accuracy left them no opportunity to bring their own weapons into play.

Professional hardmen they might have been, but nothing they had faced before prepared them for the Executioner in killing mode.

Bolan's third and fourth shots caught the guy on Holder's left, coring into his head. The hardguy flew backward, his shattered skull leaking its contents, mouth open in a silent shout of protest, his fading thoughts unable to comprehend what had happened.

The third man threw himself forward, landing belly down on the wet ground. He had done this numerous times before, but always under battle conditions, in jungle or desert, where the ground was a little more forgiving. This time he landed on hard, unyielding concrete, and the impact jarred him. It also caused him to lose his grip on the SMG for a second or two.

Those seconds allowed Mack Bolan to aim the Beretta and punch another pair of slugs through the hardman's skull, driving his head forward into the hard ground. The gunner lay flat, one leg moving in slow kicks, the only sign of life. Then that stopped.

The wild revving of a car engine alerted Bolan to the presence of the pursuit cars. He ran forward, holstering the 93-R, snatching up one of the discarded MP-5s and leveling it as he neared the archway.

The closest of the two cars jerked into motion. The driver had dropped into reverse and was tooling away from the archway, tires slipping on the wet ground.

Bolan reached the opening as the car, followed by the second, began to reverse away from the archway. He cradled the MP-5 in both hands and sprayed the windshield of each vehicle. Glass starred and blew inward, shredding the faces of the drivers and their passengers. Bolan closed in, firing a second burst into each car to make certain his targets were finished.

The second car continued rolling backward, the engine howling. It turned suddenly and bounced up over a curb, the rear end smashing through a false storefront before coming to rest.

The rain continued sluicing down over Bolan as he walked by the silent cars and through the empty studio backlot. He spent ten minutes searching the deserted streets until he found Clair Tomkins. She lay facedown, arms outstretched. Rain had washed away a lot of the blood around the twin holes between her shoulders. Her face was turned to one side, pale strands of her blond hair clinging to the wet skin. Bolan was glad that her eyes were closed so he couldn't see them staring at him.

Turning on his heel, Bolan made his way back to the big soundstage where he had first found her. He retraced his steps to the silent offices and found Lawrence Pennell still curled up on the floor. He took hold of Pennell's collar and dragged the man to his feet.

"You can't touch me," Pennell said, his voice ragged and hoarse. There was a large bruise on his throat where Tomkins had struck him. "You have no—"

Bolan slammed him back against the wall, jamming the muzzle of the MP-5 against the man's throat.

"Do you want to see how I can't touch you?"

He pushed Pennell ahead of him, directing the man with jabs of the H&K's muzzle, out into the rain and across the silent studio lot. Minutes later they were back inside the administration building. Pennell found the way himself then, knowing where Bolan wanted to go. He led the Executioner back to the office where Bolan had seen the wall charts and computers. Inside, the warrior shoved Pennell into a chair, then he checked out the guy who had taken his bullets in the legs. The man was unconscious, but still breathing.

"Give me an explanation," Bolan said, perching on the edge of a desk and indicating the office layout.

"I don't have to say a bloody thing to you," Pennell said. He seemed to have regained a little of his courage.

"Maybe a few names will jog your memory. Han Nor. Victor Suliman. Marcus Glastonbury."

"Am I supposed to know them?"

"A hard look will probably turn up more than a slight connection to them. It'll be interesting to check out your financial holdings."

"You're mad, Belasko."

"I'm also right. Don't think you can talk your way out of this one, Pennell. The names are coming together. We even have Rostok in the frame now—Yuri Rostok, the Russian with access to ex-Soviet nuclear warheads."

Pennell began to show interest. It was plain that Bolan's knowledge had shaken him. He hadn't expected such a precise linking of all the players.

"What's your excuse for selling out?" Bolan asked.

The man stared at Bolan for a few seconds, slowly realizing that his position, his power, was not going to gain him a thing from this man. The only certainty was the power that Bolan held in his hands.

Pennell slumped in the chair, running a hand across his pale, bloody face.

"They made me a good offer," he said. "The kind only a damn fool would turn down. It's as simple as that. I've always been used to the good life. Couldn't change. Problem was, it got harder to maintain. It's easy to spend money but not so easy to make it. So when Marcus came along with a suggestion that I meet up with Nor and Suliman on Suliman's yacht in Saint-Tropez, I thought, why not see what they have to offer? And they offered plenty, just for a little work on the side—information, guidance so they moved in the right direction on deals. Coming right down to it, Belasko, it was business, pure and simple."

"You didn't see the harm? That what you were doing was wrong?"

"The offer made sense," Pennell said. He smiled at the look in Bolan's eyes. "I do hope you're not going to go all moral on me, Belasko. Arms dealing is a growth industry worth billions. Every manufacturing economy in the world is dealing, including Great Britain and America."

"That clears your conscience?"

"Nothing to clear, old boy." He shook his head. "Another bleeding heart. God save me from you people. Take a look around you, Belasko. The world is a bloody armed camp, with revolution, civil war, organized crime on a huge scale, ethnic cleansing. I like that one, but I prefer the Nazi expression. They were simply exterminating the undesirables. The point I am trying to get across is the simple one about supply and demand. All we have done is to extend the range of goods on offer.''

"Nuclear warheads on ICBMs?''

"A few hundred years ago they said the gun was an invention of the Devil and would bring the end of the world. Well, we're still here. You can't stop progress, man. So why not capitalize on it? Surely you see the sense in that. It's the American way. See a sale and make it. If we didn't do it, someone else would. It's a natural progression—from guns to bombs to missiles. What's the difference?''

"The difference is someone nuking your own backyard.''

"Christ, Belasko, we've lived under that threat since Hiroshima. And if I recall, that was an American bomb. The nuclear threat has been with us all our bloody lives, and we're still here. The strength behind nuclear weapons is the implicit threat, the standoff scenario. If everyone has them, who is going to chance using theirs?''

"The theory works when you deal with reasonable governments.''

"Sure,'' Pennell mocked, "the exclusive Nuke Club. Only the big powers are allowed to have them. Keep it in the family and hold the world by the balls. Keep everyone else down. Well, not any longer, Belasko. Now the big stick is being offered to anyone who comes up with the cash."

"So you'll sell to anyone. The lunatic fringe, terrorists, drug cartels, warring factions within a country so desperate to win they'll risk nuclear suicide. Will you people risk that just for money?"

"Makes the world go round, old boy."

"The way you're dealing, it could end up a cinder crisp. Then what will all your money do for you?"

"I don't see it coming to that," Pennell said. "The nuclear threat has always worked as a deterrent. No reason it shouldn't do the same again." He gave a shrug. "If the big bang comes, so what, Belasko? Nobody lives forever."

"Why the murder of the undercover unit?"

Pennell shrugged. "They were starting to get too close. It was an object lesson. A warning, if you like, to leave us alone. A show that we're not some little gang to lock up and throw away the key. There was a similar example in your country. Three nosy FBI agents pushing their luck. A few dead makes everyone take notice. Forget negotiation. Don't tell people to stay away. Just kill a few."

"What about Nor and Suliman? Have they gone to close the deals?"

Pennell held his stare, a thin smile on his lips.

"You can't reach them. You're too late, Belasko. They're free and clear."

"And leaving you to carry the can."

"It hasn't come to that yet."

"I don't see them riding over the hill to rescue you. Face it, Pennell, you're on your own."

Bolan crossed to one of the telephones and punched in a number, his eyes never once leaving Pennell. He waited, impatient, feeling a growing concern over the dealings of Pennell's organization.

"Update," he said when Brognola came on the line.

"Able Team located and freed Hanson's family. Blancanales took a couple of bullets. He's in surgery now. We won't know the outcome for a few hours."

"We can't lose him," Bolan said. "He deserves better."

"The latest from Phoenix Force is they've stopped the test being sabotaged. A rogue board had been put into the THAAD control system. It would have recognized the incoming test missile as a friendly and allowed it through. The idea was to make the system look useless. They also took a couple of prisoners. One is singing so hard they can't stop him. It looks like all our strands are coming together, Striker. You have any input for us?"

"Right now I'm at the communications center of the operation over here. The rear guard has been handled. I've got the guy who's been breaking all our security, passing information to the opposition. He tipped them off I was coming and had a hand in arranging the killing of the undercover unit.''

"I notice you haven't mentioned the main players," Brognola said.

"They're not here. I figure they've moved on to where the main action is."

"Try Libya," Brognola suggested. "Think about it, Striker. It all adds up. Our missing computer genius, Kurt Englemann, has been sighted on the Libyan coast. The British SIS have been interested in the activity along the coast for some time. They did some cooperative work with the NAVSTAR satellite people and came up with some interesting seagoing movement there. They tracked a number of freighters coming and going. The ships had come in from North Korea, dropping anchor outside territorial Libyan waters. The satellite monitors picked up smaller ships going out to these freighters and taking on cargo from them, then returning to land. The satellites watched the movement of this cargo inland."

"Did they track it to a destination?"

"Only partway. They lost the convoy after the first day due to a combination of weather conditions and satellite delay. But the general line of travel was toward the Libyan desert. The analysts took an educated guess and put the destination down as Qatar Oasis, designated Camp Nine."

"Didn't the Libyans have some kind of research facility there some years back?"

"That's the one. It looks like it might be in business again. There was some information sent to SIS from a deep-cover agent about activity on the old airstrip near there—planes coming and going, delivery cargo that was being moved on to Qatar Oasis. Could be the warheads being shipped in by Rostok."

"Let's go back to Englemann. Where is he now?"

"Libya still, we believe. Camp Nine. Surveillance sent back photos of a mobile trailer at the camp. It was pretty sophisticated for one of those bases. It had its own generator and it was fitted with an air-conditioning unit."

"To keep a stable temperature inside for someone to work on computers?"

"I don't think it was for freezing TV dinners," Brognola said.

"We need a rebriefing," Bolan said. "And you need to move some people in here fast. There's a roomful of information here we can't afford to lose."

"Leave that with me, Striker. We've been in touch with the prime minister. He's aware of the undercover unit being compromised. He's already putting together his own group to head the British end of the operation. I need your location, Striker. The minute I get the word, I'll contact you again and let you know who to expect."

"Make it fast," Bolan said. "I have at least one wounded man needing medical attention. Maybe others."

"Striker, you okay?"

"I lost my contact in the facedown, a young policewoman. They shot her in the back while we were separated. I couldn't help her."

"Striker, you can't save the whole damn world, no matter how much you want to. Some of the good ones are going to die, too."

"I know that," Bolan said. "It's knowing that makes it all the harder."

TWO HOURS LATER Bolan was in the presence of the special group sent in by the British government. The eight-man team was led by a no-nonsense man named Beckett. He took one look at the communications room and nodded to Bolan.

"I think you've found us the pot of gold, Belasko. And by the way, I'm bloody sure that isn't your real name. Not that it matters." He turned to stare long and hard at Pennell. "Pennell *is* his name, and I'll make certain he doesn't get a chance to slip out of this."

Pennell sat upright, his face darkening with fury. "We'll see, Beckett. Once I speak to my solicitor, things will change pretty quickly."

"No chance, Pennell. This isn't a speeding offense we're talking about. If I have my way, you'll be held on a charge of treason against Her Majesty's Government. Abuse of your position. Consorting with known foreign agents. And an accessory to the murder of the undercover unit led by Inspector Rawson, including the murder of policewoman Clair Tomkins. If I had my way, you'd be up against a wall right now.''

Pennell fell silent. He slumped back in his seat, not even making any protest when one of Beckett's people handcuffed him to the chair's frame.

''By the way,'' Beckett said to Bolan, ''I have to tell you that your people are on their way from Washington and France.''

''Thanks,'' Bolan said.

He took the mug of coffee offered by one of the group and dropped into a seat facing the wall covered with paperwork. Tired as he was, Bolan needed to glean every piece of information he could from the array of charts and lists. He was aware that Beckett was also studying the information. For long minutes the two men took in the scattered details, sifting them until a cohesive picture formed.

Finally Beckett said, ''I was given a brief rundown on the background to all this before we came in. So I had a sketchy idea what was going on. It didn't mean all that much until I tied it in with this stuff. It makes sense now, Belasko. The thing is, I don't really want to believe what I'm seeing. I don't have any illusions about this being true. The problem is accepting that truth, because it's a bloody nightmare.''

"Yeah," Bolan said. "In broad daylight. You know what we're looking at, Beckett, don't you? A mail-order list for nuclear missiles. Phone in your requirements, transfer the funds to a safe account, give a delivery date and location, then sit back and wait for your goods to turn up."

"Pretty basic summary, but on the mark," Beckett agreed. "So what do we do about it?"

"My brief was to find out what Han Nor was up to and put a stop to it. That still holds. I'd say that priority has just jumped a couple of notches."

"I take it the people coming in will be handling whatever needs to be done?"

Bolan nodded. "I'll be going with them. We'll do whatever it takes. And we won't be worrying about taking prisoners if it comes to a fight."

"I should bloody well hope not."

Beckett turned as one of his people called him, leaving Bolan to study the final pieces of information pinned to the wall.

Bolan felt a chill run down his spine as he took in the clinical details on the charts. Someone had written the cold facts and figures concerning requirements and delivery as if he had been writing a shopping list. There were a half dozen regimes listed that were far from friendly with their neighbors, and the United States, in particular. The distribution list took on a sinister aspect as Bolan's eyes roved back and forth. If any two of those countries decided to start throwing missiles at each other, the resultant hostilities could easily result in mass destruction and lingering radiation.

Han Nor and his business partners had embarked on a reckless path that was bound to lead to widespread disaster. But only if they were allowed to continue along that path.

It was going to be up to Stony Man to wield its collective fist. The mission brief had been to stop the sabotage against the THAAD project. That was still a priority. But the fact that the interference with the development project was only part of Nor's scheme meant that stopping *him* was paramount.

"ELECTRONIC DATA and deep-cover intelligence have provided us with a sharper picture of what Han Nor, Suliman and Rostok have been up to," Barbara Price said, facing the Stony Man assembly.

Phoenix Force was there, having been flown into Great Britain from France. Price was a member of Brognola's team for the U.S., along with Jack Grimaldi and Huntington Wethers. The swift assembly of the mobile team paid tribute to the professional skills of the SOG's personnel.

Since his arrival Wethers had been sitting at a computer terminal, breaking into the data there.

Now his findings were providing the Stony Man team with background information.

"Add to that the information we've picked up from this center, and we can make an accurate judgment concerning the aims of Han Nor's organization."

"Plain and simple," Brognola said, "they're in the arms business. But way above the guy who goes around selling AK-74s, or even the latest hand-held rocket launcher. This crew is into the big stuff. And by that we mean Korean long-range missiles that will be armed with ex-Soviet nuclear warheads.

"Information supplied by British intelligence has been matched by some of our own information concerning Rostok. He's now been identified as being the driving force behind smuggling weapons and ammunition to the Bosnian Muslims. He's been buying the arms all over the place, then flying them in despite the U.N. embargo. The guy has no conscience. If he can sell guns to the Bosnians, he could just as easily sell them a missile and mobile launcher."

"Why hasn't the U.N. stopped him?" Calvin James asked.

"Because of the way he's been flying in his cargos," Price explained. "He ships the weapons to an island off the Croatian coast, out of U.N. jurisdiction. They can monitor the flights in but can't do a thing to stop them. From the island the weapons are ferried to the mainland, loaded into trucks and driven into Bosnian territory. There's photographic evidence that one of the regular aircraft flying the stuff in comes from Iran. It's an Ilyushin 76-TD, ex-Soviet military. That same aircraft makes trips into Iran to deliver weapons from Rostok's arsenal.''

''We also know that Victor Suliman has been talking recently to the Iranians,'' Brognola said. ''And new photographs recently released to us show him on board his yacht in Saint-Tropez with a couple of Iranian nationals. The interesting thing is that Rostok was there and so was Han Nor.''

''This gets grimmer all the time,'' Manning said.

''I need a bloody fag,'' McCarter grumbled. ''Can't we stop all this damn pussyfooting around? If no one else can't or won't do anything about this bunch of maniacs, it's obvious it's down to us. So let's get on with it. Just give us our assignments, Hal, and put us on a bloody plane.''

''I was coming to that, David,'' Brognola snapped. ''Just sit down and be quiet. If you don't have the willpower to quit smoking, stop giving us all a hard time.''

McCarter leaned forward in his seat, jabbing a long finger at Brognola, his face grim.

''You know what I think, Yank,'' he said.

The room became still.

"I think you're bloody right," McCarter continued. "Bugger this health kick. I'm going to have a smoke."

With that he sat back and pulled a pack of Player's from his jacket, lit one and trailed a long plume of smoke from his lips along with a deep sigh of satisfaction.

The tension eased and even Brognola smiled.

"Now perhaps we can get back to normal," he said.

"That'll be the day," Calvin James said softly, glancing across at McCarter, who sat happily wreathed in tobacco smoke.

"We have two objectives," Brognola said. He turned to Barbara Price.

"We're waiting for clarification from British SIS," she continued. "They're getting very close to confirming that Qatar Oasis is where the Libyan-Nor tie-up is operating from. Once we have that as a go, Phoenix Force will be covertly inserted into the area to take out the installation. Part of their mission will be the termination of Kurt Englemann's computer lab and his production of rogue computer boards for installation into the THAAD control computers. We have full authorization from the White House to designate this as a search-and-destroy mission."

"Jack will be around in Dragon Slayer to make a pickup from Libyan territory upon completion of the mission," Brognola added.

"At the same time as Phoenix Force makes its hit, Striker will be in Saint-Tropez to deal with the European branch of the organization," Price said. "Any questions?"

McCarter held up his hand. "Is there anywhere around here a bloke can get a can of Coke?"

"How are you getting us into Libya without being spotted?" Katz asked.

"A high-altitude parachute drop at night," Price said.

There was a collective groan from the Stony Man commandos.

"Sorry, guys, but it's the only sure way of getting you down without being seen. We're going to try to drop you about eight to ten miles out from Qatar Oasis. With luck you should be in place by dawn. Once the strike is completed, you'll give Jack a prearranged signal, and he'll come in to pick you up."

"Sounds pretty easy when you say it like that," Manning commented.

Price didn't flinch as she looked him in the eye. "Too tough for you to handle?" she asked.

Manning grinned. "Not if you figure we can do it."

"I've arranged equipment through Beckett," Brognola said. "Tell him what you need, guys, and he'll have it shipped in."

"When do we leave?" Katz asked.

"Tonight, so get some rest."

Katz stood. "Is a final briefing an hour before we move out okay?"

Price nodded. As Phoenix Force left the room, she turned to Bolan, who had been sitting quietly, listening.

"Any questions, Striker?"

"The mission objective was THAAD. How far was Nor going with that?"

"Oh, he had big plans there, too," Price said. "He wanted to sabotage the system at the design and construction levels, which included replacing circuit boards with the ones created by Englemann. It was a program of disruption to make the system appear inefficient so that the NATO alliance would give it the thumbs-down."

"We saved the best until last," Brognola said. "Nor wanted to have THAAD discredited in the West. But at the same time he was blackmailing Walter Hanson into handing over design disks so that the Koreans could duplicate and build THAAD for their own defense system."

"And sell it, of course, to their own chosen clients," Price added.

"We got this from one of the guys Phoenix Force took prisoner in France," Brognola explained. "As far as I know, he's still talking."

The big Fed crossed to where Huntington Wethers sat, busily stroking keys as he delved deeper into the data base of the computer system. Jack Grimaldi sat hunched over an unrolled map, making notes.

Price leaned across, staring into Bolan's eyes.

"Hard few days, huh?"

"Something like that."

"Or is it the girl, Clair?"

Bolan's thoughts were reflected in his eyes. "She was too young to die the way she did."

"Mack, she chose what she wanted to do. I'm sure she was aware she would be putting her life on the line. We all are, but I guess none of us ever really believes it will happen. It's hard. What can I say? You feel for her. That's good because someone has to care. Someone has to be there to say she died doing what she believed in. It doesn't make up for what happened. But at least it means her sacrifice is recognized. And that is important."

Bolan stood. "How about I buy you a cup of coffee, lady? I think you just earned it."

"Why, thank you, sir, so do I."

CHAPTER TWENTY

Libya, North Africa

They made their drop in the darkness before dawn, free-falling until five hundred feet, then floating in utter silence and touching down on Libyan soil within yards of each other. This was by no means the first parachute drop Phoenix Force had made. Nor would it be their last. Though they were all proficient, each man said his own form of thanks for a successful touchdown.

The first task was to roll up and bury their parachutes, oxygen masks and packs. That completed, they checked out their equipment and adjusted their backpacks. Weapons followed. Their main assault weapons were Uzis with extra magazines. Each man also carried his personal handgun and backup weapon. They were also equipped with knives and stun and fragmentation grenades.

Gary Manning and David McCarter both had Barnett Commando crossbows firing bolts loaded with cyanide capsules. Once injected into the bloodstream, the deadly poison killed almost instantly.

Calvin James carried a LAW rocket. It was his assignment to take out the base's radio shack once the strike got under way, preventing any reinforcements from being called in.

The members of Phoenix Force also carried compact transceivers, enabling them to stay in contact during the operation. Katz had a signaling device that would alert Jack Grimaldi that they were going in. Grimaldi would relay that back to base and then start his run in over Libyan territory to make his pickup. The device also acted as a marker beacon, allowing Dragon Slayer's sophisticated tracking system to home in precisely.

As well as his standard equipment, Gary Manning was hauling along a half dozen explosive devices. The packs were fitted with timers that needed only setting and activating.

"Everyone set?" Katz asked.

The rest of Phoenix Force acknowledged. With Katz in the lead and Rafael Encizo bringing up the rear, they moved off into the darkness, walking south toward Qatar Oasis.

The terrain was dry and dusty, semidesert, but with enough vegetation to prevent it from being totally barren. The air at this hour was reasonably cool, but the Phoenix commandos knew that once the sun rose, the temperature would soar. It was the reason they needed to reach the oasis by dawn.

The second reason was that it would be to their benefit to strike early, before the desert base was on full alert. Men suddenly roused from sleep would be less efficient, their reactions slower. Phoenix Force needed the element of surprise. If they were allowed that luxury, their strike could be over quickly and they could be out of Libya before anyone realized what had happened.

The success of the operation depended upon close timing. Mack Bolan was due to make his own single-handed strike at Victor Suliman's yacht at the same time Phoenix Force went into the Qatar Oasis base. It was hoped that both ends of the operation could be shut down simultaneously, preventing one section from warning the other. As Phoenix Force and Mack Bolan carried out their strikes, Hal Brognola would be contacting the Russians and tipping them off to Yuri Rostok's illegal trading in nuclear warheads. If the whole operation went as planned, the weapons consortium would be completely taken out.

Hertfordshire, England

HAL BROGNOLA SAW Barbara Price lean forward, face taut with concentration as she listened to the voice coming through the headset she was wearing. He moved across the room to where she sat, and as he reached her she glanced his way.

"Phoenix Force should be on Libyan soil by now," she said. "That was the pilot of the Galaxy. They're clearing the area. Still at twenty-five thousand feet and heading back to Aviano Airbase."

Brognola turned to check the map pinned to the wall. His gaze followed the course the C-5 Galaxy had taken from England, across European airspace to its earlier touchdown in Italy. After a brief rest and refuel the giant airplane had taken off for another flight. This time the destination had been the airfield on the island of Sardinia, where Jack Grimaldi and Dragon Slayer had been off-loaded. The Stony Man pilot would be making final preparations for his solo flight into Libya to pick up Phoenix Force upon the completion of their mission, which was now under way.

Price's voice, low and steady, interrupted the Fed's silent reflection on recent events.

"Striker confirms he's in position—on standby to move the moment we hear Phoenix has gone on the offensive."

She leaned back in her seat, shaking loose her mane of hair.

"Now all we can do is wait," she said.

Saint-Tropez, France

AN HOUR AFTER Phoenix Force's touchdown in Libya a dark-clad figure slipped from the deck of a motorboat in Saint-Tropez harbor and lowered himself into the warm Mediterranean. Dressed in a rubber wet suit, a waterproof bag holding his weapons, Mack Bolan swam silently, making for the long, sleek craft that belonged to Victor Suliman.

The powerful motor cruiser, named *Celleste,* was sixty feet long, painted gleaming white and powered by twin Rolls-Royce marine engines. Intelligence data provided by the British SIS had also informed Bolan that the yacht's communications included a radio able to send and receive over long distances. One of those destinations would be Libya.

The Executioner had a wait ahead of him. His intention was to hit the *Celleste* at the same time Phoenix Force went into Camp Nine at Qatar Oasis. Timing was to be as close as possible so that no warning could be passed from one target to another.

Bolan carried a compact transceiver that linked him to his backup, a team of British SIS operatives sitting it out on board the motorboat he had just left. They in turn were linked to Jack Grimaldi, the Phoenix pickup. Once Grimaldi got the word from Phoenix Force, he would relay a simple signal that would be relayed to Bolan. On that signal the Executioner would make his own strike.

All very neat and tidy, Bolan thought, as he swam slowly through the soft dawn, his gaze fixed on the distant cruiser. The trouble with sophisticated equipment was its fallibility—the unexpected breakdown at a crucial moment. Despite the advances in electronics, there were times when the simplest device would decide to malfunction, and those breakdowns could be costly—sometimes fatal.

At the end of the day Mack Bolan would, if necessary, fall back on the most reliable indicator of judicious timing—his own gut feeling. Something would tell him when it was time to make his move, and he knew from past experience that instinct often had it over electronics.

He paused, treading water in the shadow of a gleaming hull. He could feel vibrations through the hull, the beat of music coming from somewhere on board the vessel. People were still enjoying themselves, relaxing, while he, Mack Bolan, was taking himself along yet another side road on his trip to the hellgrounds.

Bolan glided through the still water without a sound, barely disturbing its tranquillity. Up ahead, on board the cruiser, were the leaders of the consortium that was planning to trade in missiles and nuclear death.

The observation team that had been watching the cruiser all day, in anticipation of Bolan's arrival, had told him that Han Nor and his bodyguard were on board, along with Victor Suliman and Marcus Glastonbury. Bolan had been shown photographs of them during the final briefing in England.

Bolan's equipment had traveled with him. In the waterproof bag clipped to his waist were his Beretta and Desert Eagle. He also had a Ka-bar knife, a thin wire garrote and a number of thermite incendiary devices.

Bolan reached the last craft before the cruiser, which was anchored a good three hundred yards away from the closest vessel. Riding the slight swell of the water, he could see the soft glow of lights showing from the main cabin.

He rested for ten minutes, then eased away from the shelter of the launch and pushed out at a steady pace, concealed by the thin sea mist drifting across the harbor. Some way out he felt the pull of the undertow, the restless movement of the ever-changing sea. Bolan adjusted his direction, compensating for the drag of the current, and brought himself back on course. He rested, turning on his back, keeping the cruiser in sight, then paddled with hands and feet to stay in line with it.

He moved toward the stern of the cruiser, aiming to come in beneath the overhang of the *Celleste*'s hull. He spotted the dinghy, fitted with an outboard, tethered to the stern on the end of a line, and decided to make use of it. There was canvas pulled over the top to prevent seawater from flooding the small craft. Bolan loosened the ropes at the stern of the dinghy and hauled his waterproof bag up out of the water. He rolled it into the dinghy, then grabbed the side and pulled himself on board. He reached up to pull the canvas sheet back into place and lay in the soft darkness, feeling the dinghy roll and fall against the tide.

Bolan unzipped the bag and pulled out his weapons. He got out of the wet suit. He wore his blacksuit underneath. His rubber-soled combat boots were in the bag, and he slipped them on and laced them up. Then he eased on the shoulder rig for the Beretta and the high-ride belt and holster for the Desert Eagle. The sheathed Ka-bar was already looped on the belt. Bolan slipped the garote into a zip pocket. The thermite devices hung from a pouch also on his belt. He checked the transceiver. Then he made certain that both handguns were fully operational. Spare clips for each autopistol went into blacksuit pockets.

Bolan checked the fluorescent face of his waterproof watch. It was coming close to zero hour.

But then he heard the pulse of the cruiser's engines and the rattle of the anchor being raised. The dinghy rocked as the cruiser took up the slack.

Bolan tensed as he felt the dinghy moving forward, pulled by the powering cruiser.

It was leaving harbor.

He remained calm. There wasn't a great deal he could do. His only option was to wait, then get on board somehow. The change in plan didn't detract from his mission. Whether they were in the confines of Saint-Tropez harbor or on the open sea, the passengers on board Suliman's cruiser were still going to receive a visit from Mack Bolan.

Libya, North Africa

As PHOENIX FORCE neared Qatar Oasis caution became the prime consideration. If the intelligence reports and the educated guesses *were* correct and there was a missile store at the site, then it followed that the people running the setup would be paranoid about security.

Han Nor, Suliman and Rostok knew the penalty for trading in such weaponry. The kind of hardware they were dealing in went far beyond the traditional wares of the arms dealer.

Trading in nuclear missiles would be roundly condemned by every stable government. Passing out nuclear missiles with the casual ease of someone handing around salted peanuts would mark the dealers as pariahs. The very thought of unstable regimes, or terrorists, with their own nuclear capability would fill the world with dread. Not only was it irresponsible, there was the possibility that any use of the weapons would drag in other countries.

The niceties of protocol would not apply here. The desert site was under the control of men with little regard for human life—as they had already shown—so Phoenix Force would meet fire with fire, bringing more than a little hell to the illegal missile factory.

Dawn was breaking to the east, pushing back the black mantle covering the landscape. Light split the dark shadows, pushing into the hollows and the folds in the land.

Hugging the earth, no more than a few hundred yards from the site, Phoenix Force began to assess the situation.

Katz and Manning scanned the area with powerful binoculars taken from their backpacks. Calvin James sat close by sketching a rough layout on a small pad, noting the sentry positions as Katz and Manning called them out.

McCarter unstrapped his Barnett crossbow and checked it out. He repeated the check for Manning's identical weapon. He stretched out beside Katz and took sightings through the scopes mounted on top of the crossbows, ranging them in. It was the Brit who picked out the lean, blond-haired figure crossing from one of the clusters of tents to a long portable trailer. He quickly fine-focused the telescope, homing in on the man's face.

"Englemann," he said. "Bloody Kurt Englemann."

Katz swiveled his binoculars, bringing the computer expert into view. He watched Englemann mount the steps, speaking briefly to the pair of armed guards before he pulled open the trailer's access door and went inside, closing it behind him.

"I'd say, gentlemen, that we do appear to have come to the right place," the Israeli announced.

"Take a look at this," Manning said.

Katz and McCarter trained their instruments on the spot Manning indicated.

Beyond the clump of tall, curving palms and the wide pool that gave Qatar Oasis its name, there was a low-lying block of buildings. The bulk of the buildings lay below ground. The flat roofs were dotted with vent pipes and conduits that snaked across the ground to the water and gas tanks that were also partly buried. To one side of the building complex stood a tractor with an attached trailer. On the trailer were four long, cylindrical shapes, covered by a camouflage canvas.

"If they're not bloody missiles, I really will give up smoking," McCarter stated.

"Promise us anything, David, but not that," Encizo said, glancing up from his Uzi.

The Mediterranean Sea

WITH NO SIGNAL having come through and the deadline past, Mack Bolan decided there was little point in waiting. The *Celleste* was almost two miles out now, moving at a steady pace. The sea was clear and empty all around.

Lifting the bow section of the canvas covering the dinghy, Bolan checked out the cruiser. The armed guard he had seen walking the deck was not in sight. Bolan figured this was as good a moment as any to board the cruiser.

He grasped the line that held the dinghy in tow and began to pull it in. The moment he was close to the stern of the cruiser, Bolan stood up, caught the rope close to the stern rail and pulled himself clear. He went hand over hand, covering the final few feet in seconds, gripping the stern rail and pulling himself on board.

As Bolan's head and shoulders cleared the rail, he saw the armed guard, no more than a couple of yards away. The man was in the act of lighting up a cigarette, and as his eyes fixed on Bolan he stopped what he was doing to stare in complete surprise.

The last thing the man on deck had expected was an armed boarder to come climbing over the stern rail.

Bolan recovered the fastest, his right hand snatching the Beretta from its shoulder rig, snaking the weapon around to aim it at the startled guard.

Flinging aside the cigarette he was lighting, the guard went for the H&K MP-5 slung over his shoulder. His fingers closed over the nylon strap, began to grip it, then relaxed as a trio of 9 mm slugs hammered into his chest, cleaving a traumatic path to his heart.

As the guy crumpled to the deck, Bolan dropped to a crouch as he scanned the vessel. The stern deck was clear, but Bolan's view of the midsection was restricted by the cabin structure.

He moved quickly, not wanting to waste the time available. A situation of this kind could alter drastically in moments, so it was in his interest to make the most of his present freedom of movement.

Closing on the cabin, Bolan sensed rather than heard the presence of a second man. The guy's head and shoulders came into view, pale light striking the cold steel of the MP-5's barrel. Bolan saw the guard's head turn, eyes raking the cruiser's stern section.

The Executioner's fingers were already hooked around the handle of the Ka-bar. He slid it from the sheath, turning the point of the blade upward.

The guard, still searching for his buddy, took a cautious step forward, craning his head as he began to sense something might be wrong. He didn't get a chance to take the thought further.

Bolan's hand pushed the upturned knife in a short, decisive thrust. The tip of the blade went in just where jaw and throat merged, not far from the left ear, slicing easily through soft flesh and tissue. It slid by bone, up to the hilt. Bolan twisted the knife, cutting back to sever the carotid artery. Blood began to pulse from the wound in soft, dark surges. Making low, tremulous gasps, the guard sank to his knees, curling into a fetal ball as his lifeblood spread rapidly across the deck.

Bolan moved along the starboard side of the cruiser, pushing the Ka-bar into its sheath. He gripped the Beretta two-handed, the muzzle tracking ahead of him, searching for any possible opposition.

Daylight was advancing quickly now, diminishing the shadow surrounding the wheelhouse. Bolan, no more than ten feet away, picked up a flicker of movement, seeing it grow into the full-blown outline of a man as he stepped away from the wheelhouse, his MP-5 already angling in toward the Executioner.

Bolan swung the 93-R, stroking the trigger. The pistol chugged out its triple-burst, sending 9 mm tumblers into the guard's body. Black specks flew out from the man's shirt, and he fell back against the wheelhouse. The cruiser rolled slightly, the motion propelling the guy away from the wheelhouse. He slammed against the deck rail, lost his balance and went over the side with a strangled yell. In the instant before he hit the water his finger curled back against the MP-5's trigger. The SMG released a short but noisy burst.

The racket was a warning signal to everyone on board the cruiser, and Bolan switched to full offensive mode, aware that his presence would soon be public knowledge.

As he eased by the wheelhouse, the sliding hatch opened and a figure lunged at him, wielding a hardwood club. Bolan ducked beneath the ill-timed swing, hearing the club thump against the bulkhead.

He swiveled his body, hooking his left elbow into the clubber's lower ribs, drawing a gasp of surprised agony. He followed with a short, crippling punch that hammered into the man's throat. The guy stumbled back, clawing at his throat, gagging. Bolan grabbed the front of his shirt and yanked the guy forward, whipping the Beretta around and clouting the man across the side of the head. He went down soundlessly.

Pulling away, Bolan forged ahead, searching for access to the lower deck of the cruiser.

An armed man stepped out from a hatch, clutching a heavy autopistol. He turned the weapon on Bolan and began to fire, his shots going wild, chewing large slivers of wood from the bulkhead. One slug did clip the underside of Bolan's left arm, grazing the skin but not drawing blood.

The burn of the slug drew a swift reaction from Bolan. He raised his left foot and slammed it against the edge of the open hatch, sliding it along its track. The solid edge of the hatch crunched against the gunner's hand, pain forcing him to open his fingers and drop the gun. He began to curse Bolan wildly, his free hand plucking at something in his belt. Bo-

Ian saw the gleam of a knife blade cutting the air. Drawing back, he triggered a burst, blowing the man back down the companionway to the lower deck.

Bolan followed him down.

An autoweapon thundered loudly from the confines of the interior, slugs chewing away ragged chunks of polished wood. As Bolan reached the bottom of the companionway he threw himself full length, the Beretta tracking ahead.

Hesitant movement midway along the passage provided Bolan with his target. He offered a burst of 9 mm slugs and was rewarded by the sight of an armed figure slumping into view, blood already pumping from ragged throat wounds. The dying man fell across the passageway, his face pressed up against the opposite bulkhead.

Ahead of Bolan, raised voices expressed surprise and alarm.

They were coming from beyond the double doors at the far end of the passage. Bolan sprinted along the passage, hit the doors with his left shoulder burst through, snatching the Desert Eagle from its high-ride holster.

He had a quick glimpse of Han Nor and Marcus Glastonbury. To one side was Victor Suliman.

Along one side of the large cabin was a bank of monitor screens, with a computer console flanking the display.

The occupants of the cabin all turned as Bolan burst into the room.

Only Glastonbury appeared to be unprepared. The handgun he held looked out of place in his slim, pale hand. The others were bringing their weapons to readiness.

Han Nor, his broad face still impassive, was the first to fire. His handgun spit a gout of flame that lanced in Bolan's direction, smashing glass off to one side.

Suliman, his eyes gleaming with excitement, began to trigger the large silver pistol in his slim hands. His shooting was wildly inaccurate, the recoil of the weapon too much for him to control.

Bolan's first shot caught Han Nor in the left shoulder, knocking him off balance. The Korean maintained his silence, only his eyes registering that he had been shot. The second and third 9 mm slugs first drove him to his knees, then knocked him over on his back.

The Desert Eagle tracked in on Victor Suliman, a single bullet striking the arms dealer between the eyes. The back of Suliman's head exploded out across the cabin, blood debris spattering the wall as the man crashed to the floor, squirming in his final moments, before death claimed him.

In the scant seconds it took for his companions to die, Marcus Glastonbury watched in mounting horror. This was not something he had ever been involved with before. Sudden, violent death was not part of his life. He was a dealer, a fixer, a man who arranged deals for others. He turned his gaze on the tall, dark-clad figure, and extended the hand holding the pistol Nor had given him.

He didn't even know how to take off the safety, let alone use it. Surely his dark-clad adversary would see that and understand. As he would understand that Glastonbury's involvement had been nothing more than advisory. Whatever had taken place had been out of his control, and though he had known about it, no blame could be attached to himself.

The expression of disbelief in Glastonbury's eyes was lost on Bolan as he triggered a triple-burst from the Beretta that cored in through the expensive suit the man wore and wrenched his pounding heart apart. Glastonbury staggered back, aware of the blood flowering across his chest, but still unable to accept he had been shot. It was only when the pain hit and he found he was lying on the floor, unable to speak or move, that he knew he was about to die. But it was too late then.

Whatever their singular or collective ambitions, the conspirators forfeited them all in the final moments of their lives. The dealers in death and destruction succumbed to their own mortality, fate decreeing that they be prevented from realizing the fruition of their scheme by an awesome blitz delivered by the Executioner.

As his weapons clicked empty, Bolan ejected the spent magazines and reached for spares. He had just pulled out a fresh clip for the Desert Eagle when he caught a glimpse of movement.

He turned, his eyes taking in the threatening bulk of Han Nor's bodyguard coming out of the corner of the cabin, where he had been standing silently.

And then the hardman slammed into him with the force of a runaway train. Bolan was flung across the cabin and crashed against the bulkhead, his guns spilling from his fingers. He barely had time to draw a breath before the bodyguard was upon him, callused hands snatching at his throat, fingers with the power of steel clamps digging into his flesh, cutting off his air supply.

CHAPTER TWENTY-ONE

Libya, North Africa

"Okay," Calvin James said, "this is what we have." He held the pad so everyone could see it. "The entrance to the workshop complex is here. The trailer, here, is where we saw Englemann go. Off to the extreme right is the radio bunker. From the equipment on the roof, I'd say they have a satellite link, so they can transmit over one hell of a range. That needs taking out first, once we remove the sentries, to prevent their sending out any calls for help. The last thing we want is a full force of the Libyan army coming over the hill.

"We have four sentries on roving patrol around the perimeter, and two pairs on static guard, here by the trailer. Two more are at the entrance to the complex."

"They need to be dealt with first," Katz said. "Gary and David, that's your job. Quick and silent. We need to move fast. I want this over and done with before too many people are up and about."

McCarter had already equipped himself with his crossbow and a quiver of cyanide-tipped bolts. He clipped his Uzi to his harness, checked that his spare ammunition was secure and nodded to Katz.

"Gary?" Katz asked.

The burly Canadian, carrying his crossbow, gave the thumbs-up.

Katz checked his watch. The others waited for his signal and synchronized their own watches.

"How long do you want?" Katz asked.

McCarter and Manning exchanged a silent glance, seeming to read each other's thoughts.

"We're short on time," Manning said. "We'll work it in fifteen. If we haven't taken them all out by then, we still go in."

"Rafael, Gary, you follow me when we do go in," Katz said. "We take the complex. Gary, you place the charges. David, you join up with Cal. Let him hit the radio bunker first, then I want the trailer and Englemann down and out. No compromise on this. Understood?"

"We understand," James said.

Manning handed McCarter one of the explosive packs. The Brit placed it in his backpack.

"Move out," Katz ordered.

Manning and McCarter took opposite directions, using the last of the gray dawn light to close in on the site. They were both excellent shots, so extreme closeness wasn't necessary. They would also be helped by the fact that there was no air movement, so there wouldn't have to be complicated range adjustments for drift. The Libyan dawn was still and breathless, holding the promise of yet another hot day.

Manning's line of travel brought him in from the western edge of the oasis, close to the water hole itself. He was able to belly down in the thick desert grass growing around the small grove of trees surrounding the pool. As he settled, loading up his crossbow for the first shot, Manning relied on a mental image of the sketch James had shown them, and he was able to pick out his first target as the first of the roving sentries appeared.

The man was dressed in light khaki fatigues, wearing a *keffiyeh,* though the fold that should have covered his lower face hung loose. An AK-74 was slung from his shoulder. He trudged across the hard-packed sand with the mechanical pace of a man ready for his shift to end.

Manning cradled the crossbow against his shoulder, adjusting the telescopic sight until his target came into sharp relief. He tracked the sentry to the extreme perimeter of his area, where the man paused to check the empty terrain beyond the site. Easing the AK-74 on his shoulder, the sentry took a moment to stretch, loosening the stiffness in his joints, and that was when Manning fired.

The bolt struck just below the sentry's left ear. He jerked at the sharp pain, slapping a hand to his neck, sure that he'd been stung. By the time he realized it was not a bite, the cyanide took hold. The sentry wavered, knees going. He fell flat on his face and lay still after a few seconds.

Manning reloaded, changing position slightly so that he was ready for the second sentry as the man came into sight around the curve of a long dune. This man could have been the twin of the guy Manning had just dropped—same clothing, identical weapon. The only difference was that this sentry was carrying his AK-74. And he was sharper-eyed than the first sentry.

Just as Manning picked him up in his sights, the man spotted his downed partner. To his credit he didn't panic, but simply stopped in his tracks, bringing his weapon up to firing position before he scanned the area. His professional stance gave Manning an easy target. Drawing down on the sentry, Manning stroked the trigger and the crossbow expelled its missile without alerting anyone. The sentry stiffened as the bolt hit him in the upper chest. He slapped at the object protruding from his shirtfront, trying to knock it free. He died still trying.

DAVID MCCARTER'S crossbow released its bolt with a subdued whoosh. The shaft buried itself in the neck of the target, breaking open to release its deadly cyanide, and the roving sentry became one of the walking dead for a few seconds. Stiffening in silent agony, the man's spine arched in a convulsive spasm. He toppled and struck the ground without a sound.

Aware of the silent clock that was running, McCarter had been forced to eliminate this man with his partner close by. The Brit had prepared for a second shot by having the next bolt laid out on the ground next to him. The moment he'd fired, McCarter cocked the crossbow and scooped up the bolt, dropping it into position. The crossbow was back to his shoulder, eye against the telescopic sight, while the dead sentry's partner was still trying to figure out what had happened.

The guy leaned over to check his partner, saw the feathered bolt protruding from his neck and realized there was an attack in progress. He opened his mouth to yell, but instead emitted a gargling gasp as McCarter's second bolt cored into his throat, spilling its poison into his bloodstream. The agony he experienced remained within him, unexpressed. He slid to the ground, darkness returning to claim him. This time it was not the black of night but the eternal shadow of death.

On his feet and moving, McCarter had his crossbow cocked and loaded by the time he dropped to his knees in a shallow depression. Stretching his long frame across the sand, McCarter scanned the area.

Ahead of him was the long trailer where Kurt Englemann was working his computer expertise. The two guards lounging against the steps, sharing a few words and a smoke, were plainly European. Even in the poor light McCarter saw that one of them had red hair. Unlike the roving sentries, these two were clad in tan camou fatigues and carried H&K MP-5s. They also sported handguns in high-ride holsters.

Adopting the procedure he had used on the two sentries, McCarter drew down on the first guy, placing the bolt directly between the shoulders. The man coughed, falling forward into the unprepared arms of his partner. As the guy tried to extricate himself, McCarter reloaded, came up on one knee and triggered the crossbow just as the man pushed his dead partner aside, pulling his SMG into the firing position. The fourth bolt McCarter fired sliced into the man's chest. He uttered a stunned grunt, stumbling back against the trailer steps.

Moving on, McCarter skirted a couple of parked Land Rovers and crouched in the shadow of a battered truck. From beneath the truck he was able to look out across open ground directly at the entrance to the complex. The guards there were engaged in an animated conversation. The distance was too far for McCarter to make out what they were talking about, but it didn't appear to be anything urgent.

He was still watching when one of the sentries fell to the ground. His partner looked around, unsure of what to do because he hadn't heard a shot.

McCarter pulled the crossbow to his shoulder, sighting quickly, and shot the man through the back of the neck. He fell forward, over his downed partner, jerking a few times before the cyanide kicked in and took him.

Discarding the crossbow and quiver, McCarter unlimbered his Uzi. Then he took out his transceiver and keyed the button.

"All clear at this end," he said. "It's a go."

"Acknowledged," Katz replied. "Take your targets."

McCarter spoke again.

"Cal, you read me?"

"Yeah," came back James's voice. "Where are you?"

"Old truck just beyond two Land Rovers."

"I got you. On my way."

WITH ENCIZO ON HIS HEELS Katz moved in on the site. The fact that Manning and McCarter had taken out the sentries didn't mean they were going to have it easy. Getting into an enemy camp was often the easy part of the job. It was dealing with the personnel inside and then getting out that caused the most bother. Katz didn't dwell on the matter. He put his effort into covering the ground as quickly as possible.

The sand underfoot restricted movement. It was a surface that moved beneath the feet, dragging a man back instead of allowing him to keep a steady pace. Sometimes it felt like running through soft mud.

Katz could feel his heart starting to pound, his breath catching in his throat. No use denying it, he was getting too old for this kind of operation. He could fight with the best, and beat them to a standstill. Weapons were something he understood. Tactics, too. But as a man grew older, no matter how genuine his intentions, how noble his purpose, reactions slowed. Stamina lessened.

Katz shook off his mood of reflection. Damned if he wasn't starting to think like an old man! He sucked air into his burning lungs and plowed on, fixing his gaze on the entrance to the complex. The bulky figure of Gary Manning appeared, joining Katz and Encizo.

Keying his transceiver, Katz spoke urgently into the mouthpiece.

"Cal, you read me?"

"Yeah."

"We go the minute you take out the radio bunker."

"Coming up," James replied.

The seconds stretched into infinity. Katz began to get impatient. He forced himself to stay calm.

And then the dull explosion ripped the morning calm wide open. There was a flash of light, followed by a plume of smoke. Katz turned and saw the radio bunker vanish, debris scattering in every direction.

"Come on!" Katz yelled to his Phoenix partners, and they raced across the open compound. The distance lessened quickly, and before he knew it Katz was standing at the wooden door to the complex. No more time for thought. Only action.

He raised his booted foot, slamming it against the door and shoving it open.

"Let's do it!" he shouted, and went ahead of Encizo and Manning.

JAMES DROPPED INTO the sand beside McCarter.

"Took your bloody time," the cockney muttered.

"Well, I'm here now, so why waste time?" The black commando grinned.

McCarter rolled out from under the truck, his long legs carrying him toward the trailer. He reached the vehicle seconds ahead of James. The pair made sure their weapons were up and ready.

McCarter reached up to free the access handle that would admit him to the trailer.

He heard James yell a warning, and turned in time to see three armed men running toward them.

"School's out," James muttered.

He turned and opened fire, his Uzi cutting a swathe through the advancing terrorists. One went down instantly, skidding across the ground, his chest leaking blood. The other two split apart, one shaking a bloody hand.

McCarter's Uzi added its noise. The Brit's initial volley took out the man James had winged. The stream of slugs chewed ragged holes in the guy's torso, spinning him off his feet and dumping him facedown in the sand.

The third man opened fire, his AK-74 exploding with a harsh, distinctive sound. Bullets gouged the sand at the feet of the Phoenix pair, falling short because the running man hadn't compensated for his rapid movement. He didn't get a second chance. McCarter caught him with a short burst that took off one side of his face and snapped his head around. The screaming man dropped his rifle and clutched his shattered head. McCarter put him out of his misery with a second burst.

From across the area more shooting flared up as Katz and the others met resistance within the complex.

"They're going to need us," James said.

"I know. I bloody know," McCarter snapped.

He plucked a grenade from his harness and pulled the pin. Tossing it under the trailer, he motioned for James to get clear.

They cleared the danger zone just before the grenade went off, filling the dawn with a brilliant flash and a cloud of smoke. The trailer rocked. Moments later the door burst open and an armed man in camou fatigues appeared on the top step. He saw McCarter and James and opened fire.

James returned fire, stitching the guy with 9 mm slugs. He fell back inside the door. Together James and McCarter ran for the open trailer door.

The terrorist was sprawled across the entrance. McCarter had to step over him.

The interior was brilliantly lit, and chilly compared to the outside. The hum of the air-conditioning could be heard above all the other noise.

The trailer had been outfitted as a computer lab. The whole of the interior was filled with a dazzling array of equipment—monitors and consoles, printers and backup units.

The blond-haired man seated at the main console was already halfway out of his padded chair, shoving it back. He began to turn, his lean face rigid with anger, lips drawn back from his clenched teeth. His right hand was already lifting the 9 mm SIG-Sauer P-226 that rested on the desk beside him. He swung the muzzle of the weapon round, lining it up on McCarter.

The Brit, having already recognized Kurt Englemann, angled the Uzi toward the man. His finger stroked the trigger, and the weapon misfired.

"Bloody hell!" McCarter rasped, then felt someone slam into him, pushing him out of the way.

Calvin James's SMG chattered loudly in the confines of the trailer. The stream of 9 mm slugs caught Englemann chest high, lifting him and tossing him back across the trailer. The pistol in Englemann's hand discharged its single shot into the ceiling, shattering one of the light tubes. Crashing against a cabinet, the rogue computer expert was pitched forward, facedown on the floor, his back a bloody mess of shredded flesh and bone where the Uzi's burst had torn through his slim torso.

McCarter turned to glance at his partner.

"That was too bloody close," he said. "I owe you one, chum."

The grin on James's face was undisguised.

"Don't worry, I won't let you forget it. Now set that charge Gary gave you so we can get the hell out of here."

Aboard the Celleste—*off Saint-Tropez*

MACK BOLAN'S RIGHT HAND reached down to close over the handle of the sheathed Ka-bar. He knew he had no more than seconds to defend himself. The hardman's fingers were squeezing his neck without letup, and Bolan was aware that if the pressure increased, he would be unconscious.

It was a life or death situation.

Bolan's or the Korean's, and the Executioner had no intention of losing his.

He yanked the knife free, pulled his arm back and plunged the blade deep into his enemy's left side, below his ribs. As the keen blade sank in up to the hilt, Bolan twisted and cut, opening the deep gash. Blood began to pour from the wound and the man's body arched in pain.

Bolan freed the knife and plunged it in again and again. The powerful Korean resisted initially, but he couldn't withstand the injury. His grip on Bolan's throat slackened and he took a couple of faltering steps back. Blood was pulsing from the ragged wounds in his side.

The Korean clamped one huge hand over the bloody area. Despite his pain, he moved quickly, his right arm sweeping around in a blur, the back of his thick hand clouting Bolan across the side of the face. The force of the blow spun Bolan across the cabin, and he lost his balance and fell to his knees.

Shaking his head to clear the fog of pain, Bolan sensed his adversary coming up behind him. The warrior dropped forward into a shoulder roll. On his back, he looked up to see the Korean's threatening bulk looming over him.

Bolan kicked out with his booted foot, catching the man in his wounded side. The Korean uttered a grunt of anger, bending to reach for Bolan. This time Bolan's hard-delivered kick smashed his enemy's broad face, crushing his nose and shattering some teeth.

Howling with pain, the Korean backed off. Bolan dropped his legs to the floor, set himself, then scythed his right leg in a powerful sweep that knocked the man's feet from under him. He crashed to the cabin floor and lay dazed.

Pushing to his feet, Bolan took long strides across the cabin, where he scooped up the Desert Eagle. He snapped in a fresh mag, cocked the heavy pistol and, still down on one knee, turned his upper body as he heard the man clambering to his feet. The muzzle of the .44 Magnum tracked in on the Korean. Bolan shot three of the 240-grain hollowpoints into his adversary's deep chest, ripping his heart to shreds, dumping him back on the cabin floor.

Bolan crossed to the computer setup. He stared at the machines for a moment, then calmly blew them apart with the Desert Eagle. Searching the cabin, he found a box of disks. Bolan dumped them, along with those from the drives of the computers, into a waste bin. Taking one of the thermite devices, he pulled the pin and dropped the canister into the bin. He turned and made for the door. As he stepped outside he heard the sharp crack of the detonator exploding. A brilliant white light blazed from within the cabin as the thermite charge began to erupt.

Bolan located the companionway that led down to the engine room. He found the fuel tanks and placed two more of the thermal devices. Pulling the pins, he made a swift exit, and heard the detonators blow just as he reached the top of the companionway.

Bolan made his way back up to the deck.

As he made the hatch a gun crackled from the wheelhouse. Conscious of the time slipping away before the thermite ignited the fuel supply, Bolan didn't hesitate. He holstered the Desert Eagle and took out the Beretta. Snapping in a fresh magazine, he laid down a steady volley that shattered the wheelhouse windows, then ducked out from the hatch. Running along the deck, Bolan pulled the pin on the last thermite device, and as he closed on the wheelhouse he tossed the package in through one of the windows.

The brilliant gush of light from the device drew all attention away from Bolan, and he used the moment to move along the deserted deck to the stern of the *Celleste.* Bolan swung over the rail, pulled the dinghy in close and dropped into it. He cut the line with his ka-bar, shedding the canvas weather sheet, and settled by the outboard motor. It burst into life on the third pull. Bolan took the dinghy around in a tight circle, turning up the power.

Over his shoulder he could see smoke starting to billow from the main cabin and then from the wheelhouse. Figures emerged from the wheelhouse, one man slapping at the flames flaring from his sleeve. Then there was a deep boom of sound and more smoke, accompanied by flame, flared from belowdecks. The cruiser faltered as the engines shut down. The fire spread quickly. The men on deck leapt into the water. A second explosion took out part of the starboard hull, and the cruiser began to list badly.

Bolan picked up the sound of an engine. When he checked he saw it was his backup crew in the motorboat.

When they pulled him on board, one of the SIS men said, "The signal came through."

Bolan shook his head, smiling grimly.

"Does that mean I can go ahead?" he asked.

Behind them the cruiser began to go under, bow first. A mass of huge bubbles rose to the surface as the vessel vanished from sight, leaving only a scattering of debris on the oily water and a drifting cloud of dark smoke that stained the clear, blue Mediterranean sky.

Qatar Oasis, Libya

ARMED MEN, both European and Arab, raced to confront Phoenix Force as they breached the complex.

Katz, bracing his Uzi against his steel prosthesis, triggered the first volley. The stream of 9 mm slugs cut down two moving figures, tearing into flesh and shattering bone. The men went down, spilling their weapons and their blood across the dusty concrete.

A few feet behind the Israeli, Manning and Encizo fanned out, bringing their own weapons into play, scything the enemy with a deadly spray of 9 mm death.

The defending force, despite superior numbers, found they were facing a formidable foe. The sheer intensity of the Phoenix Force attack drove them apart like blades of grass before a strong wind.

The complex echoed to the crackle of gunfire and the screams of the dying.

Reaching the main complex area, Katz took in the scene before him.

The setup was not as sophisticated as a regular weapons workshop, but Katz saw that it could do the job. Long metal benches held the cradled warheads, enabling the technicians to adapt the locking collars that would secure them to the Korean missiles. The cone-shaped warheads, gleaming softly in the diffused light from the overhead lamps, reminded Katz of the destructive power within those metal sheaths. He was fully aware of the damage just one of them could wreak, let alone the numbers Han Nor's group was offering for sale.

Slinging his Uzi from his shoulder, Katz pulled a grenade from his harness, yanked out the pin and tossed it across the work area. The exploding grenade blasted two armed men off their feet and shattered a bank of electronic equipment. He followed the first grenade with others, tossing them across the work area, then bringing his Uzi back into action as he weaved his way between the racks and benches.

Close by, Manning and Encizo were tackling their own problems.

The Cuban had gotten himself pinned down in a corner by two armed men. They were spaced far enough apart to catch Encizo in a cross fire, and though he was protected behind a low cinder-block wall, he was unable to move into the clear, or get a chance to fire back.

Encizo placed his back to the wall, replaced the magazine in his Uzi, then pulled a stun grenade from his harness. He pulled the pin and leaned out to throw the grenade at his attackers. The grenade landed short, but rolled the final few feet before it went off. The glare of light and the gush of smoke, accompanied by the pounding explosion, caught the pair unprotected.

Encizo allowed the noise to fade before he peered around the edge of the wall. His tormentors were reeling from cover, hands rubbing at their deafened ears, eyes blinking and watery. The Uzi in the Cuban's hands dispatched the pair before they could regain their senses.

Moving on, Encizo joined up with Gary Manning, providing backup for the Canadian.

"Where do you want to plant your explosives?" he asked Manning.

Ducking for cover behind a metal drum, Manning fed a fresh magazine into his Uzi. He traded shots with the figures darting around the work area, then said, "Generator room on the far side. Support beam to the right there. I want to leave one under that missile trailer outside when we leave."

Encizo plucked a couple of grenades and pulled the pins. He lobbed the explosives across the work area, ducking back under cover before they detonated. As the explosions downed a number of the opposition and scattered others, Encizo raked the area with autofire, then tapped Manning on the shoulder.

"Let's go," he said. "This place is getting uncomfortable."

The Phoenix pair broke cover and dashed across the work area. Encizo provided cover for Manning, allowing the Canadian to slip in through the door of the generator room and place one of the explosive packs under the stationary diesel engine that powered the generator. Manning had set the timer for five minutes. The Canadian had also fitted an interrupter contact in the circuit. If the pack was located and someone tried to disable it, the explosive would detonate prematurely.

Easing out of the room, Manning scouted the work area, pinpointing the major support column that rose overhead. That was his next target.

That was when he picked up movement nearby, and saw a pair of armed men, both European, easing out from the shadows behind a stack of metal canisters. One of the men was directing his partner, and Manning realized they were targeting Katz.

There was no time to warn the Israeli, and Encizo was looking in the opposite direction.

Manning grabbed his shoulder-slung Uzi and leveled the weapon. He triggered a burst that took out the lead man, knocking him back into the stacked canisters. The man's partner, his H&K arcing around, locked eyes with Manning for the briefest of moments.

Both men opened fire.

Manning's volley cut through the other's midsection. The man slumped to his knees, finger pulling back against the trigger of his SMG. The released stream of slugs rattled against the wall close to Manning, one of them bouncing back and tearing into the back of the Canadian's left shoulder. Manning gasped at the bite of the flattened slug.

"Come on, Gary, lean on me," Encizo said, aware of his partner's injury.

Ignoring Manning's protest that he was fine, the Cuban took charge. One arm went around Manning's waist to support him, leaving Encizo's right arm free to use the Uzi. He snugged it against his side as he moved the Canadian across to the support pillar Manning had designated as his next target. Locked together, the Phoenix pair slid to a stop at the base of the concrete pillar, Manning sinking to his knees.

"I'll cover if you can manage," Encizo said.

"I'll be fine," Manning replied.

He pulled out an explosive pack and wedged it under the base of the pillar. Peering at the timer, he keyed the buttons to set the delay. Almost ready to activate, he suddenly realized he had allowed only forty seconds instead of four minutes. Shaking his head, Manning rekeyed the timer. He took a long look before he was satisfied he had it right this time, then depressed the activate button. The readout flashed, the seconds changing rapidly.

"Okay," Manning said.

When he tried to stand up, his legs threatened to cave in under him. The pain from his shoulder was increasing, and his left arm was already numb.

"Looks like you'll be in for some R & R when we get back," Encizo remarked as he hauled the Canadian to his feet. "The things you'll do to get time off."

Manning grinned, or imagined he had. He wasn't certain anymore. He leaned against the sturdy Cuban, feeling the complex spin around him.

Katz fell in beside Encizo, still trading shots with the surviving defenders. The Israeli's decision to attack early had paid off. The work area had been manned by a skeleton crew, and they had been slow to respond to the surprise appearance of Phoenix Force. Even so, an armed man was still a threat, and Katz refused to relax his vigilance.

Covering Encizo and Manning, he moved in the direction of the entrance. The last of his grenades downed two defenders as they made a last-ditch attempt to block the way.

Flattened against the wall close to the entrance, Katz took one of Manning's explosive packs and placed it against the door. He set it for one minute.

"Be a good idea if we got out of here," he suggested.

"Give me a hand, Katz," Encizo said, his tone urgent.

Manning had slumped unconscious. The Canadian's shoulder was a mass of pulped and bloody flesh where the flattened bullet had ripped into him.

Moving up to the pair, Katz helped Encizo to pull Manning upright. He keyed his transceiver.

"Phoenix One. We have a wounded man. Need help."

As if to acknowledge Katz's appeal, there was a sudden increase in gunfire from outside the complex.

CHAPTER TWENTY-TWO

Libya, North Africa

David McCarter and Calvin James had been close to the complex entrance when there had been a sudden influx of armed men. Roused by the noise of conflict, the bulk of the terrorist force began to emerge from their tents. Half-dressed, some still groggy from sleep, they nevertheless joined their companions to defend Qatar Oasis.

"Bloody great," McCarter grumbled. "Now we've woken the neighbors."

The Brit was not fazed by the reinforcements. Little, if anything, threw McCarter. Despite his outwardly brazen and throwaway attitude, McCarter was a skilled, combat-wise veteran. When it came to the real thing, the cockney had few equals.

Without hesitation McCarter pulled grenades from his harness and began to lob them in the direction of the advancing defenders of Qatar Oasis. He laid down a withering line of explosions, scattering the defenders. As the dust cleared it was easy to see the devastation McCarter's grenades had left behind. At least five men were down, with others reeling from the detonations or nursing minor and major wounds.

"Up and at 'em, lads," McCarter yelled, letting loose with his Uzi. He took out two of the terrorists before Calvin James joined the assault, his own autoweapon crackling.

Between them the Phoenix pair pushed the dazed defenders back toward the tents, and at the same time they worked their way closer to the entrance to the complex.

Suddenly Katz and Encizo appeared, dragging Manning between them. The burly Canadian made some attempt to help himself but he was obviously weak from his wound.

"Clear the entrance," Katz yelled.

McCarter and James kept up a steady stream of fire, punctuated with grenades. They kept the camp's defenders from closing in.

The explosive device Katz had planted just inside the entrance detonated abruptly. The explosion took out the front of the complex, and a thick cloud of smoke and dust billowed out across the compound. Debris showered the area.

The explosion provided cover for Phoenix Force's retreat. They fell back to where a number of vehicles were parked, using them to conceal their immediate moves.

"Cal, see what you can do for Gary," Katz said as he and Encizo lowered the Canadian to the ground.

James, who was the team's medic, knelt beside Manning and used his knife to slit open the Phoenix pro's camou jacket. He took a quick look at the wound, glancing over Manning's head to where Katz was watching.

"Looks messy," James said. "Whatever hit him must have been out of shape already. It's dug a nasty hole. Looks like bone broken, too. Right now all I can do is try to stop the bleeding and patch him up. He'll need medical help as soon as we can get it for him."

"Do what you can," Katz said.

From within the complex Manning's explosive charges detonated. The deep rumbles were followed by numerous other explosions, and the Phoenix team felt the ground tremble beneath them. The roof of the complex lifted, cracked, and flame and smoke gushed out, throwing debris high into the air.

"Gary wanted to place a charge under those missiles," Encizo said. "Looks like we missed them."

McCarter, who had been laying down covering fire, glanced over his shoulder.

"You got any of those packages left?" he asked.

"David, forget it," Katz snapped.

"And have him moaning we didn't finish off the job? Not bleedin' likely."

McCarter took the pack that Encizo handed him. He reloaded his Uzi, moved to the front of their cover vehicle and scanned the terrain.

"Katz, see if you can raise that tardy Yank pilot and tell him to get that chopper in here fast."

"Damn it, David, I don't want you risking your neck on some foolish whim," Katz said.

"You know I just love it when you're forceful," the Brit said, then ducked under the high chassis of the truck they were hiding beside and vanished from sight.

"Company coming," Encizo said, trading shots with a number of advancing terrorists. Bullets were burning the air, clanging off the metal of the vehicles.

Katz moved beside the Cuban and they laid down a volley of withering fire that took out two men instantly, dumping their bleeding bodies on the dusty ground.

The others went to cover, and for a moment or two the firing slackened.

Katz pulled out his transceiver and changed the frequency to that of Dragon Slayer. He wasn't sure whether the transceiver's range would carry to the chopper, but he had to try.

"Ground Force to DS One. Are you receiving? Are you receiving? Over."

The transceiver hissed. Katz adjusted for maximum transmitting power and tried once more. Again the transceiver hissed. He was about to switch off when a faint voice broke through.

"DS One to Ground Force. I'm on my way. ETA approximately fifteen minutes."

"Try to make it in ten. We have a casualty here. Needs immediate evacuation."

"You got it," Grimaldi replied. "I'm stepping on the gas. Over and out."

McCARTER SKIRTED the wrecked complex, using the thick clouds of smoke issuing from it to hide his approach. Twice he felt the ground underfoot shake as further explosions took place. He could still hear the rattle of autofire, though the rate was slower than it had been earlier.

He eased by some chunks of shattered concrete, peering through the coils of heavy smoke. He could taste the stuff, too. It had an acrid, oily feel to it.

A lean figure loomed out of the smoke ahead of him—too quickly for McCarter to avoid. It was a bearded terrorist, clad in stained desert fatigues and carrying an AK-74.

McCarter saw the terrorist turn the muzzle of his rifle. He didn't pause to think what he was doing. Dropping forward, McCarter rolled over once, coming up with his Uzi crackling and driving a short burst of 9 mm fire into the man's body. The terrorist fell over backward, his weapon firing at the sky.

Two other figures materialized from the smoke, weapons probing ahead of them. Still crouching, McCarter unleashed another burst from the Uzi, cutting into the terrorists before they saw him. The bloodied figures twisted in agony, bodies punctured by the slugs. One hit the ground on his knees, fighting against the pain, and triggered a single shot from his AK. The slug ripped through the left sleeve of McCarter's shirt, scoring a shallow gash in the flesh of his arm. McCarter jerked the Uzi around and laid a heavy burst into the terrorist, slamming him to the ground. McCarter heard the Uzi click on an empty breech. Pushing to his feet, muttering in a low monotone, the Brit continued on his way, more determined than ever to complete his task. He slung the Uzi over his shoulder by its nylon sling and pulled out his Browning Hi-Power.

He was clear of the complex entrance now. Pressed tight against the wall, he made out the shape of the trailer holding the Korean missiles.

A yelling figure burst into view—a smoke-blackened terrorist, brandishing an AK with the bayonet attached. Either the man was out of ammunition, or delirious. He lunged at McCarter. The Phoenix pro rolled to one side. The steel tip of the bayonet struck the wall, sparks flying. Before the man could pull back, McCarter launched a hard kick, driving the toe of his boot into the guy's stomach, doubling him over. The gagging terrorist was still trying to pull himself erect when McCarter triggered a single shot from the Browning that caved in the side of the man's skull.

McCarter ran on, reaching the trailer and throwing himself to the ground beneath it. He wriggled to the far side, pulling himself upright, and wedged the explosive pack in between the curving cradles that separated the top and bottom missiles. His fingers keyed in a twenty second sequence.

McCarter hit the button, turned and dived back under the trailer. He emerged from the other side and lost himself in the smoke still pouring from the wrecked complex. He retraced his steps, making his way back to where the others had been hidden by the parked vehicles.

He was preparing for a final dash across open ground when he heard the roar of a vehicle engine. McCarter turned to check out the sound and saw a Jeep lurch into view.

There were four men in the vehicle. In the rear were two people the Brit recognized from photographs. One was Jordan Delacourt, the American who had been providing the muscle for the organization. Next to him was the gaunt-faced Yuri Rostok, the Russian who had been supplying the contraband warheads.

The other two in the vehicle were armed mercs, probably from Delacourt's group.

From behind McCarter came the heavy blast of the explosive package detonating. The explosion was powerful, sending metal debris into the air, followed by a raging fireball. The shock waves knocked McCarter to his knees.

The blast attracted the attention of the men in the Jeep, and as their heads turned they saw McCarter's reeling figure as the Phoenix commando struggled upright.

"That's one of them!" Delacourt screamed.

The Jeep's tires spun in the soft sand as the man behind the wheel jammed his foot down on the pedal. It was that action that saved McCarter's life. The man beside the driver had drawn down on the

Brit and was about to fire when the Jeep lurched forward. His shot went wild.

McCarter by this time had realized how vulnerable he was out in the open. He also knew he had nowhere to run. So he stood his ground and fought back.

Unhampered by a bouncing, swerving vehicle, McCarter was able to aim and fire his Browning with care. His first shot hit the driver in the head, knocking him sideways. The driverless Jeep veered to the side and came to a jerky stop.

The driver's partner pushed to his feet, laying his H&K over the frame of the windshield, and tried for a second shot. He was still unlucky. McCarter had already shifted aim, sighting along the Browning's barrel. He triggered two close shots, driving a pair of 9 mm slugs into the man's chest. The guy slumped back, falling over the back of his seat and colliding with Yuri Rostok as the man tried to scramble from the Jeep.

Jordan Delacourt jumped clear on the other side, unclipping the leather holster he wore and pulling his stainless-steel .45-caliber Detonics autopistol. Moving around to the front of the stalled Jeep, Delacourt triggered a shot at the tall figure, cursing as he missed.

McCarter felt the wind of the bullet pass his cheek. He half turned, crouching, his Browning tracking the source of the shot.

The two men fired at the same time.

McCarter grunted as the .45 slug clanged against the Uzi slung from his shoulder, driving the weapon into his ribs with bruising impact.

He saw Delacourt fall away from the Jeep, dropping from sight. McCarter ran forward, making a wide detour of the vehicle until he could see the merc leader. Delacourt was on his hands and knees, the big autopistol dangling from his right hand. Blood was leaking from the body wounds the 9 mm slug had opened. Delacourt's head snapped up as McCarter came into his field of vision, then he raised the Detonic's muzzle.

McCarter didn't hesitate. He shot twice, into Delacourt's body, the slugs coring into the merc's heart. Delacourt arched back in agony, then collapsed with the looseness of death, facedown in the Libyan dirt.

"David!"

The warning call was followed by the crackle of autofire.

McCarter looked around in time to see Yuri Rostok slumping forward, his chest torn and bloody. The H&K MP-5 he had taken from the dead merc in the Jeep slipped from his fingers.

Beyond the Jeep Katz ran forward, his Uzi still raised.

"Thanks," McCarter said as he rejoined the Israeli. "But I was doing okay."

Katz shook his head. McCarter would never change. As irreverent as ever. But still one of the best to have at your side in a battle.

"You were?"

McCarter nodded as they trotted back to where the others waited.

"Three out of four, Katz. Not bad going for a wounded man."

"Wounded?"

McCarter showed his bloody sleeve.

"You don't think I would let Gary get all the sympathy, do you?"

Katz remained silent. He had to because there was no answer at all to that.

"How's Gary doing?" McCarter asked as soon as he crouched beside James. "Will he be okay?"

The Phoenix medic shrugged. "He's strong. But that's a nasty wound. We won't know just how bad until he can be operated on. It's certain he'll be out of action for a while."

McCarter sat with his back against the wheel of the truck they were using for cover.

"He's got to be okay. Make sure, Cal, or I'll come and haunt you."

"How?" James asked.

"I'll move in with you."

"Now there's a threat I wouldn't take lightly," Encizo said from where he was keeping watch.

"Quiet," Katz said.

He was listening to his transceiver.

"Got you in sight. Smoke showing. ETA three minutes."

"Acknowledged," Katz said. "Check out the area as you come in. See if our friends down here are regrouping. It's gone too quiet for my liking."

The Phoenix warriors took advantage of the lull to reload all their weapons. James remained with Gary Manning, who had lapsed into unconsciousness again. The others took up positions where they could watch the outlying areas of Qatar Oasis.

The drifting smoke made observation difficult and might have been concealing the advance of the defenders.

The next 180 seconds slipped by very slowly.

Calvin James moved to where McCarter knelt.

"Let me take a look at that arm," he said.

"It's nothing."

"David, don't be an asshole."

"In England we say arse."

"I know what they say in London," James said. "So don't be one."

McCarter allowed him to roll up the sleeve. The bullet had torn out a ragged chunk of flesh, leaving a messy wound that was still seeping blood. James cleaned the arm and put on a temporary dressing.

"That was a crazy stunt to pull," James said after a moment's silence. "Going out on your own."

McCarter raised his head to look at the black warrior. "Bloody lovely bang, though," he said.

The rising beat of a helicopter's rotors reached their ears. Moments later the long, sleek outline of Dragon Slayer appeared. The matt-black combat chopper, designed and created exclusively for Stony Man, slid out of the clearing sky to hover over the site.

"We're just below you," Katz informed Grimaldi. "In among the vehicles parked to the right of the complex."

"Got you," the pilot's voice came back through the transceiver. "I'm coming in. Make it fast, guys, 'cause you have visitors moving in from the west side of the camp. Ten, maybe twelve, gathering just by the tent area."

The chopper sank to the ground. The passenger-compartment hatch was already open.

"Cal, you and Rafael handle Gary," Katz said. "David and I will cover you. Don't stop for anything. Just get him on board. Now go!"

James and Encizo slung their weapons over their shoulders, then bent to pick up Manning. They made sure they were comfortable, waited for McCarter's signal, then broke cover and ran across to where Grimaldi had put the chopper down. The combat helicopter was facing in the direction of the tent area, visible through a hazy veil of drifting smoke.

"Our turn, David," Katz said.

McCarter nodded and followed the Israeli.

By the time they cleared the vehicles, James and Encizo were already lifting Manning into Dragon Slayer.

Midway across, a ragged burst of autofire split the air. Bullets chewed at the ground around McCarter and Katz, kicking up sand and stone chips. Through the curtain of smoke McCarter could see distant figures advancing. For once he resisted the temptation to stop and fight.

The need was not there. The air was suddenly ringing with the explosive roar of the 30 mm chain gun, part of Dragon Slayer's armaments payload. Spitting out death at a rate of 600 rounds per minute, the relentless power of the cannon tore apart anything that stood in its path. McCarter had a quick vision of the terrorists scattering, many of them going down under the tremendous power of the chain gun, bodies torn to bloody rags.

Ahead of him Katz stumbled, almost falling. McCarter reached him and grabbed his arm, pulling him to his feet and giving him a boost up into the helicopter. As McCarter hit the cabin floor Grimaldi boosted the power and Dragon Slayer lifted off in a swirl of rotor fog. Turning the chopper, Grimaldi made a wide circle, then took a run at the camp, loosing off a couple of rockets from the pods. The missiles streaked down to turn the parked vehicles into a tangled mass of twisted metal, flames shooting up from ruptured fuel tanks. Then the black chopper soared over the camp, climbing as Grimaldi went for altitude.

Peering through the side window, McCarter watched Camp Nine dwindle in size until all he could see was the black smoke staining the sky above it. Then even that vanished. He flopped back against the padded couch and watched James bending over Gary Manning.

On the other side of the compartment, Katz and Encizo, their weapons on the floor between their feet, visibly slumped as the tension drained out of them. They were streaked with dust and smoke, and their faces showed the exhaustion that was starting to take hold.

"Hot coffee in the flasks back there, guys," Grimaldi called from his position up front.

For once McCarter didn't ask if there was Coke. Coffee, hot, cold or indifferent, sounded bloody welcome right there and then.

EPILOGUE

Stony Man Farm, Virginia

Barbara Price pushed the file across the War Room table, then reached out to pick up her mug of coffee.

"Is the update complete?" Hal Brognola asked.

Price nodded. "I completed the final draft a half hour ago."

The Fed sat staring at the file.

"Too many good people died because of those bastards," he said. "And we didn't come out without casualties."

"At least our guys are still alive. Out of commission for a time, but alive."

Brognola sighed. "You're right. I saw Gary and Pol yesterday. They're coming along. Slow but sure."

"What did the doctor say about Gary's shoulder?"

Brognola unwrapped a fresh cigar.

"The bones will mend. He was lucky no nerve ends were damaged. That shoulder is going to be painful, but it won't hold him back, if I know Gary."

"Pol?"

"He has more lives than any damn cat I ever knew. They dug three bullets out of him and he's already complaining about the hospital food."

"According to David, he got it worst of all. You'd think his arm had been shot off."

Brognola grinned.

"I have to meet with the Man later. He needs a final briefing on the outcome. There are going to be some behind-the-scenes ass-kicking sessions. The President's had some heat already from the North Koreas and Libya, but he's on top of that. Considering what they've been up to, neither government wants any of this made public. It'll be dealt with strictly through diplomatic channels."

"Sounds like they're getting off lightly," Price said.

"What they do have are red faces," Brognola said. "They were caught and given the big-stick treatment. The Koreans have already disowned Han Nor, saying he was acting on his own. The British have Lawrence Pennell locked up so tight he'll forget what daylight is."

"And I see that the Russians are rounding up Rostok's partners, as well."

Brognola nodded. "They were extremely embarrassed by the whole thing. Apparently Rostok had been stringing them along for two years, but they never suspected his black-market dealing included nuclear warheads."

"According to surveillance reports the satellites haven't monitored any more activity around Camp Nine."

"The latest update has the place deserted. But they'll keep it under long-term scrutiny."

"Unless someone else comes up with the same idea."

Brognola's response was to bite down hard on his unlit cigar.

"My rundown doesn't go into any detail on the THAAD project."

"Now that Walter Hanson is back on track, the project appears to be settling down again." Price stood up. "You need me for anything right now?"

"No. You take a break."

"I might just do that."

"Do what?" asked a familiar voice.

Mack Bolan stood in the open door of the elevator. He looked tired, a little battered, but at ease in casual clothes.

"Why, let you take me to dinner," Barbara Price said, quickly recovering from her surprise.

"Sounds good," the warrior said. "If I'm on stand down."

"You are," Brognola said. "Welcome home, Striker."

Bolan nodded. "Good to be back."

Brognola shuffled the papers in front of him.

"Go on, you two, get out of here before I change my mind."

The elevator doors closed behind Bolan and Price.

Brognola sat in the silence for a time. Finally he rose, scooped up his files and crossed to the elevator. Before he stepped inside he switched off the lights, leaving the War Room in darkness.

But for how long? he wondered.

And knew the answer straightaway.